CHRISTOPHER BUSH was born Charlie Christmas Bush in Norfolk in 1885. His father was a farm labourer and his mother a milliner. In the early years of his childhood he lived with his aunt and uncle in London before returning to Norfolk aged seven, later winning a scholarship to Thetford Grammar School.

As an adult, Bush worked as a schoolmaster for 27 years, pausing only to fight in World War One, until retiring aged 46 in 1931 to be a full-time novelist. His first novel featuring the eccentric Ludovic Travers was published in 1926, and was followed by 62 additional Travers mysteries. These are all to be republished by Dean Street Press.

Christopher Bush fought again in World War Two, and was elected a member of the prestigious Detection Club. He died in 1973.

By Christopher Bush

The Plumley Inheritance

The Perfect Murder Case

Dead Man Twice

Murder at Fenwold

Dancing Death

Dead Man's Music

Cut Throat

The Case of the Unfortunate Village

The Case of the April Fools

The Case of the Three Strange Faces

CHRISTOPHER BUSH

CUT THROAT

With an introduction
by Curtis Evans

DEAN STREET PRESS

Published by Dean Street Press 2017

First published in 1932 by William Heinemann

Cover by DSP

ISBN 978 1 911579 77 9

www.deanstreetpress.co.uk

INTRODUCTION

THAT ONCE vast and mighty legion of bright young (and youngish) British crime writers who began publishing their ingenious tales of mystery and imagination during what is known as the Golden Age of detective fiction (traditionally dated from 1920 to 1939) had greatly diminished by the iconoclastic decade of the Sixties, many of these writers having become casualties of time. Of the 38 authors who during the Golden Age had belonged to the Detection Club, a London-based group which included within its ranks many of the finest writers of detective fiction then plying the craft in the United Kingdom, just over a third remained among the living by the second half of the 1960s, while merely seven—Agatha Christie, Anthony Gilbert, Gladys Mitchell, Margery Allingham, John Dickson Carr, Nicholas Blake and Christopher Bush—were still penning crime fiction.

In 1966--a year that saw the sad demise, at the too young age of 62, of Margery Allingham--an executive with the English book publishing firm Macdonald reflected on the continued popularity of the author who today is the least well known among this tiny but accomplished crime writing cohort: Christopher Bush (1885-1973), whose first of his three score and three series detective novels, *The Plumley Inheritance*, had appeared fully four decades earlier, in 1926. "He has a considerable public, a 'steady Bush public,' a public that has endured through many years," the executive boasted of Bush. "He never presents any problem to his publisher, who knows exactly how many copies of a title may be safely printed for the loyal Bush fans; the number is a healthy one too." Yet in 1968, just a couple of years after the Macdonald editor's affirmation of Bush's notable popular duration as a crime writer, the author, now in his 83rd year, bade farewell to mystery fiction with a final detective novel, *The Case of the Prodigal Daughter*, in which, like in Agatha Christie's *Third Girl* (1966), copious references are made, none too favorably, to youthful sex, drugs and rock and roll. Afterwards, outside of the reprinting in the UK in the early 1970s of a scattering of classic Bush titles from the Golden Age, Bush's books, in contrast with those of Christie, Carr, Allingham and Blake, disappeared from mass circulation in both the UK and the US, becoming fervently sought (and ever more unobtainable) treasures by collectors and connoisseurs of classic crime fiction. Now, in one of the signal developments in vintage mystery publishing, Dean Street Press is reprinting all 63 of the Christopher Bush detective novels. These will be published over a period of months, beginning with the release of books 1 to 10 in the series.

Few Golden Age British mystery writers had backgrounds as humble yet simultaneously mysterious, dotted with omissions and evasions, as Christopher Bush, who was born Charlie Christmas Bush on the day of the Nativity in 1885 in the Norfolk village of Great Hockham, to Charles Walter Bush and his second wife, Eva Margaret Long. While the father of Christopher Bush's Detection Club colleague and near exact contemporary Henry Wade (the pseudonym of Henry Lancelot Aubrey-Fletcher) was a baronet who lived in an elegant Georgian mansion and claimed extensive ownership of fertile English fields, Christopher's father resided in a cramped cottage and toiled in fields as a farm laborer, a term that in the late Victorian and Edwardian era, his son lamented many years afterward, "had in it something of contempt....There was something almost of serfdom about it."

Charles Walter Bush was a canny though mercurial individual, his only learning, his son recalled, having been "acquired at the Sunday school." A man of parts, Charles was a tenant farmer of three acres, a thatcher, bricklayer and carpenter (fittingly for the father of a detective novelist, coffins were his specialty), a village radical and a most adept poacher. After a flight from Great Hockham, possibly on account of his poaching activities, Charles, a widower with a baby son whom he had left in the care of his mother, resided in London, where he worked for a firm of spice importers. At a dance in the city, Charles met Christopher's mother, Eva Long, a lovely and sweet-natured young milliner and bonnet maker, sweeping her off her feet with a combination of "good looks and a certain plausibility." After their marriage the couple left London to live in a tiny rented cottage in Great Hockham, where Eva over the next eighteen years gave birth to three sons and five daughters and perforce learned the challenging ways of rural domestic economy.

Decades later an octogenarian Christopher Bush, in his memoir *Winter Harvest: A Norfolk Boyhood* (1967), characterized Great Hockham as a rustic rural redoubt where many of the words that fell from the tongues of the native inhabitants "were those of Shakespeare, Milton and the Authorised Version....Still in general use were words that were standard in Chaucer's time, but had since lost a certain respectability." Christopher amusingly recalled as a young boy telling his mother that a respectable neighbor woman had used profanity, explaining that in his hearing she had told her husband, "George, wipe you that shit off that pig's arse, do you'll datty your trousers," to which his mother had responded that although that particular usage of a four-letter word had not really been *swearing*, he was not to give vent to such language himself.

Great Hockham, which in Christopher Bush's youth had a population of about four hundred souls, was composed of a score or so of cottages, three public houses, a post-office, five shops, a couple of forges and a pair of churches, All Saint's and the Primitive Methodist Chapel, where the Bush family rather vocally worshipped. "The village lived by farming, and most of its men were labourers," Christopher recollected. "Most of the children left school as soon as the law permitted: boys to be absorbed somehow into the land and the girls to go into domestic service." There were three large farms and four smaller ones, and, in something of an anomaly, not one but two squires--the original squire, dubbed "Finch" by Christopher, having let the shooting rights at Little Hockham Hall to one "Green," a wealthy international banker, making the latter man a squire by courtesy. Finch owned most of the local houses and farms, in traditional form receiving rents for them personally on Michaelmas; and when Christopher's father fell out with Green, "a red-faced, pompous, blustering man," over a political election, he lost all of the banker's business, much to his mother's distress. Yet against all odds and adversities, Christopher's life greatly diverged from settled norms in Great Hockham, incidentally producing one of the most distinguished detective novelists from the Golden Age of detective fiction.

Although Christopher Bush was born in Great Hockham, he spent his earliest years in London living with his mother's much older sister, Elizabeth, and her husband, a fur dealer by the name of James Streeter, the couple having no children of their own. Almost certainly of illegitimate birth, Eva had been raised by the Long family from her infancy. She once told her youngest daughter how she recalled the Longs being visited, when she was a child, by a "fine lady in a carriage," whom she believed was her birth mother. Or is it possible that the "fine lady in a carriage" was simply an imaginary figment, like the aristocratic fantasies of Philippa Palfrey in P.D. James's *Innocent Blood* (1980), and that Eva's "sister" Elizabeth was in fact her mother?

The Streeters were a comfortably circumstanced couple at the time they took custody of Christopher. Their household included two maids and a governess for the young boy, whose doting but dutiful "Aunt Lizzie" devoted much of her time to the performance of "good works among the East End poor." When Christopher was seven years old, however, drastically straightened financial circumstances compelled the Streeters to return the boy to his birth parents in Great Hockham.

Fortunately the cause of the education of Christopher, who was not only a capable village cricketer but a precocious reader and scholar, was taken up both by his determined and devoted mother and an idealistic local elementary school headmaster. In his teens Christopher secured a scholarship to Norfolk's Thetford Grammar School, one of England's oldest educational institutions, where Thomas Paine had studied a century-and-a-half earlier. He left Thetford in 1904 to take a position as a junior schoolmaster, missing a chance to go to Cambridge University on yet another scholarship. (Later he proclaimed himself thankful for this turn of events, sardonically speculating that had he received a Cambridge degree he "might have become an exceedingly minor don or something as staid and static and respectable as a publisher.") Christopher would teach English in schools for the next twenty-seven years, retiring at the age of 46 in 1931, after he had established a successful career as a detective novelist.

Christopher's romantic relationships proved far rockier than his career path, not to mention every bit as murky as his mother's familial antecedents. In 1911, when Christopher was teaching in Wood Green School, a co-educational institution in Oxfordshire, he wed county council schoolteacher Ella Maria Pinner, a daughter of a baker neighbor of the Bushes in Great Hockham. The two appear never actually to have lived together, however, and in 1914, when Christopher at the age of 29 headed to war in the 16th (Public Schools) Battalion of the Middlesex Regiment, he falsely claimed in his attestation papers, under penalty of two years' imprisonment with hard labor, to be unmarried.

After four years of service in the Great War, including a year-long stint in Egypt, Christopher returned in 1919 to his position at Wood Green School, where he became involved in another romantic relationship, from which he soon desired to extricate himself. (A photo of the future author, taken at this time in Egypt, shows a rather dashing, thin-mustached man in uniform and is signed "Chris," suggesting that he had dispensed with "Charlie" and taken in its place a diminutive drawn from his middle name.) The next year Winifred Chart, a mathematics teacher at Wood Green, gave birth to a son, whom she named Geoffrey Bush. Christopher was the father of Geoffrey, who later in life became a noted English composer, though for reasons best known to himself Christopher never acknowledged his son. (A letter Geoffrey once sent him was returned unopened.) Winifred claimed that she and Christopher had married but separated, but she refused to speak of her purported spouse forever after and she destroyed all of his letters and other mementos, with the exception of a book of poetry that he had written for her during what she termed their engagement.

Christopher's true mate in life, though with her he had no children, was Florence Marjorie Barclay, the daughter of a draper from Ballymena, Northern Ireland, and, like Ella Pinner and Winifred Chart, a schoolteacher. Christopher and Marjorie likely had become romantically involved by 1929, when Christopher dedicated to her his second detective novel, *The Perfect Murder Case*; and they lived together as man and wife from the 1930s until her death in 1968 (after which, probably not coincidentally, Christopher stopped publishing novels). Christopher returned with Marjorie to the vicinity of Great Hockham when his writing career took flight, purchasing two adjoining cottages and commissioning his father and a stepbrother to build an extension consisting of a kitchen, two bedrooms and a new staircase. (The now sprawling structure, which Christopher called "Home Cottage," is now a bed and breakfast grandiloquently dubbed "Home Hall.") After a falling-out with his father, presumably over the conduct of Christopher's personal life, he and Marjorie in 1932 moved to Beckley, Sussex, where they purchased Horsepen, a lovely Tudor plaster and timber-framed house. In 1953 the couple settled at their final home, The Great House, a centuries-old structure (now a boutique hotel) in Lavenham, Suffolk.

From these three houses Christopher maintained a lucrative and critically esteemed career as a novelist, publishing both detective novels as Christopher Bush and, commencing in 1933 with the acclaimed book *Return* (in the UK, *God and the Rabbit*, 1934), regional novels purposefully drawing on his own life experience, under the pen name Michael Home. (During the 1940s he also published espionage novels under the Michael Home pseudonym.) Although his first detective novel, *The Plumley Inheritance*, made a limited impact, with his second, *The Perfect Murder Case*, Christopher struck gold. The latter novel, a big seller in both the UK and the US, was published in the former country by the prestigious Heinemann, soon to become the publisher of the detective novels of Margery Allingham and Carter Dickson (John Dickson Carr), and in the latter country by the Crime Club imprint of Doubleday, Doran, one of the most important publishers of mystery fiction in the United States.

Over the decade of the 1930s Christopher Bush published, in both the UK and the US as well as other countries around the world, some of the finest detective fiction of the Golden Age, prompting the brilliant Thirties crime fiction reviewer, author and Oxford University Press editor Charles Williams to avow: "Mr. Bush writes of as thoroughly enjoyable murders as any I know." (More recently, mystery genre authority B.A. Pike dubbed these novels by Bush, whom he praised as "one of the most reliable and resourceful of true detective writers", "Golden Age baroque, rendered remarkable by some extraordinary flights of fancy.") In 1937 Christopher Bush became, along with Nicholas Blake, E.C.R. Lorac and Newton Gayle (the writing team of Muna Lee and Maurice West Guinness), one of the final authors initiated into the Detection Club before the outbreak of the Second World War and with it the demise of the Golden Age. Afterward he continued publishing a detective novel or more a year, with his final book in 1968 reaching a total of 63, all of them detailing the investigative adventures of lanky and bespectacled gentleman amateur detective Ludovic Travers. Concurring as I do with the encomia of Charles Williams and B.A. Pike, I will end this introduction by thanking Avril MacArthur for providing invaluable biographical information on her great uncle, and simply wishing fans of classic crime fiction good times as they discover (or rediscover), with this latest splendid series of Dean Street Press classic crime fiction reissues, Christopher Bush's Ludovic Travers detective novels. May a new "Bush public" yet arise!

Curtis Evans

Cut Throat (1932)

DURING THE FALL and spring of 1930-31--when ideas likely were germinating in Christopher Bush's crafty and fertile mind about *Cut Throat* (1932), the seventh Ludovic Travers' detective novel--the devastating impact in Great Britain of the global Great Depression was casting British politics ever further into disarray. Beset by crisis upon crisis, the weak and unpopular Labour government of Prime Minister Ramsay MacDonald continued to flag, propped up only with Liberal and Conservative acquiescence. Yet Stanley Baldwin, leader of the Tories since 1923, himself was under immense pressure. Powerful right-wing press lords--Max Aitken, 1st Baron Beaverbrook, owner of the *Daily Express* and *Evening Standard*, and Harold Harmsworth, 1st Viscount Rothermere, owner of the *Daily Mail* and *Daily Mirror* and younger brother of the late press titan Alfred Harmsworth, 1st Viscount Northcliffe--united in an effort to oust him as party leader over the issue of free trade. In the 1929 general election, Lord Beaverbrook had launched the Empire Free Trade Crusade, a political movement designed to promote free trade among member states in the British Commonwealth while erecting tariff walls, including a so-called "tax on food," against the rest of the world. In 1930 he joined Lord Rothermere in forming the United Empire Party, a dagger aimed at Baldwin's political heart. The shadow conflict between Baldwin and the press lords came to a head in a hotly-contested and much-publicized March 1931 by-election contest in an affluent constituency in London's West End. There Beaverbrook and Rothermere's man, Sir Ernest Petter, ran an Independent Conservative campaign on behalf of "Empire Free Trade" against rising Tory star Alfred Duff Cooper, a Baldwin supporter. Just two days before the by-election, in what historian William D. Rubinstein calls "one of the most famous political speeches of the twentieth century" (see Rubinstein's *Twentieth-Century Britain: A Political History*), Baldwin dramatically denounced the newspapers of the press lords as "engines of propaganda for the constantly changing policies, desires, personal wishes... of two men" and the two men themselves as power-hungry prostitutes: "What the proprietorship of these papers is aiming at is power, but power without responsibility—the prerogative of the harlot throughout the ages." After Baldwin's so-called "harlot speech," Duff Cooper won the election, effectively saving the career of the opposition leader. Baldwin went on with Ramsay MacDonald in August to form a National Government, which won a remarkable landslide victory in the October 1931 general election.

In addition to being a corker of a detective novel, Christopher Bush's *Cut Throat*, which saw publication in the spring immediately following the 1931 general election, is reflective of early Depression-era domestic politics in the United Kingdom, particularly in its highlighting of the political ascendance in between-the-wars Britain of the press lords. Much of *Cut Throat* concerns two fictional newspaper tycoons, elderly Sir William Griffiths, who recently divested himself of the *Mercury*--"so Cobdenian that it creaked," fatalistically comments Ludovic Travers of the newspaper (referencing Richard Cobden, the mid-Victorian Liberal thinker and free trade ideologist)--and punningly-named Lord Zyon, owner of the *Evening Record*, with which the now defunct *Mercury* has been amalgamated. Drawing on the *Record*'s slogan, "Free Trade with a Difference," the enterprising Lord Zyon has created the protectionist "Work-for-All Crusade," which he plans to formally launch, against an "enormous background of Union Jacks," at a grand rally at the Albert Hall. On account of his extensive economic expertise, Ludovic Travers--author, as any Bush mystery fan by this time surely knew, of *The Economics of a Spendthrift* and other highly brainy yet charmingly written treatises--has been personally invited by Lord Zyon to attend the rally, though he believes that "in the panacea which his lordship was prescribing for the nation's ills there should be far less syrup and more Epsom salts."

Travers arrives at the Albert Hall, where he learns from Lord Zyon that Sir William Griffiths has sent him a note informing his lordship of his unexpected conversion to the "Work-for-

All" cause. In the note Sir William has promised Lord Zyon not only that he would most certainly be on the platform but that he has sent to the Hall a hamper filled with evidence of illicit dumping, personally secured by himself. (The economic term "dumping" refers to predatory pricing of exports in international trade.) Sir William's hamper duly arrives at the Hall and inside it there indeed is evidence of dumping--but not quite the sort of evidence that people were expecting. Upon opening the hamper Lord Zyon discovers, amid a scattering of cabbage leaves, Sir William's corpse, his throat cut from ear to ear.

Could the murder of Sir William Griffiths in such a brutal and demonstrative fashion have been some form of domestic terrorism? "A burnt offering! Mightn't there have been a fanatic so frantic in his devotion as to have presented that sacrifice?" asks Travers in a flight of fancy. "The slain body of a man who more than any other stood for reaction: the old, obstinate creeds of Free Trade and the weary shibboleths of a dead political age?"

To this theory Superintendent George Wharton of the Yard, who has been called into the case, scoffs. However, he allows Travers--or more accurately Travers's man, Palmer--to drive him down to Sir William's Devonshire country house for further investigation. There the pair interview Sir William's nephew and heir, the intrepid—or so publicity has it--world explorer Tim Griffiths, only recently returned from outer Mongolia; Sir William's uxorious financial secretary, Bland; Bland's distressingly vulgar wife ("What on earth had she been before Bland married her," a bemused Travers wonders. "Barmaid? Chorus girl? Third-rate schoolmarm?"); Bland's chess-playing pal, local vicar Reverend Cross; Sir William's housekeeper, Mrs. Rigg; and Sir William's "soft-footed" and "slimy" (Travers's words again) butler, Daniels. Also participating in the investigation is Chief-Inspector Norris, Wharton's "right-hand man," of whom we shall hear more in future novels, and an intrusive crime reporter named Sanders, who always seems somehow to wheedle his way into a crime scene.

When required at one point in the novel to dally with Mrs. Bland (for the good of the investigation, of course), Travers may come off to readers as a tad priggish, though he gives Bush mystery fans glimmers of hope that there might be some form of a romantic fling in his future. ("Given the right woman—and every other propitious circumstance—all sorts of things might happen," reflects Travers after his ordeal by flirtation with Mrs. Bland. "But this was appalling!") Additionally, in *Cut Throat* Bush again gives scope to his extensive familiarity with classical music, including Ravel's then cutting edge composition *Bolero*, first performed only four years prior to the publication of the novel. "All drum taps and things," remarks Travers, "Works up to a tremendous climax." To which the more prosaic Wharton responds "Gets on your nerves a bit."

Overall *Cut Throat* is beautifully-constructed and hugely-entertaining detective novel, with some unexpected moments of melancholy concerning the troubled social condition of Great Britain in the early Thirties. "All this case seems nothing but times!" wails one fretted investigator late in the novel, but the alibi problem Bush presents his readers is one of the finest such from the Golden Age, which is saying something, given the high standards of detection in those years. As the crime fiction blogger Nick Fuller once aptly observed, Christopher Bush "was to the unbreakable alibi what [John Dickson] Carr was to the impossible crime."

Chapter One
WHARTON PROPHESIES

Ludovic Travers was sitting in his private room at Durango House that August afternoon, feeling on quite good terms with himself. That, in some ways, was notable. Most people at that moment were probably rather irritable. It was hot—extraordinarily hot—and precious few were in town who could get out of it.

Travers was, however, as those knew who knew him best, a compound of paradoxes. In the first place there was no need for him to work at any time, let alone on a sweltering afternoon of August. He had far more money than he was ever likely to spend, irrespective of what his directorship of Durangos brought him in; irrespective too, of the royalties on those two classics of his—*The Economics of a Spendthrift* and *The Stockbrokers' Breviary*—and on a couple of more than adequate textbooks. At the moment too, he was seeing another manuscript through the press—though that wasn't the cause of his peace of mind.

Travers then was that rarity who likes work— congenial work—and the more of it the better. At the moment, the managing director was away, concluding his annual holiday in Norway, and the whole of that ramification of Publicity and Enquiry, known as Durangos Limited, was under the immediate control of himself. The atmosphere of the place was therefore one of leisurely industry, with the knowledge that in a few days Sir Francis would be returning to take over the reins and his own annual go-easy would begin.

As for life in general, the club was habitable. The places where he and his kind most congregated were now most miraculously airy and spacious, and freed of those who liked killing things, or who regarded sun-bathing in August as the twentieth-century equivalent of the elixir of life. But there was no sun-bathing about Travers himself at the moment. The blinds were drawn and the electric fan was humming. In his favourite attitude in an easy chair, he looked rather like an elongated lamp-post, legs stretching away into space, tips of his fingers together and eyes closed beneath the horn-rims. What he was thinking was that he'd been extraordinarily lucky.

He smiled like a benevolent ascetic. To get hold of thirty people who were definitely coming to the dinner, was an amazingly good piece of work for August. The Odysseans had rallied round magnificently; Coates, for instance, coming down from Scotland and Petter crossing from Deauville. Then the list of personal guests was as attractive-looking a collection as they'd ever bagged. His own big gun—George Wharton—was about as original a bird as the Odysseans were ever likely to see—or hear. George, proposing the health of the chairman, ought to be worth hearing, even though that chairman did happen to be Travers himself.

Then came a frown. There was his own speech, as chairman and president in one. Heaven knew what he was going to say; and heaven alone knew, for the matter of that, why they'd ever pitchforked him into the presidency. Damn little he'd travelled in his time, and it seemed rather cool for a fellow like himself to get on his pins and pronounce a benediction—or even a panegyric—on a chap like Tim Griffiths, who'd not only crossed the Sahara from side to side, but had just put in eighteen months endeavouring to find apparently in the wastes of China places to put a foot where no white foot had ever been put. China . . . Travers lingered over the word. What subtle allusions could be brought in? Mandarins . . . Ming . . . pigtails. . . . Then the telephone-bell rang!

"Yes. Speaking. . . . Oh, yes! How are you, Steve? . . . At the Regality. . . . Really important? Or are you pulling my leg? . . . Right-ho! I'll be over straightaway!"

Travers frowned heavily as he hung up. That'd been Stephen Pendry. Something most damnably urgent, which he didn't feel like mentioning over the phone. Surely something wasn't going to go wrong with the show, after all the trouble people had taken! Travers fretted vaguely as he made his way to the cloakroom. Stephen was a reliable old cuss—and an extraordinarily good fellow. About the best man there was at the film-making game, too. Travers smiled. That'd be it. Something had gone wrong over the stuff they'd taken on the expedition.

. . . No! that couldn't be it. Perhaps Steve had a brain-wave about some sort of a private show—an exhibition of the film—somewhere after dinner. Perhaps he was going to suggest running off a few reels in the dining-room of the Club.

Coming out of the glare of the sun into the coolness of the Regality, Travers was blinking his way from the bureau towards the elevator when Steve Pendry hailed him. He wasn't looking any too jovial.

"Good of you to come over, Ludo. Had tea?"

"Oh, rather! Half an hour ago. . . . What's all the trouble?"

"Come along in here!" He led the way to a corner of the drawing-room where palms—profuse as everything else in the Regality—made a species of bower; got Travers seated, then drew his chair in close.

"There's hell to pay upstairs!"

Travers' eyes popped open. "Er—I don't follow."

"That bloody swine Griffiths is up to his tricks again." He saw the look of blankest astonishment; then explained. "He's tight—or he damn soon will be!"

Travers was all of a flutter. "But . . . I say, this is awful! . . . I hadn't the faintest idea!"

"Of course you hadn't!" said Pendry, and shot it out like a man who has to relieve his feelings or bust. "You, and the Press, and old Silbermann, and the Odysseus Club; you make me tired! . . . Sorry, Ludo! I didn't mean that. Awfully sorry! . . . You don't know what I'm trying to get at."

Travers looked at him. "You mean . . . Griffiths isn't all he's cracked up to be?"

Pendry hesitated; not because he didn't want to say too much, but because he wanted to be careful how he said it.

"I wouldn't say that . . . exactly. I mean, I don't know for certain what he was like on that first show of his—though I heard rumours. Firth told me how he'd cut up in Africa; what a hell of a time they had with him . . . and I didn't believe him. I thought he'd got some private grouse of his own."

Travers nodded, sympathetically—and patiently.

"What was the trouble then? Not drink, surely! I mean, a man can't go in for that sort of thing and . . . Well, you know what I mean."

"He always could mop it up," growled Pendry. "One of those cantankerous swine who can't stand their liquor . . . though that wasn't it altogether with us. Too damn top-heavy. Wanted to boss the whole show."

Travers smiled. "Well . . . if he was paying for it!"

"Paying for it! Where'd you get that idea?"

"Well, I mean I thought it was generally understood."

Pendry waved his hands about. "That's what I was telling you! You people don't know! Griffiths went through that pile of his before the show started. Silbermann was behind us. If I and Malone hadn't gone—Silbermann'll tell you that himself—there wouldn't have been any show at all. Malone and I backed Silbermann for most of what we've got. I admit we'll get it all back over the film—or we ought to."

"But surely Griffiths can call on money! I mean, what about his uncle?"

"Uncle be damned!" said Pendry. "The old man's never parted with a bean. It's his own money he's been spending; the money his mother left him. He used to tell us all about it in his genial moments; blast him! The real honest-to-God truth is this. He put the proposition up to Silbermann, and Silbermann fell for it. Griffiths was to go on the expedition to give it a touch of class. He was the talkie hero; you know—posing against yaks and temples and mastodon mounds. 'Famous explorer—Tim Griffiths'—and all that bilge. Silbermann fixed the whole thing up, then found Griffiths had no money . . . and that's how the three of us were left to hold the baby."

"Yes, but Silbermann knew you and Malone well enough. I mean, it wasn't any gamble he was taking."

"That isn't the point," said Pendry obstinately. "Knowing how things were, Griffiths ought to have pulled his weight. What *did* he do? I had to run off reels when *he* felt inclined! I, mind you! Cross him and he'd sulk for days; then Malone and

I would have the whole show on our hands. The last effort was when we found he'd shipped half a dozen cases of rot-gut from a Russian at Tashkend on the way home. We carted him round on poles till we found what it was. Then he and I had a stand-up scrap and I scuppered the lot. After that he sulked for a fortnight—not that we gave a damn; then he found out we were doing pretty well without him, so he came round and apologized—about as offensively as any one could apologize. He said he'd been all cut up about some damn girl or other."

"Girl!" Travers frowned back. "Wasn't there some talk about him and Silbermann's daughter?"

"That's the one! Apparently he got a letter with the mail at Tashkend. That'd be about a couple of months ago. We crossed over yesterday morning, as you know, and he was all right then—if you let him have his head. Malone and I went off with our people and got here for lunch as arranged. Griffiths has been here all the time. Just after lunch he came in—he was a bit rocky then. Malone asked him what the hell he thought he was doing, and didn't he know where he was going tonight; then he cut up rough and told us both to go to hell—and you people as well."

Travers flushed slightly. "Where's he now?"

"Upstairs. Malone's there—holding the fort and trying to knock some sense into him. If it hadn't been for you fellows I'd have let him stew in his own juice."

Travers rarely lost his temper, but he certainly felt like it at the moment. "Does he think he's a person of sufficient importance to be so damnably—"

"That's just what I told him!" cut in Pendry. "So did Malone. 'You cheap skate!'—that's what we told him. 'If you were twice as good a man as you've ever thought you were, you'd be honoured if the Odysseus Club took a damn of notice of you!' That's what we told him. 'Nansen and Scott; that's the sort of person the Odysseus Club has entertained. And here's you—a fourth-rate screen actor!'" Then Pendry swore some more.

Travers suddenly felt an alarm of quite a different kind. "But yours was a first-class show, wasn't it? I mean, you were doing really big work?"

Pendry smiled wryly. "If you call making a first-class talking film of unknown Mongolia good work, then you're right!"

"Yes . . . but the papers—"

"Papers! . . . Publicity! Silbermann's publicity for the film. He kidded all you people into thinking it was an expedition for exploration purposes. When did all this bally-hoo about Griffiths start?"

"Don't know. . . . Month or so ago, perhaps."

"Exactly! Silbermann got those cylinders six weeks ago. The film may be shown in a month's time—or less. Where's your sense, Ludo? Silbermann flooded the Press and made you people think Tim Griffiths a hero."

Travers thought hard and thought quickly. Then he made up his mind. "I'm not standing for seeing people like Hugh Coates and Johnny Allsopp and Roger Petter let down like this—irrespective of the Club itself. You and Malone will be there, of course?"

"Oh, rather! Extraordinarily grateful and honoured—"

"That's all right then," nodded Travers. "'Sudden indisposition' will do for Griffiths. Mind you, if I'd known a week ago when we got in touch with you, what I know now, I don't think there'd have been any show at all. I don't see why we should make free publicity for Silbermann. We'd probably have asked you along, Steve. It's about time you had some recognition—"

Pendry waved him short. "Rubbish! I'm just a bloke who earns an honest living."

Travers got to his feet. "I'll have a word with Griffiths. Can you call off Malone for a minute?"

. . . .

Travers said afterwards that when he'd finished with Griffiths he felt like getting into a hot bath. If there was anything he loathed it was subterfuge; and to spend a quarter of an hour telling Tim Griffiths what a fine fellow he was, and asking him if there was anything he specially wanted referred to, and lying about what this person and that had said, and getting the Silbermann story out of him and telling him there wasn't a woman in the world worth an unnecessary drink . . . well, it was a pretty loathsome business. Of course it wasn't all as crude as that. Few men had more delicate courtesy and natural charm of manner than Travers, and it would have taken a bigger lout than Tim Griffiths to stand up against a deliberate, attack of the kind Travers launched. But it was pretty horrible—Griffiths, beefy and too well-fed, a bit baggy under the eyes, aping an importance which he somehow felt necessary to suit with the unassumed superiority of Travers; and Travers, feeling white-hot inside, chatting away with all the deference and friendliness he'd have shown to a white man like Steve Pendry.

The end of it was that Travers' man, Palmer, was rung up to bring round the necessary garments. The whisky was removed and Travers had a second tea. Pendry and Malone were given their cue and were gradually drawn in, and altogether things looked better.

"If I were you," said Travers solicitously, "I'd go very easy to-night, Griffiths. Short drinks and fever are a pretty bad combination, and you're looking none too good. Tell you what I'll do! I'll ring up Chester and get him to pass the word round."

Then Travers rang up Superintendent Wharton, of Scotland Yard, and changed their rendezvous to the Odysseus Club itself. Seven o'clock found them all in the smoke-room, where Pendry and Malone followed in the wake of Travers and left Griffiths to it.

"Let him have the limelight," said Travers. "You fellows don't give a damn. Once this show's over he can go plumb to hell as far as I'm concerned."

"That's the stuff!" said Pendry. "We'll go back to the hotel to-night, but to-morrow—"

"He won't be there himself to-morrow," Malone reminded him. "Don't you remember he said he was going down to his uncle's place, first thing? That's what's been upsetting him—so he says."

As a matter of fact, the whole thing was an extraordinary success, except perhaps for Travers, who was more or less on tenterhooks the whole time. Perhaps, too, the sympathy for

Griffiths—so obviously not yet fully recovered from his fever bout —had something to do with the wonderful reception

There were few in that room who had ever clapped eyes on George Neville Wharton, one of the really big noises at Scotland Yard, and known as The General to the force at large. What they saw was something rather disconcerting. Perhaps Wharton's other nickname—given by a detective-sergeant who frequented the movies—might explain him. Give Chester Conklin another six inches, and you'd have George Wharton; the same mildly-surprised face, the same vast, weeping moustache that curved over the mouth, the same spectacles on the end of the nose and the same peering motion that looked clean over the top of them.

Wharton began very slowly. "I understand that I'm supposed to be proposing a vote of thanks to your excellent chairman, Mr. Ludovic Travers. Some of you know him as an author; some know him as a financial expert; some know him as an after-dinner speaker of very mixed merits. With your permission, gentlemen, I'll tell you what we think of him—and know of him—at Scotland Yard!"

He kept them going after that, not perhaps so much by what he said as by how he said it. He, too, had his contribution to make to the theme of romance; the other fellow's job, as he defined it. There were those apparently who thought Scotland Yard—his own job—romantic. Wharton shook his head. And there were apparently those who thought the life of an explorer romantic; who'd give a lot to swap jobs with their distinguished guests of that evening. Then Wharton ended much as he'd begun—on a note of obvious raillery.

"Mr. Travers has reminded us that Mr. Griffiths and Colonel Pendry and Doctor Malone have, at any rate, had what very few of us can ever hope to have—they have experienced, in fact, every the gamut of human emotions. If one is to believe Mr. Travers, therefore, life holds no further excitement for them. What a prospect gentlemen, for these distinguished guests of ours! The rest of their lives must be passed in complete stagnation. If I may put it that way, they will yawn themselves from one week to another!

"But I once knew a man, gentlemen, who also had had most of the thrills there are in life, and he told me there was one thrill he never wanted to have repeated. It was the thrill of being hunted!" Wharton smiled grimly. "Far be it from me to suggest that that one thrill yet remains to be experienced by our guests of this evening. That thrill is this. Let them—any one, of them—be suspected of a downright, hundred per cent, murder. Let them have the law—the inefficiency of which we hear so much about these days—well on their heels. If they want a bigger thrill than that, gentlemen, then my name's not Wharton!"

And Wharton proposed his vote of thanks and sat down.

....

Just after midnight, Travers and Pendry and Malone were having a final yarn and nightcap in Travers' huge apartments at St. Martin's Chambers, where they'd adjourned after the main excitement of the evening. The conversation, as it was bound to do, got round again to Tim Griffiths.

"I don't see why he shouldn't stab old Sir William for a hefty allowance," Malone was saying. "He's the only nephew. He'll get the whole bag of tricks when the old man dies."

"I'm not so sure!" said Travers. A couple of drinks above normal always loosened his tongue.

He'd been chattering away most of the evening, and the morning would find him blushing for his overnight loquacity.

"Bit close, is he?"

"Close! He's an Armenian! And why shouldn't he be? After all, if you've sweated blood for years to make money in a perfectly legitimate way, why hand it over for some young fool to throw down a drain! There aren't many men who'd have made the Associated Press what it is . . . or was when he sold it. And he's a good plucked 'un. It took some pluck to scrap the *Mercury*!"

"The *Mercury*!" Malone was surprised. "You don't say the old *Mercury*'s gone!"

"Over a year ago," said Travers. "Just before he sold out, in fact. It was so Cobdenian that it creaked. Griffiths only kept it alive because it was part of the Nonconformist conscience. Everybody knew it was tottering, so he did the wisest thing—scrapped it and amalgamated with the *Record*. They called it the double-barrelled name till the *Mercury* clientele was all roped in, then the *Mercury* was dropped altogether."

"Pretty tough luck on the poor devils who lost their jobs!" said Pendry.

"It was. That's one of the finest things in journalism; I mean there isn't a paper, whatever its politics, that doesn't resent a disappearance of that kind. I believe some of the staff got on the *Record* or the *Evening Record*." He shook his head. "Still, it was a bad business, as you say."

"What did Griffiths get for the whole caboodle? You ought to know, Ludo!"

Travers smiled. "I ought to . . . but I don't; at least, precisely. In any case, Sir William Griffiths didn't get it. He was merely the controlling interest in a syndicate. . . . I can find out the exact figures, if you're interested."

"Not to that extent," said Pendry. "Who bought it, by the way?"

"Another syndicate. Lord Zyon's the big noise. They're doing extraordinarily well." He smiled. "It's funny . . . really. You see, old Griffiths' idea was that people would pay for their souls. He tried to keep the *Mercury* going on those symposium articles—'Is Religion Dead?' or 'Do Mothers Pray?'— with contributions from all the old gang, from the Sally Sisters down to the Bilious Bishop. Lord Zyon's gone one better!" Here Travers wagged his pipe solemnly. "If ever you two young lads have any money to invest, put it into industrials. People must buy bread and drink tea and use soap. That's where Griffiths was wrong. People can do without souls. What they can't do without is work! That's why the first thing a shrewd fellow like Zyon did, when he took over the *Record*, was to start the 'Work-for-all' campaign. Haven't you heard of the Work-for-All Crusade?"

Pendry smiled. "Mongolia hadn't!"

"No! I forgot that! . . . Well, you can take it from me that it's the best bit of journalism this century's seen."

Pendry glanced at the clock, then got to his feet.

"You can call it what you like, Ludo. It terrifies me. When I was first in the game, you knew what a paper was. You knew what it stood for. where to find it . . . and the people who wrote for it. This modern idea of a newspaper is . . . well it's blasphemous!"

Travers laughed. "Why worry? The remedy's in your own hands! . . . When are you fellows coming to town again?"

"We'll be here most of the time now, till the trade-show. Why?"

"You blokes are a bit rusty," said Travers. "Why not let me keep you seats for Zyon's great show at the Albert Hall? Ten days' time. Grand meeting of Inauguration and Consecration of the League! There'll be a couple of ex-Prime Ministers, a fistful of ex-Chancellors, and the Bilious Bishop, and his lordship . . . and myself!"

"Damn funny!" chuckled Malone. "Well, Ludo! Thanks for the refreshments and all that!" He turned to Pendry. "What about sending Ludo a ticket for the trade-show, when it comes on? Like to see the film, Ludo?"

"I'd love to! Let me know and I'll be there like a shot."

At the elevator there was a final echo of the evening.

"Excuse my putting unpleasant thoughts into your heads," said Travers, "but didn't I gather that Griffiths was going away to-morrow?"

"Yes . . . thank God!" said Malone. "His uncle's place—somewhere in Somerset. You might be amused to know he's taking the old boy along a collection of weapons and junk. It cost us in freight charges about ten times what it's worth."

"Bread on the waters!" said Travers, and saw them into the elevator.

CHAPTER II
"SIR WILLIAM WILL BE THERE!"

IT WOULD HAVE BEEN a matter of extreme difficulty to find a couple of financial magnates so inherently and visibly different as Sir William Griffiths, the man who built up the Associated Press—and Lord Zyon of Wimberley, the man to whom he sold it.

Sir William was another of those people with a passion for work; he had to be up and at it. The diminutive frame of him—five foot three and a hundred and twenty pounds—was the only one that could have housed his mercurial, fiery little temperament. His black eyes burned out of a face that was high-cheeked and lean; the ragged, diaconal beard on chin and neck seemed to have been grown to save time and neglected to save more. Honours, he had not two penn'orth of use for. When he purchased his baronetcy the eagerness had been on the side of the vendors rather than himself; and during his control of the Associated Press he could have been anything for the asking.

Ostentation he abominated. There had to be the house in town. After all, one must keep up a certain style and entertainment is a necessary thing, but that was the measure of his ostentation. What he liked in his leisure was his own company; the Cottage—if one can call a twelve-roomed house a cottage—at Mulberton, a day's or a week's fishing in the Exe, or in winter a quiet jog to the meet and perhaps a reasonable run that would clear a man's lungs and give him an appetite. The evening of a day like that was the only time that ever saw him really quiet, and then he would drowse in a chair till the hour of ten saw him in bed.

With those of his kind, Lord Zyon was all gentleness, suavity and polish. When he lost his temper, or with his servants, the veneer was apt to go rather quickly. Griffiths exploded in a white-hot rage, then subsided, losing no polish, because he made no pretence of having any to lose. Lord Zyon had the love of his race for art, for music and for colour. He was colourful himself—a delightful shrimp-pink from under the last crease of his chin over to the back of his utterly bald head; except, of course, for the black moustache nestling well under the shelter of the nose. In shape he was like a pear on legs, and there seemed to be considerable portions of him which he never saw but by reflection.

In his own way he had remarkable ability. He could unerringly pick the men by whose judgment he was determined to abide. Take the new blood he had put into the *Record*, after he had settled on the policy of that paper. And when circulations soared, so that even the *Patriot* grew alarmed and the *Wire* palpitated, he let the credit go where it was due. When he took as the *Record*'s slogan—"Free Trade with a Difference"—and inaugurated the Work-for-All League, he took good care not to make a fool of himself. That was why he picked the brains of the economists before he drew up the manifesto of the newest party. That also accounts for the presence that morning of Ludovic Travers at the Albert Hall.

Travers had, of course, been consulted by his lordship—and more than once. *Could* anything be done about this deplorable business of unemployment?

Travers gave his ideas for what they were worth. Would Mr. Travers entertain the idea of writing a condensed report? Mr. Travers did so. Later on, when the famous manifesto was published, he recognized in the features of the infant some faint resemblance to himself. Then, on the morning of the great day, Lord Zyon had rung up personally from the Albert Hall. *Could* Mr. Travers possibly come along for a matter of minutes? Travers went.

He had a look round; admired the enormous background of Union Jacks; admired the altar-like erection at which the Bilious Bishop—nickname of the *Patriot* for his lordship of Camden—was to officiate; smelt the flowers; agreed with the proposed placing of the massed bands of the Guards, and congratulated his lordship generally. Then in the private room the real business was tackled. The *Patriot* had had that morning a most disturbing leader on a point which his lordship was actually proposing to tackle in his speech. Would Mr. Travers mind exposing, very clearly, the fallacy in the *Patriot*'s arguments? Travers, recognizing that in the panacea which his lordship was prescribing as cure for the nation's ills there should be far less syrup and more Epsom salts, hinted so fairly bluntly and got to work on the emendation. It was best part of twelve o'clock before it was all over. Travers accepted the invitation to lunch.

At half-past twelve the limousine drew up outside Lord Zyon's superb house in Park Terrace. Every-thing was looking cheery. The striped awnings glowed before the windows, and the boxes, gay with begonias, smiled out across the few feet of gravel that lay between the wrought-iron railings and the windows themselves. Lord Zyon, however, was plainly feeling none too happy. Travers could sympathize. His debut that night as a really public speaker was to be in the presence of a nation and an Empire, of whom more would be likely to scoff than remained to pray. Moreover, just as they were leaving the Albert Hall, Mortimer—the financial secretary—had rather tactlessly showed his lordship a ribald gibe in that morning's edition of the *Wire*, to the effect that the audience that evening would certainly be a packed one, since the discharged employees of the *Mercury* alone would suffice to fill the building!

Percival, the butler, took their hats and gloves. "Pardon, m'lord, but Major Heather would like to see your lordship on a matter of urgency."

"Where is he?"

"In the library, m'lord."

"Hm! Tell him I'll see him in the dining-room in a minute. Come along, Travers!"

His lordship's man followed them to the lavish cloak-room. Five good minutes later they moved into the dining-room. Percival followed.

"Will you have lunch immediately, m'lord?"

Lord Zyon waved a pudgy hand. "In a minute! In a minute! . . . Morning, Heather! What's your trouble? . . . You know Mr. Travers."

Heather, the social secretary, smiled gracefully, with that delightful charm indeed for which he was paid. A ball-bearing in an oil bath, as Travers once called him.

"No particular trouble, sir. A message arrived at midday—precisely midday; a very urgent message, so it was said. From Sir William Griffiths."

"Griffiths!" His lordship raised his eyebrows, wobbled uneasily and looked inquiringly at Travers. Travers avoided the look. "What on earth does he want?"

"Well, sir, I'll give you the message exactly as I took it down. You see, sir, it wasn't quite in my province so I thought it just as well to take it down verbatim."

His lordship grunted impatiently. "All right! All right! Get along with it, Heather!"

Heather nodded deferentially and consulted the pad.

"It was Sir William's secretary, sir—he didn't say which secretary—ringing up and asking if he might speak to you. I told him you were at the Albert Hall, arranging and supervising certain vitally important matters in connection with to-night's—er—meeting, and would he prefer to speak direct. Then he asked when you'd be in, and I told him twelve-thirty. It was then that he said it was so urgent he couldn't wait, and would I give you the message—this message."

He passed over a typewritten sheet. The other raised his eyebrows, adjusted a pair of pince-nez, then began reading aloud. Travers politely sidled away a yard or two and admired the Chippendale.

"Sir William Griffiths' compliments and he would like Lord Zyon to know that he will most certainly be on the platform to-night. . . ."

He broke off. "You hear that, Travers? Extraordinarily good! Don't you think so?"

"You expected it? I mean, you asked him?"

"No! I don't think I did," said his lordship very slowly. "I hadn't really thought of him in that—er—context. Extraordinarily good, of course, a man like that being with us!"

"Rather than against us!" smiled Travers.

"Precisely! Precisely!" He resumed the reading.

". . . will be on the platform to-night. There is one particular aspect of this evening's meeting concerning which Sir William would like to make a practical suggestion, and he has already ventured to put that suggestion into practical form. The subject of dumping will undoubtedly be referred to this evening by more than one speaker. Sir William has for some time been paying deliberately arranged visits to certain of the larger and more popular stores, and has collected evidence in direct form. This he has had suitably arranged and labelled so as to be self-explanatory and he is sending it by special hamper direct to the Albert Hall. . . ."

His lordship broke off in dismay. "You quite sure this is right, Heather?"

Heather nodded confidently. "Quite sure, sir. As I told you; I told Sir William's secretary that it wasn't my province, and got him to speak slowly. And I repeated it to him after I'd got it down."

Lord Zyon frowned more heavily still, glared at Travers' back, glared at Heather, then resumed—

". . . by special hamper direct to the Albert Hall. Sir William is certain that Lord Zyon will be able to make a most impressive use of the contents of the hamper in conjunction with the case against unrestricted dumping and its influence on unemployment. Sir William adds that he will most certainly see Lord Zyon at the meeting or before."

The final part, of course, was much more satisfactory. His lordship nodded. "He didn't say exactly when?"

"No, sir. That concluded the message."

"I see. . . . Push the bell, will you? . . . Most amazing business this, Travers! What's your idea?"

Percival entered, followed by a couple of footmen with the beginnings of the meal. Travers was dexterously placed on his lordship's right. He temporized over the question.

"I can't say that I have any ideas . . . at the moment. The thing is, is Sir William a sufficiently valuable ally? Is he worth placating—and would it be unwise to antagonize him?"

"We must certainly have him," said his lordship emphatically. "You know, I suppose, what he's doing at the moment? Confidential, of course, but you know?"

Durangos could afford to pay for information. Travers certainly did know—at least, he knew a merger was in process of formation; that Sir William was preparing to do for the haberdashery business—for shirts and socks—what other far-seeing people had done for tobacco and traffic. Still, he was guardedly non-committal.

"Yes, I think I've heard something about it. . . . But with regard to to-night. Do you mean to incorporate Sir William's experiment in your own speech, or did you think of putting up a wholly new speaker to tackle it?"

"Hm! Depends, I think." He had an idea— two ideas—three ideas. "We'll have the hamper along here and go into the whole thing. . . . Perhaps you could say something about it—after we've seen Sir William, of course. . . . Percival! Get me Sir William on the phone!"

Percival was a goodish time. The meal progressed normally to the cold meats and the potatoes baked in their jackets. The butler came back looking rather flurried.

"Sir William isn't in town, m'lord."

"Not in town! Where is he?"

"The butler informed me, m'lord, that Sir William went down to Mulberton a few—"

"Mulberton! Where's Mulberton?"

"It's a little town in West Somerset," said Travers quietly. "In the Exe Valley."

"Thank you. . . . Go on, Percival! What the devil are you waiting for?"

"Certainly, m'lord. Sir William went down to Mulberton about a fortnight ago, m'lord; for his principal vacation, I gathered, and has not returned to town since. They don't expect him before another fortnight, m'lord."

Zyon turned half angrily, half helplessly. "Perfectly preposterous! What's the idea?"

"The hamper's probably come on by train," suggested Travers. "Sir William has probably been amusing himself in his leisure by doing the labelling and so on, to which his message referred. He's coming to town to-night especially for the meeting. That's why he wasn't certain when he'd see you." The air cleared. The meal progressed as far as the Stilton; then—another idea.

"Percival! Get the Albert Hall! . . . No! Mortimer won't be there. . . . Yes! Get the Albert Hall! Somebody'll be there. Ask if a hamper has arrived . . . and have it sent on here at once. . . . By taxi if necessary."

On his return this time, the butler was much more at ease.

"A hamper *has* arrived, m'lord, and is being sent. It should be here in a matter of minutes, m'lord." The air cleared still further. The conversation almost degenerated into chatter. Then they moved off to the smoke-room, cool as a grotto and smelling faintly of old leather and terrifically expensive cigars. On the very heels of the coffee came the hamper, borne by a couple of footmen, Percival superintending from the rear. His lordship waved for it to be placed on the Persian rug, as a fourth corner to the triangle of chairs; gestured the hirelings away, then heaved himself out of his chair to have a look at it.

It was an almost new hamper, wicker-work still yellow. Stout rope lashed it round cunningly; three strands across and one lengthwise. Two labels stuck up from the ends, the printed writing so large that from where he sat Travers could read—

"Lord Zyon,
The Albert Hall,
LONDON."

and in red at the top—"Personal"—and again in red, at the bottom—"Urgent."

His lordship appeared, however, none too happy in his contemplation of Sir William's thoughtfulness. The hamper looked crude. It offended his sense of the fitting. Then he saw something that first surprised, then horrified.

"Good God! Is that a cabbage leaf?"

A cabbage leaf it was, protruding from under the lid. His lordship made a grimace, then began to feel very annoyed with the hamper. The annoyance brought a further query. He scowled at Heather.

"If he's motoring up from Somerset, why the devil didn't he bring the damn thing with him?"

Heather smiled placatingly. "That, I can't say, sir. Sir William is rather—er—direct, sometimes."

"Direct be damned!" Vaguely he felt the wretched hamper cutting clean across the comparative peace of mind he had felt when he entered the doors of his house an hour or so before.

"And what the devil are cabbage leaves for? People don't dump cabbages! . . . What's the idea, Travers?"

Travers was enjoying himself immensely. It was on the tip of his tongue to suggest that in the Promised Land—the portals of which his lordship was proposing that night to open—there was surely room for cabbages among the milk and honey. As it was he did smile slightly.

"Why not open it, sir . . . and find out?"

It was perfectly amazing how the air once more cleared. Heather and Zyon smiled at each other. Travers hopped up, fumbled for and found a pocket-knife. His intentions were spotted in time for such a breach of the proprieties to be happily prevented.

"No! no! no! Mr. Travers! . . . Er—Heather! Ring for Percival!"

The butler entered, received his instructions, and also found a pocket-knife. A few carving movements and the rope was through. A heave of the hamper and the butler had gathered up the loose ends of rope. Travers all at once noticed something extraordinary and grabbed an end.

"Rather peculiar this, sir! The back of the label's blank!"

They didn't see the point. Travers held the label over.

"You see! . . . It didn't come by rail or there'd have been the Company's label on the back. Sir William must have changed his mind and brought it up by road after all!"

"Then he might be here at any time!"

"Well—it rather looks like it."

His lordship grunted, then waved. "All right, Percival! . . . Let's have a look what's in it, Heather."

The major whipped back the lid. Nothing was to be seen but a few cabbage leaves, resting on a mass of sacking. He looked up blankly. Travers smiled.

"He's certainly packed it well! . . . Carry on, major! Let's see the worst!"

Heather felt round the edges, grasped the sacking at opposite corners to retain the cabbage leaves, then all in one movement got to his feet and whipped off the sacking. Then he stopped suddenly. Lord Zyon, looking down, saw nothing but a mass of black with one white blotch. Travers, peering round his lordship's shoulder, saw the same blackness and what looked like a melon in the corner of the hamper. Heather began to breathe rather quickly. He made a queer noise—then stammered out something. His lordship's eyes goggled as he stepped back, clutching Travers' arm.

"My God! . . . What is it?"

The question was one of hope against hope. He knew very well what it was—the body of a man, curled round artistically, head in one corner and knees drawn up to touch the chin. Perhaps the whisking away of the sacking had lessened the pressure on the head, for all at once it began to move. It shot upwards so that the face with its staring eyes looked at the ceiling.

Travers held his breath, then suddenly felt very sick. Zyon drew further back towards the mantelpiece.

"Don't touch it, Heather! . . . Don't touch it!" and he gasped.

Travers all at once found himself going forward. He looked down at the face. Under the chin was a blackish mass of matted hair. On the collar was a red patch and a long streak. Across the throat was a gash. He shut down the lid, then moved back—not knowing quite what he was doing, till Zyon clutched his arm again.

"Who is it, Travers?" and he pointed.

Travers moistened his lips. "Sir William Griffiths—that's who it is!"

"But it can't be!"

Travers looked at him. "I tell you it *is*!"

"Griffiths!" Heather stared as if he were looking clean through the wall beyond. "You remember what that secretary said? He said Sir William would be on the platform to-night! That's why—"

"That'll do!" said Travers curtly. "Go out— run like hell and get a policeman!" He glanced at Zyon's face. "You'd better sit down, sir. I'll get Percival to bring in some brandy."

He shepherded him to the nearest chair, swivelled it round with back to the hamper and saw him seated. Then he nipped out to the hall. A footman was there, looking through the open front door by which Heather had already vanished.

"You!" snapped Travers. "Tell Mr. Percival to bring back that rope and the labels he took out of the smoke-room. Bring them to me, in the library. Hurry up!"

In the library he rang up Scotland Yard. Super-intendent Wharton was in. One minute and he was through. Another minute and he was hanging up.

Percival was standing by with the rope ends and the labels. For the first time for years—so one imagined—he was looking surprised.

"The things you asked for, sir. . . . Anything the matter, sir?"

"Plenty!" said Travers. "Take his lordship some brandy . . . in the smoke-room."

Percival scurried off. Travers stood there thinking . . . and the thought that suddenly came to him was fantastic enough to make, him hold his breath for a moment at the sheer horror of it. Heather was right! Whoever the swine was who had done it, he'd tried to stage a cold-blooded piece of cynicism that was terrifying—insane—obscene! *Sir William should have been on the platform that night!* A meeting of consecration . . . the high, cathedral-like dome of a roof . . . the altar-like erection . . . the priest . . . and the sacrifice! Again he moistened his lips nervously, fumbled for his glasses, replaced them, then went slowly back to the smoke-room.

CHAPTER III
THE LUCK TURNS FOR SANDERS

HEATHER WAS fortunate in finding his policeman.

He ran full tilt into one at the corner of Park Mansions, spluttered his story, then set off back the couple of hundred yards, adding further explanations as he got his wind again. The pair of them took at a run the four steps that led to the front door, then the door was closed behind them—and by a third man. He had joined them during the last fifty yards of that rapid walk, had padded up the steps behind them, and slipped through the door and was now closing it with head averted. Percival and a footman came into the hall at the same moment, and there was a sort of general mix-up.

"His lordship in the smoke-room?" Heather asked quickly.

"Yes, sir!" Percival regarded the policeman impassively.

"All right! You'd better be handy in case you're wanted. Come along, officer!"

Travers added to the mix-up by appearing at the smoke-room door.

"Oh, Heather! Will you be so good as to get Sir William's town house again. Get hold of that secretary by hook or by crook—the one who rang up. Get all the information you can! I'll see to the officer."

Heather drew off to the library. Travers turned back to the smoke-room, the officer on his heels and the stranger close up. Percival took him for a necessary concomitant of the law; the officer took him for a member of the household who had a perfect right to go wherever he was going. Lord Zyon was far too upset to be more than barely aware of his presence. Travers, taking him for a plain-clothes man who had been with the policeman, saw no reason to say anything. The stranger, realizing that the colossal bluff had worked, effaced himself against the wall of the smoke-room, where he stood by the door, hat in hand.

"Lord Zyon is very distressed," explained Travers. "It's been a great shock."

"Who'd you say, sir?" asked the officer.

Travers explained further. Out came the notebook.

"Spelt with a 'y,' isn't it, sir?"

"That's right."

"And who might you be, sir?"

"My name's Travers." He spelt it. Down it went.

"And who was the gent who came to fetch me, sir?"

Travers explained that—and watched the note-taking. When he sent Heather for a policeman, it had been more with the idea of getting him out of the way than of having him return with a real live officer of the law. Ringing the Yard made all that unnecessary. The officer, in fact, was a white elephant, and looked like being a nuisance.

"If it interests you," added Travers, "I've already rung up Scotland Yard. I'm a personal friend of Superintendent Wharton. He'll be here in a few minutes."

Travers watched the pencil heavily pressed.

"Friend—of—Superintendent—Wharton."

The notebook was closed.

"And what's all this about a body in a hamper, sir?"

Travers turned back the lid. The other had a look, then shook his head solemnly.

"Know who he is, sir?"

"Yes . . . Sir William Griffiths."

The other's eyes opened wide. "What! the millionaire, sir!"

"That's right. . . . The financier." He took off his glasses and blinked away as he polished them. "Of course I don't want to interfere with what may be your duties, but if I were you I'd leave all this to the Yard people. If you prefer to wait till Superintendent Wharton gets here . . ."

The officer looked hard at Travers, then ran a quick eye over his lordship. The matter-of-factness of the one and the obvious importance of the other; the opulence of the room and the smooth efficiency of everything, all had a cumulative effect that was irresistible.

"Very good, sir! . . . Perhaps I'd better ring up the station, sir."

"Do, please!" said Travers. "Come along to the library!" and he led the way. The stranger opened the door for them, then closed it. When Travers got back, almost at once, there he was kneeling by the hamper and making a rapid survey of the contents. Then he picked up the sacking that lay incongruously on the rug, and shook it. He gave Travers a long look. Lord Zyon, from his chair across the room, watched the pair of them.

"Cabbage leaves! . . . They came . . . with that?"

Travers nodded. "The sacking was wedged round the body and the leaves were on top."

"But why cabbage leaves?"

"Gawd knows!" said Travers testily. He turned to his lordship, now looking much his old self again. "How're you feeling now, sir?"

"Better, Travers . . . thanks. Very good of you to—er—see us through like this."

"That's all right, sir. As soon as the police get here, the whole thing'll be over in five minutes, as far as you're concerned." He turned back towards the fireplace. The plain-clothes man was now bending over the hamper.

"I say! I don't think I'd touch anything if I were you!"

The other got to his feet. "How'd this hamper get here?"

Travers told him in very few words, and ran his eye over him at the same time. He was best part of six foot and somewhere in the late thirties. His clothes were shabby rather than workaday. But his face was the startling thing. The clean-shaven cheeks were drawn in, then curved out to the grooves that ran down the thin, hard mouth, while the grey eyes were those of a fanatic. Travers felt them boring into him, till he turned his own away. And yet there was nothing offensive about the man; nothing but a hard efficiency that was disconcerting. His voice was like himself—hard and direct, but courteous for all that. Travers felt a sudden alarm.

"Who *are* you, by the way?"

The question was ignored. He pointed to the hamper. "He's in evening dress. That looks suggestive!"

"I asked you who you are!" repeated Travers. "Are you a plain-clothes man?"

The other shook his head. "No! . . . I'm a reporter . . . on one of his lordship's papers."

"Reporter!" Travers was knocked clean off his perch. Lord Zyon scrambled up hastily.

"What's that you say? A reporter?"

The other stood his ground as his lordship came forward.

"What's your name?"

"Sanders, sir."

"One of *my* papers, you say?"

"Yes, sir . . . The *Evening Record.*"

His lordship glared. "Then you've got in here under false pretences!"

There seemed to be some danger of people losing their sense of proportion. Travers cut in quickly.

"That's all right, sir! Sanders was only doing what he's paid for. . . . May I deal with him?" He turned to the reporter. "How'd you get in here?"

Sanders looked him clean in the eye. "I was sent round on the chance of seeing Lord Zyon and getting some late information about to-night; then I saw a man rush out of the house and come back with a policeman." He shrugged his shoulders. "So I bluffed my way in."

"I see," said Travers, and nodded. "The *Evening Record* ought to be proud of you. . . . But—er—don't you think you'd better go now, before the Yard people get here? . . . They might keep you here."

The other's face showed the first sign of anything that lay beneath the surface. "That's very sporting of you, sir."

He cocked an ear as Heather's voice was heard with the policeman's in the hall, then moved like a streak across to the window. In a jiffy he whipped it up, put his foot to the sill and leaped across the window-box to the gravel. He stuck his head in again.

"Sanders is the name, if you want to try the *Evening Record* to verify," and he was gone. Travers went quickly across and closed the window again.

....

What happened to Sanders, is best related here, in its context.

A quarter of an hour after he left Lord Zyon's house by means of the window, a taxi drew up outside the gigantic building which housed the bulk of the Associated Press, including the *Record* and its evening satellite. Sanders had the door open twenty yards before the taxi slowed. He was out like lightning, shoved half a crown into the driver's hand and was round the corner and into Pike Lane at such a pace that the driver scarcely saw the whisk of him. At the subsidiary porch which forms the special entrance for the *Evening Record* he actually pushed the uniformed attendant on one side, bolted through the swing-doors and made for the elevator.

On the third floor he skirted the restaurant and circled round to the News Room. At one of the glaringly yellow tables a fluffy blonde sat typing.

"Where's Mr. Rodman?" snapped Sanders.

The girl gave a start, then smiled. "My word! you did give me a turn! . . . Who was it you wanted?"

"Mr. Rodman! . . . Hurry up! It's urgent!"

"I think he's in his room." She got up. "What name, please?"

Sanders was already across the room. "Never mind the name!"

He pushed out into the corridor, listened for a moment at Rodman's door, tapped, then looked in. The News Editor was there, jawing away at a reporter and re-enforcing his remarks with a series of jabs of his pencil. He stared at Sanders as if he didn't recognize him, then his eyes opened wide. "Sanders! . . . What on earth next!"

Sanders had grabbed a chair and was dragging it with him in his progress across the room.

"I've a story for you, Rodman—the biggest you've ever handled. Straight from the horse's mouth!"

Rodman looked at him. As he sat there, straddling the chair, there was a directness about Sanders that was impressive. Rodman turned to the reporter.

"All right, Trott! Cut that down, then turn over to Bill. . . . Get a move on!" He waited till the door closed. "Well, what's the story?"

Sanders leaned his arms across the chair-back. "Anybody rung up about me?"

"About you?" Rodman shook his head.

"Right! Then I'll tell you the story as soon as we've had an understanding. If this turns out big —and it's going to be a bigger thing than you've ever dreamed of in your life—then where do I come in? Do I handle it—or not?"

Rodman looked uncomfortable. "Well . . . what is it? Come across, and I'll tell you."

The other shook his head. "Oh, no! I'm giving you this chance because you're a good sort. And you've been lucky. When the *Mercury* sank, you got shifted over here. Oh, no!"—he waved his hand—"I'm not jealous. I wasn't then—and I'm not now. I was damn glad. As I said, you were a good sort. Only, you see, I wasn't lucky. I don't want to whine, but I've had a pretty rotten time. You don't know that."

Rodman looked up to catch the other's eyes burning into him. He lowered his own. "Perhaps I do know. . . . But you mustn't blame me. I've had my work cut out to hold down this job—"

"Who's blaming you? But you can do something now. Do I handle my own story—or don't I?"

"It's a crime story?"

"It is—and the biggest for years. All the inside dope is yours . . . now! Wait till Spruce gets round to the Yard Press Room and you'll have what they hand you out—and that'll be damn-all."

Rodman wasn't prepared to throw his Special Crime Reporter to the lions without at least a protest.

"If you take over, it's going to be pretty hard lines on Spruce."

"Hard lines!" Sanders sneered. "Your idea of what constitutes hard lines and mine differ slightly." He got up briskly. "Sorry and all that, but I don't give a damn about Spruce. It's my terms or nothing. One minute and the story goes to the *Wire*."

Rodman shot out his hand for the pad.

"Right-ho! Have it your own way."

Sanders sat down again. "Just a moment. You've got heaps of time for the 6.30, and you can't make it before. Just one other thing before I begin . . . a personal one. You know what this game is; why I've got to sit here, like a swine . . . trying blackmail. Terms—money terms—I leave to you, because you'll do the right thing. . . . But there's something else. If we make a big thing of this—and we shall!—how do I stand for a permanent job?"

Rodman leaned back in his chair and looked at him. Something queer seemed to have come over Sanders since he'd seen him last. Why the devil couldn't he see reason?

"Why are you acting like this? Do you think I can guarantee my own job? . . . Have a little sense, man, for God's sake . . . I'll do what I can. I can't say more than that."

"That's good enough for me," said Sanders quietly. "But not the reporters' room, mind you! There was a time when I'd have been glad to have that . . . but I'm not crawling back there now. That goes then?"

"It goes with me! Provided, of course, you realize—"

"Damn what I realize! . . . Now listen to this. And before I begin, if anybody rings you up, you're to say I am—and was—a regular reporter on the staff."

"What's the idea?"

"You'll see in a minute. I had to bluff Lord Zyon into thinking—"

Rodman's eyes bulged like marbles. "Lord Zyon! . . . What's he . . . is he murdered?"

Sanders smiled grimly. "Not yet! Now listen to this!"

. . . .

Five minutes later the News Room of the *Evening Record* was like an ant-heap. Rodman was rushing round like a man possessed. Reporters were sent scurrying in all directions; to Park Terrace in search of fragments, to the Albert Hall for news of the hamper and to see if any reverberations of the tragedy had yet reached the scene of the evening's demonstration; even to the Press Room at the Yard for any statement that might be ready. The photographers' morgue had been scoured for pictures of the town houses of both Lord Zyon and the dead man, and the artist was already at work on the former with a super-imposed drawing which should interest and elucidate. Then, of course, there had to be photographs of his lordship and the murdered magnate. The general lay-out of the front page had already been roughed. The scoop was to be more than a scoop—it was to be a riot!—a roar that should rumble through Fleet Street like a Zeppelin bomb. Under the banner headlines, three-column captions should shriek between the photos of the two magnates. Below, sprawling across the page, was to be a drawing of the hamper, as Sanders had described it and sketched it roughly for the artist.

Spruce, the Special Crime Reporter, just back from the inquest on the victim of the Ilford shop murder, arrived in the thick of it. Rodman buttonholed him on the way to a sprint to the phone. Then when Lord Zyon *was* rung up, it was his secretary who spoke. Oh, no! the evening's plans would not be altered. The meeting would stand. His lordship would send an official communication to the paper.

Out bolted Rodman to get Sanders going and finish the pacification of Spruce—then the bell rang again. Was that the News Editor? Had the reporter Sanders come in? Rodman said he had— then added unblushingly that he'd gone again. He also asked the voice, which had coldly described itself as Scotland Yard, if there was anything they wanted done; and at the frigid negative, rang off.

Spruce was still waiting; so was the stenographer. The Special Crime Reporter was taking the matter philosophically. After all, he hadn't been any too long at the game himself, and it wouldn't do to quarrel with one's bread and butter. Sanders, coming over with Rodman, shot a look at him, then held out his hand.

"Glad to see you again, Spruce! There's going to be a big thing in this for you, as you'll see when you hear the dope. Pull me up if you want to know anything."

Luckily the story had come in at the perfect moment; nothing much to scrap except the anticipatory write-ups of the Albert Hall affair, and Spruce's inquest account to go over to column seven. It was half an hour before the machines need start, and the odds a thousand to one against a competitor having an inkling of what was happening. In the room was no sound but the click of the typewriter and the staccato of Sanders' voice as he rattled off his story with the fluency and instinct for colour that only the old hands have as second nature. As he spoke you could see the interior of the room; you heard the voices and you felt the horror. Then, almost imperceptibly, you viewed the figure of Lord Zyon rising heroically from the tragic ashes—the great financier, the man who juggled with millions, the man who moulded the views of a nation, the man at whose call came secretaries and soft-footed servants, the man who had surrounded himself with wealth expressed in impeccable taste—and yet a man struck as other men are! Overwhelmed though he was with grief at the death—the dastardly death—of an old friend, he yet could heroically set aside that grief in order to devote himself and the great organs which he controlled to the task of bringing to justice the fiend who had flaunted . . . and so on.

Rodman sat mesmerized. Spruce was like a man fascinated; not so much at the story as at the enormity of the stroke of luck that had come Sanders' way.

"My God, Sanders! It's wonderful! . . . You'll have Lord Zyon feeding out of your hand!"

Rodman gathered up the typewritten sheets, his face one immense smile.

"This'll make 'em sit up! . . . Want to look 'em over, Fred?"

Sanders apparently noticed nothing of that expressive change of address. As he rose he seemed to dominate the room. His face alone showed nothing of the general excitement; if anything the scarcely perceptible smile was indicative of ironic amusement.

"Don't think so . . . My name's not to be mentioned, by the way. Zyon mightn't be any too pleased at having his consecration bunkum pushed out."

Rodman smiled feebly as he pushed the bell for the foreman printer and got to work. Sanders looked at his watch, then sat there waiting till the room was clear again.

"Anything you want, Spruce?"

"Don't think there is. . . . Where are you going? Mulberton?"

Sanders nodded. "That's it. . . . On spec. You carry on here. Do what you like, provided you don't crowd out my stuff. That suit you?"

It was generous, and Spruce said so. Sanders gave the same dry smile.

"Anything you want, Rodman?"

"Can't think of anything. . . . Going now?"

"Yes," said Sanders. "Three-thirty from Paddington. You'll arrange with the *Daily*?"

"Oh, rather! Getting anything through tonight?"

Sanders nodded determinedly. "I'll get something through all right! If I should get stuck, you've no objection to the Taunton *Messenger* taking it and sending on? You know what country phones are like!"

"Why not? You get the stuff here. We don't give a damn how!"

Sanders still hesitated. For the first time he seemed to be losing something of that icy self-possession.

"May I see you a moment . . . in your room?"

"My dear fellow! Come along!"

They were back again in a couple of minutes. Spruce turned his back tactfully and lighted a cigarette. But he heard the tail-end of the conversation.

"Well, take care of yourself! . . . How's your wife, by the way? Mrs. Rodman was only asking after her—"

Sanders' voice cut across that kindliness like a cold douche.

"She's too late then. . . . Six months too late."

Spruce turned his head, but Sanders had gone. He looked enquiringly at Rodman, but Rodman said nothing.

"Well," said Spruce, "we're certainly going to set 'em alight, as you said. What was the matter with Sanders?"

"Wanted the usual advance!" said Rodman curtly.

"Hard-up, was he?" He flicked the ash off the cigarette. "Do you know, I'm damn glad it was Sanders who clicked like that! . . . Queer devil! . . . Had the hell of a time, by the look of him. . . . Want me to take those reports?"

All this was related to Chief-Inspector Norris before six o'clock that evening, by the various people concerned. "All this" is hardly correct. Rodman, for instance, lied heroically. He took no chances on Lord Zyon's knowing that Sanders was a free-lance reporter and not on the staff of the *Evening Record* at the time he had entered with Heather and the policeman. To be frank, moreover, Rodman was doing himself an equally good turn, since there might have been a ricochet in his lordship's annoyance. It was only when he was positive which way Lord Zyon was going to jump, that Rodman, a day later, added as a minor and additional scoop in the columns of the *Evening Record*, the story of the romantic reporter and the value of taking time by the forelock.

CHAPTER IV
ENTER THE LAW

It was a miniature regiment which descended that early afternoon upon the peaceful austerities of Park Terrace. With Wharton was Chief-Inspector Norris, his right-hand man. On him would fall the bulk of the routine work and the presentation of facts; indeed, if the affair looked like being reasonably straightforward, he would take over its entire conduct, once Wharton had given the word.

Perhaps the reason why those two worked together so well was the old one of dissimilarity. Norris was a ramrod of a man; policeman every inch of him. As Wharton once told him, if he'd had a moustache he'd have waxed the ends. But he was thorough—meticulously so. The facts that he presented were definitely facts. And he had somewhere a sense of humour, which association with Wharton had made somewhat mute, but none the less present.

Wharton, of course, was a detective in the grand manner. He loved the dramatic and the scope for acting, the manipulation of the net and the narrowing of the meshes. His memory was colossal and his tenacity inexhaustible, and best of all, when he left the beaten track to chase an intuition he rarely went far wrong. But they made a good couple—Norris all on the surface, earnest, painstaking, superbly competent; Wharton never so happy as when tunnelling; deceptively genial, missing nothing, and a living example of the aphorism that the main purpose of speech is for the concealment of thoughts.

The party crowded together in the entrance hall, Percival like a sheep dog regarding a herd of buffaloes. Then Travers appeared.

"Where's the hamper?" asked Wharton.

"In there—the smoke-room," Travers told him.

"Anybody else there?"

"No! we're all in the library. There's a policeman with the hamper."

Wharton looked round at the senior surgeon. "What about it, Menzies?"

Menzies nodded, whatever that might mean.

"Right-ho!" said Wharton. "Take what men you want and carry on. I'll be in as soon as I've got the general hang. . . . Come along, Norris! . . . and you—and you!" He picked out half a dozen men. "Now, Mr. Travers; if you're ready!"

It was doubtful what Lord Zyon thought as the party entered, but whatever he was thinking he had to do it quickly. As the main body lined up inside the door—Norris a little in advance—Wharton went forward like a shot out of a gun, hand outstretched.

"Lord Zyon, I believe." He clutched the very warm, cushion-like hand. "Most distressing affair, sir. Must have been a great shock to you." He swivelled round on Heather.

"My secretary—Major Heather," his lordship explained. Out went Wharton's fist again.

But one thing both of them were apparently recognizing—that they were in the presence of somebody who was going to get things done and with the minimum of fuss. Here was a man who obviously knew his job. The whole business was going to prove to have been a nightmare after all. The sun really *was* shining—

"Now then, gentlemen," came Wharton's voice. "Who's telling the story? You, my lord?"

"Heather, I think," said Travers. "He's got it all ready."

Heather began. He got as far as the call from the supposed secretary, then Wharton held out his hand for the copy of the message and read it for himself.

"You've checked up on this? You've spoken to Sir William's secretary over the phone?"

"Oh, yes!" said Heather. "There isn't any secretary! While Sir William's away, a sort of lady secretary calls at the house in the morning and sorts out the correspondence. She was there this morning from ten to half-past eleven." He consulted the pad. "Smithson, her name is. Miss Smithson."

"And Sir William was definitely at Mulberton?"

"Everybody says so. They had a communication from him at the town house only two days ago."

"Hm!" Wharton made a face. "Just a moment, major!" He had a word with Norris; then, "Bird and Rowley! You go to Eaton Square and get this Miss Smithson's address. Find out if she knows anything or if anybody's been asking her questions about Sir William. One of you find out from the servants if anybody's been doing the same thing round there. Report to the Yard."

"Now then, Major!" went on Wharton. "If you don't mind carrying on."

The story progressed as far as the hamper and its arrival.

"Can we find out who took it over?" Wharton asked.

"Certainly!" said Heather, and pushed the bell for Percival. It turned out to be the butler himself who'd taken the hamper over at the door. He knew his lordship was interested and had therefore seen to the job himself.

"Came in a taxi—did it?"

"Yes, sir!"

"You'd recognize the driver again if you saw him?"

"Yes, sir!"

Wharton turned round again. "Bates! you get that going! See if the same man took it over at the Albert Hall. Smith, you and Porter go along to the Albert Hall as well. Find out how the hamper got there and who took it over. Full description and everything. Get a move on!"

Then, of course, there were two—Norris and one other. Before Wharton could resume, the phone went. Heather picked up the receiver, and his conversation has already been heard. He hung up before Travers could stop him.

"About that reporter—"

"What reporter?" asked Wharton.

Travers gave a quick outline. Wharton took the receiver and his conversation has also been heard.

"Pretty smart chap that!" He beamed on the company in general, then addressed himself to Zyon in particular. "No wonder your papers are what they are, m'lord, when you've got enterprising young fellows like that about!"

Norris caught Travers' eye and winked rapidly. Travers blew his nose, then found Wharton addressing him.

"How'd he strike you?"

"Cool—and efficient," said Travers.

Wharton thought for a moment. Then he thought aloud. "He might possibly have seen somebody hanging about suspiciously before he came in. Wonder where we could get hold of him for a minute."

"Mulberton! . . . if he's all that sharp," said Norris quickly.

"You mean, chasing the story?"

"That's right. . . . In any case there'd be no harm trying to get him at Paddington."

Wharton nodded, consulted the Bradshaw which Heather found for him, then turned to Travers.

"Describe him, will you? Clothes—face—everything."

Travers gave a description; a bit flowery perhaps, but good enough. Wharton nodded over to his last man.

"You hear that, Turner? Get along to Paddington and see if you can pick him up. Find out if he saw anything suspicious and ask him at the same time if they've got anything fresh round at the *Record* office. Report to the Yard."

He looked at his watch. "Now, m'lord; we hope we shan't keep you more than a minute or two at the most. We know you're a busy man—and to-day in particular. Five minutes and we'll be gone for good. . . . This hamper. Any reason why it should be sent to you? I mean, any special connection between Sir William and yourself?"

His lordship explained, concisely and well, the deal concluded some months before. For the life of him he couldn't see any other connection between the dead man and himself.

"What about his political convictions, sir?" asked Norris.

Lord Zyon was remarkably tactful.

"Well, Sir William was a Gladstonian. A fine tradition, of course; but whether suitable for modern conditions . . . well, that's a very debatable point."

"Exactly!" said Wharton. "What we mean is, were you surprised to hear that Sir William was going to be on the platform to-night?"

"Surprised! Of course I was surprised! . . . Wasn't I, Travers?"

"You certainly didn't seem to have anticipated Sir William's being there," corroborated Travers.

"He was in sympathy with the movement with which your lordship is identified—and very fortunately identified?"

Lord Zyon shook his head. "You really mustn't ask me to describe another man's political opinions! If you want to know what the general opinion was, then I'd say he was a bigoted Free Trader. Mind you," he added hastily, "that was no reason why he shouldn't change his mind. Did he send us a subscription, Heather?"

"Ten pounds, sir!"

His lordship's shrug was eloquent. "You see!"

"But you were pleased to think he was coming?"

"Certainly I was. One sinner that repenteth, you know!" Heather tittered politely. "Also, he that's for us is not against us."

Wharton's nod was probably a tribute to his lordship's unexpected knowledge of the Authorized Version.

"What I want to get at, m'lord, is this. What was the point in that hamper being sent to the Albert Hall, and addressed to you? Now if Sir William had told anybody he was going to be there, then there'd be some point in the joke. A horrible joke—a grisly joke; but a species of joke all the same. You see the idea, m'lord?"

Apparently Lord Zyon didn't. Wharton decided to waste no more time. He held out his hand.

"That's all for the present, sir. We'll have the hamper removed at once. If I might venture to suggest it—and to you, Major—the major might remain here with the phone. The bell's sure to start ringing like wildfire as soon as that paper gets on the street. One of my men can come in and take down anything that comes through for us. . . . Good-by, sir! I hope we haven't troubled you unduly. I'd hoped to have the pleasure of hearing you speak to-night." He shook his head. Norris once more caught Travers' eye and winked rapidly. "This terrible business is going to spoil that, I'm afraid. . . . Good-by, Major! . . . You coming, Mr. Travers?"

. . . .

In the smoke-room, the body of the dead man lay curled up on a ground-sheet. On the table lay the contents of the pockets and the finger-print men were going over them. The photographers were standing by.

"Well?" said Wharton breezily.

"Dropped out of the hamper like a jelly out of a mould!" said Menzies, about as sensitive to the presence of death as a retailer of skinned rabbits. "What did it?"

"I should say a knife. . . . Must have been held very rigid; then flicked across clean . . . like that!"

"Any chance whatever of it being self-inflicted?"

"Self-inflicted, hell!" said Menzies. "He couldn't have started so cleanly and kept the knife at the same angle all the way through. . . . And there're other reasons."

Wharton grunted approval. "And how long ago do you make it?"

"Ah!" said Menzies. "Now you're asking." He made a series of faces before venturing on a tentative commitment. "Strictly unofficial and very roughly . . . between eight and ten last night."

"You're not prejudiced by the dinner clothes." asked Wharton.

"Did you ever know me prejudiced?"

"Well . . . no!" admitted Wharton. "Still, the fact remains that he *is* in dinner clothes!"

"The stomach content'll soon settle all that!" said Menzies. "What about getting him away?"

"Might as well. . . . Notice anything unusual yourself?"

Menzies got out a cigarette. "Don't know that there was. Shoes seem perfectly clean."

Norris happened to be looking at them at that very moment. Wharton went over.

"Soles absolutely unsoiled," said Norris. "He was killed indoors for a fiver!"

"Not necessarily," said Wharton. "Still they don't look as if they've been cleaned to hide anything up. They're just dirty enough. What's the colour of the soil down there? Red, isn't it?" Norris thought it was. Travers thought so too. "Put 'em aside!" said Wharton. "Run over 'em for prints, then let Harbord have 'em. Get everything there is on the hamper—not that it's much use. It's probably been messed about by half Europe. Any prints on that stuff?"

"That stuff" was a silver pencil, a notecase containing about £40 in Treasury notes, a thin, gold watch and some loose change. A few prints were reported—those of the dead man.

Wharton grubbed round for a minute or two himself, then shook his head as if satisfied.

"All I know about him is he didn't smoke. . . . Well, get everything together and go over 'em again. Leave one of those cabbage leaves behind. Let Harbord have the sacking."

Travers had to turn his head away during the re-placing of the body. Why Wharton and Norris were still waiting, he didn't know. Wharton followed the hamper out of the room. When he came back again, he seemed rather pleased.

"His nibs has gone out! The secretary's in the smoke-room. I told him we'd only be a few minutes. Talk things over here, shall we?"

"It'll certainly save time, sir," said Norris. "What about that rope and labels that were on the hamper, Mr. Travers?"

Travers fetched them. On his heels came Percival with some lemon squash! Then pipes were out and they got down to business.

"About those labels," said Wharton. "As you say, Mr. Travers, it looks as if the hamper didn't come by rail. And yet presumably he was killed in Mulberton. Was the body brought to London by road?"

"I'd say that everything depended on the call from that fake secretary," said Norris. "If it was a trunk call, then it's easy. Still, whoever he was he had the body nice and handy while he was ringing up. You remember he was careful to ask when Lord Zyon would be back—"

"Away from the Albert Hall!" corrected Wharton.

"That's it, sir! When he'd be away from the Albert Hall. The call was exactly midday. What time'd you leave there, Mr. Travers?"

"Twelve-twenty—almost to the dot."

"Then as soon as he'd phoned and learned that Lord Zyon was at the Albert Hall and coming home again at twelve-thirty, he put the body in something—a private car of his own, for instance—and took it along to the Albert Hall. He watched Lord Zyon go, then delivered the hamper. Of course he must have been a man who knew all about the meeting—to-night's meeting."

"That's not difficult!" growled Wharton. "The whole of the Associated Press has been broadcasting it for days. Let's leave this end altogether and try the other. Menzies says he was killed just after dinner last night. Now listen to this and tell me where I'm wrong. He was killed in Mulberton, or near it. Why? Well, suppose he was killed in his own house—Combe Cottage, or whatever they call it. The fact that he wore evening clothes showed he wasn't alone. There were servants in the house—"

"They might have bolted, or *he* might have bolted; I mean if there was only one servant," suggested Norris.

"We're not talking about mutiny on the high seas," said Wharton. "This is a murder case. If whoever did it, bolted, then the case is over before it's begun. . . . However, I say he *wasn't* killed in his own house, or he'd have been missed. Whoever was at Mulberton would have got anxious and rung up the town house. There'd have been a hue and cry. . . . Very well then. We must assume he wasn't killed in his own house; therefore he was killed elsewhere. But wherever he was killed, he had dinner clothes on; therefore he was wherever he'd set out to go—to the house of friends or to a hotel. But he *wasn't* killed there because they'd have missed him, just as the people in his own house d have missed him. Where then was he killed?"

"Well, sir, if we're to follow your arguments to a logical conclusion, he wasn't killed at all I He's still alive!"

Wharton ignored that. "Where was he killed, Mr. Travers?"

Travers shook his head. "Don't know!"

"He was killed *between the two*. He was killed on the way from Combe Cottage *to* somewhere. Why? Because he left Combe Cottage to go somewhere, and the people there thought he had got to where he was going to. That's why they didn't worry about him. But he never got to where he was going to. The people there didn't worry either, because they naturally imagined something had turned up to prevent him coming after all! That's why nobody missed him. Am I right?"

"You may not be right," smiled Travers, "but you're most ingenious. Your theory presupposes that he was going somewhere to dinner. You'll know that by the stomach content."

Wharton nodded. "If the stomach content says he had dined, then I'd say he was going somewhere *after* dinner—say to bridge, or for a chat."

"All right," said Travers. "We'll leave that. But why shouldn't the people where he was going have rung up Combe Cottage to ask why he didn't turn up?"

"Good! I'm glad you asked that. It tells me he wasn't going to friends after all. He must have been going to a hotel, where they wouldn't care so much. As far as they were concerned, he merely didn't turn up."

"Have it your own way," said Travers. "But your theory also presupposes that he went *alone*. Either the person he went with was his murderer or else he'd have reported him missing. A chauffeur would have known, for instance, that he'd his master somewhere—at the hotel, we'll say."

Wharton nodded.

"Now if he went alone somewhere, there are three methods of getting to a place—walking, by car or by train. But he didn't walk; that is if you accept the evidence of the shoes. He didn't go by train, because that also involves a certain amount of walking, and it also admits that he was killed on the train. That'd make all that hamper business rather awkward. Therefore he was killed in a car—and he drove himself."

"The shoes will show traces of that," said Norris. "There's bound to be microscopical traces on them somewhere."

Travers suddenly smiled. Then he began polishing his glasses.

"If I might mention it, can't you discover all this much more easily down at Mulberton itself?"

Wharton smiled too—ironically. "The impatience of youth! What do you think we've been here talking things over for? We had to get some idea where he *was* killed. When we knew we had to go to Mulberton, we still had to find out *which* of us had to go." He gave that annoying little grunt of his. "Now then, Norris I What do you think about it?"

Norris wasn't ready. "You move a bit too quickly for me, sir! . . . I should say—off-hand— there's most to do at this end."

"I don't know." Wharton shook his head. "It's the *silence* down there that I don't like. . . . And that hamper. Where'd it most likely come from? This end or that?"

Norris picked up the cabbage leaf. "I'd say this points to that end."

"If it comes to that," said Travers, "what were the cabbage leaves doing there at all?"

Norris saw which way the pendulum was swinging.

"You think you'll go to Mulberton, sir?"

"Yes. . . . I think I will," said Wharton slowly. He looked at his watch. "Hour and a half before the express. We'd better run through quickly what's got to be done this end."

"I'll leave you to it for a moment if you don't mind," said Travers. "I'd rather like to call up somebody. It might be interesting."

In the library, Heather and Wharton's men were doing themselves well over tea.

"How's business?" smiled Travers.

"Rather slack at the moment," said Heather. "We've switched some over to the Albert Hall."

"Good!" said Travers and took off the receiver. "We'll try stirring them up from this end. Shaftesbury 772!"

"Hallo! That the Travelogue Film Company? . . . Is Colonel Pendry about by any chance? . . . Right! I'll hold on."

A few moments' wait and Pendry apparently arrived. Two minutes' conversation and Travers hung up again, looking quite pleased. A temporary and flippant farewell, and he was out of the room again. In the smoke-room Wharton and Norris were still discussing details.

"Why not a broadcast appeal to-night about the hamper?" Norris was asking. "We know the weight and colour and how it was tied and the size and everything."

"Splendid!" said Wharton. "Send it out from the press-room too." He got up and stretched his legs. "Anything important send along to Mulberton police station."

"Something that ought to interest you," said Travers. "You remember Tim Griffiths?"

"Tim Griffiths? Of course I do!"

"Well, I just rang up Silbermann's—the film people. Colonel Pendry tells me that Tim Griffiths is down there, at Combe Cottage. He should have come up to town to-day—arriving to-night—but this morning they got a wire from him saying he'd been detained. The visit was a rather urgent one too."

"Hm!" said Wharton. "You mean Tim Griffiths was down there last night, whoever else wasn't. . . . And it also looks as if something had happened— that he knew about."

"Any point in my going to see Colonel Pendry personally?" asked Norris.

"Why not?" said Travers. "I'll give you the address."

Wharton nodded brightly. "Why don't you go round with Norris yourself?"

Travers looked at him. "Well . . . to tell the truth, I rather thought of going with *you*."

"Going with me!"

"That's right!" said Travers solemnly. "You see, if I take you down in the Bentley, you'll get there just as soon as in the express. If you go by train, you won't be able to get back again till midday tomorrow. If you want to go anywhere when you get there, you'll have to hire a car. Also I know Tim Griffiths many times better than you do . . . and there's quite a lot of things you'd like to know about him. Also I think I can tell you why the hamper was sent to the Albert Hall—"

"And why was it?" asked Wharton, quick flash.

Travers shook his head. "The impatience of age!"

Wharton looked at him again, then decided.

"All right. . . . Get your things together and we'll go. Don't forget, Norris. Police Station, Mulberton; anything urgent."

CHAPTER V
THE OTHER END

WHEN HE'D READ through Sanders' story of the afternoon's happenings, in one of the half-dozen copies of the *Evening Record* with which he'd provided himself, Wharton, chiefly for want of something better to do to pass the time, had listened to Travers' various arguments. He had even appeared interested if not too encouraging. Only a maniac, thought Wharton, would deliberately encourage into argument, and exposition especially, the man who held the wheel of a car that was doing anything up to eighty in the straight. At the rear of the new Bentley sat Palmer, shipped as relief driver for part of the homeward journey of a hundred and eighty miles. At the moment they were well inside schedule and Travers' scheme to make Mulberton by dark looked like coming off.

As for theories, the cabbage leaves—according to Travers—had been put in as camouflage, with edges artistically protruding, so that the hamper should seem to be packed with garden produce; the sort of hamper, in fact, that is sent regularly from an owner's place in the country to his house in town.

"You say 'camouflage,' " said Wharton. "Who was to be deceived? Not the railway people, because it wasn't sent by rail!"

"We'll know the answer to that later on," said Travers evasively. "What were the leaves? Garden cabbage—or field?"

"Why?"

"Oh I'm just hunting round for ideas. If they came from a field, we might find the actual field down there. The curious thing is that I never remember seeing a field of cabbages in that particular part. It's practically all pasture."

Then there'd been that perfectly fantastic theory about the Albert Hall. Wharton had been entertained and amused by that, till Travers began driving with one hand and gesturing with the other. Still, it had been interesting—at first. Take the scene that evening; the great building packed to the fanlights; the table draped with velvet and reared like an altar; the solemn moment when all those assembled fanatics should hear from Lord Zyon's lips the opening sentences that were to precede the consecration:

"to bow your heads with all reverence while our brother, the Bishop of Camden, repeats the articles of our faith"—or some such mumbo-jumbo as that. There would be the thousands prostrated with a fervour whose treble mainsprings were politics, religion and patriotism; above them the great enveloping dome of the roof; in their ears the intoning voice.

"Picture it!" said Travers. "The dimmed lights, the priestly cadences and the voice of an immense multitude repeating those articles of faith. And one thing lacking; that integral part of all worship and consecration—sacrifice! Mightn't there have been a fanatic so frantic in his devotion as to have presented that sacrifice? The slain body of the man who more than any had stood for reaction, the old, obstinate creeds of Free Trade and the weary shibboleths of a dead political age?"

That last had been too much for Wharton. His blasphemous ejaculation had unmistakably indicated his opinion of the rot that Travers was talking. It was not till they reached Taunton that he wondered if Travers too hadn't needed some amusement to make the journey interesting.

Once through Taunton the pace was slower. Villages became frequent; the road narrowed and zig-zagged erratically, and then there were the hills. Wharton, who had never seen that particular country, was enraptured with it; the hills covered with trees and undergrowth, the roads which hugged the valleys and skirted the tiny rivers, and above all those narrow lanes that rose almost sheer from the main road away up through high banks to cottages or farms that perched on the skyline.

"They must be a tough lot about here!" he remarked to Travers. "It'd kill me, crawling up there every time I had to go home!"

Travers laughed. "The fun begins when you're going up with a car—and meet another one!"

"Going up with a car!" He snorted. "You wouldn't take a car up there!"

"Nonsense!" laughed Travers. "It isn't the hill that counts. It's the surface."

They dropped down from the hills to where the valley widened, into a village that sprawled across a river.

"What's that?" asked Wharton. "The Exe?"

"That's right," Travers told him. "Five minutes and we ought to be in Mulberton."

The road now led through woods along the banks of the river and Travers switched on the lights. Round the last bend the lights of the little town could be seen twinkling in the dusk. Over the bridge and just inside the town he drew the car in to the curb and found himself opposite the police station. Inside the main room a sergeant was working.

Wharton introduced himself and Travers. The sergeant looked startled—then knowing.

"You've come down about Sir William Griffiths perhaps, sir!"

Wharton's eyes narrowed. "Perhaps I have. . . . What makes you think that?"

The sergeant smiled sheepishly. "Well, sir— after all the fuss to-day!"

"Fuss! What fuss?"

"Then you don't know anything, sir?"

"Never mind what I know!" snapped Wharton impatiently. "You tell us what you're talking about."

"Well, it's like this, sir. Mr. Griffiths—young Mr. Griffiths that is—rang up first thing this morning about his uncle. From what we could gather, sir, his uncle went out late last night and hadn't come."

"Out where?"

"He didn't know, sir. He seems to have gone out all of a sudden. So we've been on the look-out all day, sir. We only had about five men, taking duty men, and we've been over all the roads round—"

"He went out by car?"

"That's right, sir! The inspector's actually out now, sir. He hasn't got back yet."

"I see." He stood there thinking for a moment or two. "Got a man handy to show us up to Combe Cottage?"

"Sorry, sir; I haven't. . . . But you'll find the way easy enough. You can't miss it. Look here, sir!" and he drew out a map on a sheet of paper. "You can't go wrong, sir. First right, first right again, then first left. You'll see the house on your left, up the hill."

"Good!" said Travers. "What about ringing up?"

"Are they on the phone?" asked Wharton.

"Oh, yes, sir! They're on the phone."

"Pretty enterprising place this!" said Wharton. "Get them, sergeant, will you?" He whispered to Travers. "You speak. Make it purely personal."

The sergeant got Combe Cottage, told them to hang on and handed Travers the receiver.

"Hallo! . . . Who's that speaking? . . . Oh! I see. Well, is Mr. Tim Griffiths in at the moment?" (There was a longish wait) . . . "Not feeling very fit! . . . My name's Travers. . . . Tell him I'm coming along now, straightaway, to see him, will you? . . . Yes, now!" He hooked up the receiver almost before the last word was spoken.

"Which is the best hotel, do you think?" he asked the sergeant.

"Well, sir; the best one's back at the station, and that's a mile and a half away. Try just up on the right. They'll look after you all right there."

"We'll be back some time later," Wharton told him. "If the inspector comes in, ask him to be good enough to see me." He passed over one of the copies of the *Evening Record*. "Let him see this. . . . And not a word's to be said to a soul! . . . Understand?"

Outside, Travers had something to say.

"That was the butler speaking at Combe Cottage. . . . Tim Griffiths was in the room with him."

"How do you know?"

"As soon as I asked whether Griffiths was there, he covered the mouthpiece up quickly, and asked something. I couldn't hear what. The only thing I was certain of was Griffiths' voice answering. Do you know what he said, George? 'Not so loud, you bloody fool! Not so loud!' What d'you think of that?"

Wharton nodded. "Might be nothing in it. Let's get along. What about Palmer here?"

"Oh, yes!" Travers smiled at his own impetuosity. "Get yourself a meal, Palmer, at the hotel there. Ask them to have something waiting for us in about an hour."

He took the wheel. Wharton got in alongside, and for a minute or two they nosed the car gently along the winding, narrow streets of the tiny, little town. The first on the right was clear enough; the second on the right led back to the opposite bank of the river to that by which they'd entered the town. For some way they followed the valley—quarter of a mile perhaps—then Wharton got anxious.

"Damn fellow must have told us wrong. There can't be a road to the left—unless it's a tunnel!"

Travers switched on the headlights and almost at once they picked up a direction-post on the left. He stopped the car just short and hopped out.

"It's all right!" he called, craning up to see. "Goes to a place called Barlcombe. . . . And he said a hill."

They got the car into the narrow road and let her climb up in second.

"This isn't a hill," growled Wharton. "It's a precipice!"

Travers laughed. "Don't you worry about the hill, George! Keep a look-out on that side and see if you can see the house."

The car mounted steadily up the narrow road which wound most exasperatingly in and out. Then they caught sight of the house and drew the car in at the white gate. Wharton got out and opened it. A bare forty yards of gravel and they were drawing up at the door of Combe Cottage, a low, rambling building, covered with what looked like ivy. In the air was the heavy scent of roses. In the open door, the light flooding his back, a man—a servant—was standing.

The two approached the door together. The man seemed to be standing very still; expectantly still, so it seemed to Travers—but then again it might have been the unusualness itself that made things unusual and noticeable; the unknown house, the half-darkness, the unseen face, the light that ran out from nowhere and across the gravel, and the expectancy in themselves as to what was going to happen. Then as they got level, the man drew on one side and they saw his face, heavy, sallow, with deep-set eyes.

"You are the butler—who spoke to me on the phone?" asked Travers.

"Yes, sir!" The voice was respectful enough, though there seemed some anxiety or nervousness in it. The curious thing was that he made no move to show them in. Travers put his foot on the step. "Let Mr. Griffiths know we're here, will you?" The man hesitated. "Mr. Timothy is unwell, sir. . . . A bad attack of fever, sir."

Wharton's voice came curtly. "Very well, then! Show us to the bedroom!" and he brushed his way forward into a well-lighted room, half hall, half lounge. Travers followed—the butler at his heels. This time the man's nervousness was all too apparent. He stammered.

"Er—what shall I—er—say, gentlemen?"

"Tell him that Mr. Travers—Mr. Ludovic Travers—and a friend wish to see him. *Must* see him!"

The man gave a quick look at them, then bowed. "I'll inform Mr. Timothy, sir."

He disappeared through the door at the back. Wharton made a face at Travers, then glanced round the room. Immediately on their right was a door. To the left of that door, occupying the centre of the wall, was something that interested him—a collection of curios and weapons arranged fanwise in a gaudy mass of colour that went none too well with the sober chintzes of loose covers and curtains. Travers stared at them too—the pair of monstrous head-dresses, the lacquer shields, the heavy knives with ivory or lacquer handles, the cumbersome swords in their outlandish scabbards, the masks in glaring splashes of colour, and flanking the whole lot, a pair of enormous bones that were probably those of some prehistoric animal.

Wharton nodded over. "Those the things you were telling me about?"

"Probably!" said Travers—and listened. The door opened and the butler re-entered. He addressed himself to Travers.

"Mr. Timothy is feeling a bit better, sir. He'll be down in a moment . . . if you don't mind waiting, sir." He turned to go.

"Just a moment!" Wharton caught him at the door. "You're the butler? Sir William's butler?" The man hesitated, then gave a curious little smile. "Well, not the butler, sir. . . . I act as the butler—down here."

"You mean the official butler's in town."

"Yes, sir. That is so, sir."

Wharton's manner was not at all curt. On the contrary it was kindly; the least degree patronizing perhaps, but pleasant decidedly.

"And what are you normally, shall I say?"

The man began to lose his stiffness. His tone be-came more conversational.

"Originally, sir, I was footman with Mr. Timothy's father. When he died, sir, I was butler to the family. When she died, sir, I was personal servant to Mr. Timothy; only while he was abroad I was with Sir William."

"I see. Sort of filling in your time. . . . And whose orders are you under at the moment?"

"Sir William's, sir!" He stopped short. Outside there was the sound of steps on the gravel. They halted at the door. There was a sharp knock. The butler looked at them questioningly, then his face resumed its impassivity.

"Pardon me a moment, sir!"

He moved over to the door. Wharton drew back out of the line of vision and, catching Travers' eye, nodded him back too. The voices could be heard distinctly.

"Good evening! Is anybody at home?"

"At home, sir? Whom did you wish to see, sir?"

"Well, is Mr. Timothy Griffiths in?"

"I'm afraid he's not . . . at the moment, sir. Any message you'd care to leave, sir?"

There was a pause. "Perhaps *you* can spare me a minute or two. My name's Sanders. I'm the representative of the London *Evening Record*."

"Oh, indeed, sir!" Then Wharton's voice boomed with startling suddenness over the butler's shoulder.

"Come along in, Mr. Sanders, will you! . . . Let Mr. Sanders in!"

It was an incongruous group; Sanders blinking in the light and fingering his hat; the butler looking enquiringly and nervously, now at the three men, now at the door at the end of the room; Wharton shepherding the reporter to a seat, and Travers standing apart for the moment, wondering just what Wharton was up to.

"Sit down, Mr. Sanders. . . . You know Mr. Travers, I believe?"

Travers smiled over. Sanders looked at him queerly, and nodded. "Yes. . . . I know Mr. Travers." Then he looked at him again. "By the way, Mr. Travers, shouldn't you have been at the meeting to-night?"

Travers smiled apologetically. "Yes. . . . I'm afraid I should have been—"

Wharton's voice cut in. "What's your name, by the by?"

"Daniels, sir."

"Your surname, I mean!"

"That is my surname, sir!"

"Hm! . . . Find out how long Mr. Griffiths is going to be, will you?"

Before the man could turn, the door opened and Griffiths appeared. He stood for a moment in the door, looking round sleepily—wondering apparently what it was all about. He was looking shockingly ill; face an unhealthy yellowish-grey and eyes black and puffy. His hands were deep in the pockets of the silk dressing-gown and when he took one out to close the door behind him, it shook as if his nerves had gone all to pieces. Travers stepped forward and the first thing he caught was the smell of whisky.

"Sorry to root you out like this, Griffiths . . . but I'm afraid we've got some bad news for you."

Griffiths stared at him. His face flushed suddenly to a violent red. Daniels stood still in his tracks and it was he who did the talking.

"You've got some news about Sir William, sir?"

"Yes," said Wharton, bluntly. "He's been murdered!" He felt in the pocket of his light coat and passed over a copy of the paper. It was the butler who took it. He gave a look at the shrieking headlines, then looked at Wharton.

"Murdered, sir!"

Griffiths took the paper from him, his hand shaking; then found his voice. "What do you mean— 'murdered'?"

"His body was found to-day in London—in a hamper. The throat had been cut. The details are there."

Griffiths moistened his lips. The butler fumbled with his fingers and looked away. It was all so utterly different from what Travers had imagined that he himself appeared to be hearing the news for the first time. Sanders got out his notebook and began scribbling.

"Sit down, Sir Timothy!" Wharton went on. "Perhaps you can help us." He took a seat himself.

Daniels spoke to his master. "Anything you want, sir?"

"Anything I want?" He seemed rather bewildered. "Yes! . . . Stop here, Daniels! . . . You tell them . . . if they want to know anything."

Wharton shuffled closer in his chair, crossed his legs and leaned back. Travers remained in the unobtrusive background.

"Which of you last saw Sir William alive?"

"I did, sir!"

"And when was that exactly?"

"Exactly, sir? . . . About ten minutes to nine last night."

"I see! Well, tell me what happened. Start off anywhere you like."

The butler's account was fluent. Perhaps the fact that he'd already told his story once that day to the Mulberton police had something to do with that.

"He came in, sir, at about six o'clock as usual. He'd been out fishing all day—"

"Where?"

"Where, sir?" He looked surprised. Griffiths answered:

"Down there, in the river. He owned about a mile and a half of fishing rights."

Wharton nodded.

"He came in about six, sir, and had a few minutes with Mr. Bland—"

"Who's he?"

"My uncle's financial secretary," said Griffiths, shivering slightly and huddling into his chair.

"Carry on!" said Wharton, and asked no more questions.

"Sir William had about a quarter of an hour with Mr. Bland, sir, as he usually did when he'd been out all day, then when Mr. Bland had gone Sir William dressed for dinner. That was on at seven, sir, and he and Mr. Timothy had dinner together and I waited at table. Mr. Timothy wasn't feeling any too well, sir, and he and Sir William sat in the drawing-room till about a quarter to nine, sir; then I was rung for. Sir William told me to get the car, sir, and I got it and brought it round here to the front door. Then I fetched his tweed hat, sir, and he got in just as he was and drove off. And that's the last I saw of him, sir."

"And what about you, Sir Timothy?" asked Wharton.

His tale also was fluent and told in his usual jerky, blustering voice.

"I was asleep . . . sort of dozing. I heard him —my uncle—get up out of the chair. Then I heard him say something—sort of annoyed . . . about he ought to have seen somebody . . . and being a nuisance. Then he said, 'Where's Daniels?'—like that. So I pushed the bell and he told Daniels to get the car round straightaway. . . . That's all there was—except that I saw him go out of the door and the car drive away."

"Which way?"

"Well, I didn't see the lights so I imagined he went Mulberton way. The way you came."

"You didn't ask him where he was going?"

"I shouldn't have dreamed of such a thing. He wasn't the sort who'd have—er—liked that sort of thing."

"Quite! . . . And then what happened?"

"To me? . . . Nothing! I went to bed. This morning Daniels reported he hadn't been in all night. I sent for Bland and we talked it over. Then we let the police know."

"And what happened to you, Daniels?"

"Well, sir; as Sir William got in the car, I said, 'What time will you be back, sir?' and I understood him to say, 'Don't wait up!' Mind you, sir, I wouldn't swear to that. I thought that's what he said at the time, sir. So I locked up everywhere except the French window of the drawing-room and then I went to bed."

"Quite! . . . And you were surprised when Sir William went off *alone* in the car? I mean, at that time of night?"

"Not at all, sir! I mean, Sir William had a perfect right to go, sir, if he wanted."

"And you, Sir Timothy? You were surprised?"

He shook his head. "I don't see why I should be. . . . Even if I had been, I shouldn't have said so. You see, he was a sort of—law unto himself, as they say. He didn't like being crossed. What I mean is, if he'd wanted me to drive the car *for* him, he'd have said so. I mean, I wouldn't have dreamed of suggesting it myself. . . . Also, you know, he was sort of away and gone out of the room before I knew he *had* gone!"

Wharton nodded. Travers' voice came from the background. "What make of car was it?"

"It was a Buxton, sir."

"What year?"

Daniels' voice was somehow apologetic. "It was a bit old, sir. '26, sir."

"You were accustomed to act as chauffeur when wanted?"

"I was, sir."

"How much petrol was in the tank?"

"In the tank, sir?" He hesitated. Griffiths turned in his chair to watch him. "I couldn't really say, sir . . . to a gallon. At least six gallons, sir."

"Sir William often drive himself?"

"Down here—yes, sir. . . . Not in town." Travers' questions ceased as suddenly as they'd begun and for a minute there was one of those curious silences which seem to demand an effort of will to break them. Sanders alone appeared to notice nothing as he sat scribbling away. Then Wharton rose.

"The police at Mulberton know all this?"

Griffiths and his butler spoke together. Griffiths held the field. "Everything. . . . Just as you've been told."

Wharton nodded heavily.

"Well, Sir Timothy, it doesn't look as if we can do much good here. In the morning some of us may be along again. Nothing else you know? Nothing you suspect?"

Griffiths shook his head.

"No idea whatever where he was going?"

"None! . . . It's been an awful shock to me. It's all sort of taken me by surprise—" He broke off, shaking his head as if still bewildered.

"I understand," said Wharton. "Any other servants, Daniels?"

"A cook-housekeeper, sir, and a—"

"Where is she?"

"In the kitchen at the moment, sir."

"Any others?"

"Yes, sir. A woman comes in every day to do heavy work. Then there's the gardener, and a boy who helps him or in the house, according to where he's wanted."

"And you asked the housekeeper whether Sir William had said anything to her about his intentions?"

"He wouldn't be likely to do that, sir," said Daniels with a shake of the head. "Still, we *did* ask her this morning, sir. She didn't know anything."

"Hm! And where can we get hold of Mr. Bland?"

"Why not phone, sir?"

"Phone! . . . You mean he doesn't live here?"

"No, sir! He'd be at his cottage. He and Mrs. Bland stay there when the master's down here for any length of time."

"And where is it—this cottage?"

The butler got on the move at once.

"If you'll allow me, sir, I'll show you. You can't make a mistake, sir."

The three moved forward with the butler. Griffiths remained in his chair, leaning back with both eyes closed. Travers nudged Wharton and they turned to say good night.

"Best place for you, sir, is bed!" said Wharton, holding out his hand.

Griffiths smiled wanly and said nothing.

"Good night, Griffiths!" said Travers. "Don't worry yourself ill about this. . . . And I'm awfully sorry."

Outside on the gravel they listened to the butler's directions. Travers backed the car to the garage and turned her round. Sanders, who'd been standing with Wharton, cleared his throat.

"Any objection if I go with you, Mr. Wharton?"

Wharton clapped him on the shoulder and pushed him forward. Sanders took a seat in the rear of the car. Wharton followed him.

CHAPTER VI
MR. SECRETARY BLAND

DANIELS OPENED the gate for them. The car swung left and took the short rise that led to the top of the hill. The moon was now up, and through a clearing they caught a glimpse of the valley far below and the river like a silver streak. Then the road was immediately dark again where the trees and the steep banks hemmed it in.

"You knew me then, Mr. Sanders?" asked Wharton.

"Yes . . . I covered the Hayles case the year before last."

He passed over Wharton's polite "Really!"

"You were expecting me . . . down here?"

"Either you or some one else," said Wharton. "Luckily for us it was you. Which reminds me. I haven't congratulated you on to-night's *Record*. One of the best stories I ever read! . . . It *was* yours?"

"Yes," said Sanders indifferently. "It was mine all right."

Taciturn sort of cove! thought Wharton. The car was now going gingerly down the narrow lane. Three hundred yards or so and they came to the fork the butler had mentioned. Another hundred yards to the left and there was the house, just back from the road; a much smaller affair than Combe Cottage; white-fronted and with the moonlight full on it. Wharton tapped Travers on the shoulder and the car was stopped.

"Mr. Sanders!" said Wharton, his tone dryly official. "I'd be obliged if you'd give no indication who you are, when we get inside there. . . . And while we're about it—something else. Neither my name, nor Mr. Travers', is to be mentioned in any story you write. Is that agreeable?"

"It's to be mentioned as casual information that I've picked up."

"That's right!" said Wharton. "Draw the car in closer, Mr. Travers."

As they turned, a servant girl appeared for a moment at the gate; seemed to catch sight of them, then vanished back in the direction of the house.

"They know something!" whispered Travers.

"I told the butler to phone," explained Wharton. The three went up the garden path together, and once more a man was standing in the doorway, the light behind him.

"Are you Mr. Bland?" asked Wharton, in his voice some subtle shade of sympathy or condolence.

"That's right! . . . Come in, gentlemen, please . . . You have some bad news, I understand."

It was all very unemotional; different entirely from the scene as Travers had imagined it. Bland led them along a short passage into a large room that opened on a garden. The light was on but the curtains were not drawn, and through the French window chairs could be seen set out in a sort of rustic loggia. Bland could now be seen, too—a tallish man, gravely professional, looking indeed with his wing collar and polka-dot bow the very image of a lawyer off duty. Everything about him seemed cleanly fastidious—the perfect whiteness of his linen, the creamy whiteness of his hands and the impeccable smoothness of his hair. His manner, too, was quiet; his voice slow and careful.

"Sit down, won't you?" . . . and he waited.

"I take it you've heard the—er—disturbing news, Mr. Bland," said Wharton. "By the way, my name's Wharton; Superintendent, New Scotland Yard." He waved his hand round. "Mr. Travers . . . Mr. Sanders. . . . And the whole thing is, can you help us at all?"

"To be perfectly frank," said Bland, "I've been so amazed—I mean, until a minute ago when Daniels rang me up, I hadn't the least idea . . ." He broke off. "There was something about a hamper . . . and Sir William's body."

Wharton felt in his pocket and produced another copy of the *Record*. "I'm afraid it'll be a bit of a shock to you, Mr. Bland, but see for yourself."

One glance at the unmistakable message of the *Record*, and Bland shuffled uncomfortably in his seat. When he finally looked up, his voice was trembling.

"But this is . . . it's extraordinary!"

"I know it is!" said Wharton. "Put it away, Mr. Bland, and read it at your leisure. Let me tell you what the police know, so far."

As Wharton's story progressed it was only too plain that the secretary was utterly bewildered. Travers would have bet his life against a dead match that Bland had no more conception than the man in the moon either that Sir William had been murdered or who had murdered him. In a way, too, that was the curious thing that struck Travers in his capacity of detached observer. Bland seemed puzzled—exasperated—completely at a loss; but distressed or horrified—no. And as quickly, too, Travers recognized that his own impressions were unjust, even if they were not wrong. Bland was a paid employee, a man accustomed to facts and figures; why then expect him to behave like the faithful servant of fiction?

"It's inexplicable!" said Bland. "It's an escaped lunatic you ought to be looking for, Mr. Wharton, if you'll pardon the suggestion."

"Perhaps you're right," said Wharton. "If so, it was a political lunatic, if you know what I mean. . . . Needless to ask, you've had no communication with Lord Zyon to-day?"

"Most certainly not!"

"Naturally!" said Wharton hastily. "However, perhaps you'll give us your evidence—very briefly— and then . . ."

"Pardon me a moment!" said Travers. "I don't think I left the lights of the car on."

Bland got up.

"Please don't worry!" smiled Travers. "I think I know the way out."

He turned the door-handle. Out in the passage there was a sudden swish and a scurry. In the slit as the door opened was seen the last glimpse of a woman disappearing in the direction of the garden. Not the maid—her dress had been the conventional black. Travers turned back again.

"Likely to be any cars along here?"

"Doesn't matter if there aren't. Put 'em on and be on the safe side." Wharton rose nobly to the occasion, though what was in the wind he hadn't the least idea.

"I think I will," said Travers. He made his way out by the passage to the front door, switched on the side-lights and returned. There was no sign of a woman or even of the servant. In any case, as he was beginning to assure himself, the curiosity had been perfectly natural. Not the manners of Belgravia, perhaps—listening at keyholes—but in certain circumstances decidedly excusable.

"You can think of no reason?" Wharton was saying.

"None whatever!" said Bland emphatically. "The whole thing's a nightmare. Sir William had had no communication of any kind with Lord Zyon for months."

"He was sympathetic with Lord Zyon's political views."

Bland's face underwent a subtle change. Travers listened for the irony which he felt was coming—but the speaker changed his mind.

"You refer to the Work-for-All League?"

"Well . . . yes!"

This time Bland smiled. "Sir William was a man of level judgment, Mr. Wharton. His newspapers were newspapers—not insurance coupons!"

"Exactly!" said Wharton. "He didn't think much of it. However, will you tell us, Mr. Bland, in your own way, precisely what happened yesterday as far as Sir William and yourself were concerned."

"Yes. I think I can do that." He got up slowly, then found the cigarette-box. "I take it we might as well be a little more . . . relaxed? You'll smoke, Mr. Wharton?" He lit a cigarette himself. Travers, abnormally interested, noticed the long, sensitive fingers, the delicate poise of the cigarette, and the cool detachment of the man.

"Yesterday," said Bland reflectively. "Let me see. There was a heavy post . . . for private reasons. At 9.30—my usual time—I went over the correspondence. Certain purely business matters were discussed with Sir William, and he was out of the house by 10.30. I had a chat with Tim Griffiths, then came on here to go over the stuff I'd brought with me—that's my work-room in there. I lunched here, did some more work, had tea with Cross—he's the vicar of Barlcombe—and chatted with him and my wife till just before six. Then I left them here and went along to Combe Cottage in time for the evening post. Nothing arrived of any importance. Sir William got in just after six. I got his signature to certain letters and things, then came straight back here. That'd be about half-past. After that I didn't stir out of the house. Cross and I played chess—and had dinner, of course—till just before eleven. Then I saw Cross home and came straight back and went to bed. This morning Mr. Griffiths rang me up to say his uncle had been out all night. We discussed the situation and informed the police."

"Sir William said nothing about going out?"

"Nothing whatever. I might say I *know* . . . I mean I didn't expect him to go out."

"Excuse my pertinacity," said Wharton, "but you were going to say something about what you *knew*. Why did you *know* he wasn't going out?"

The other hesitated. "I shouldn't have said that. It was entirely a private matter."

"It has no bearing on the case?"

"Directly—not!"

"Well then, indirectly?"

"Mr. Wharton, you force me to talk about what I've no desire to discuss. All the reason I have is that Sir William told me there were certain matters he was going to discuss with his nephew after dinner. Those matters were private matters, concerning the career he hoped to induce his nephew to adopt. It occurred to me—just now, I mean—that if Sir William was going to talk, he wasn't intending to go out."

"Thank you, Mr. Bland," said Wharton gravely.

He was even thinking of an apology for pressing the matter—then came the tap on the door. Bland looked round quickly.

"Come in!"

Almost before he had spoken, the door opened and a woman appeared. There was a moment's silence, as if they expected a quick apology and the door to be closed again; then she came in and the men scrambled to their feet. She was a tallish woman, handsome enough in a blown sort of way, and somewhere—thought Travers—in the elusive thirties. Self-possessed to the point of tactlessness, was his first impression; then as she came forward with a kittenish, palpitating kind of smile, he suddenly felt a bit of a fool.

"Oh, darling! isn't it too dreadful! We've just heard it on the wireless!"

Even if the wine-coloured frock hadn't been sufficient recognition, he might have gathered from the voice who it had been that has scurried away from that door. What on earth had she been before Bland married her? Barmaid? Chorus girl? Third-rate schoolmarm?

"There, my dear! don't distress yourself!" came the voice of the uxorious Bland. He patted her on the shoulder, though never consolation seemed less necessary. She gave a dab at her eyes, then stood there biting her lip.

"Oh, Helen! this is Superintendent Wharton— and—" He forgot the rest. Wharton came to the rescue.

"How do you do, ma'am? . . . This is Mr. Travers. . . . Mr. Sanders. . . . And you're Mrs.—"

"Yes." The smile was a simper. Before Travers could move, she had settled on the edge of the wicker chair, and with hands on lap was looking round at the four of them. Wharton, a great fellow with women, put on his best society manner.

"You were saying . . . about the wireless, Mrs. Bland?"

"Oh, yes! Perfectly dreadful. It can't be true. They must have made a mistake!"

Wharton took the room into his confidence. "Well, we can't say that, can we? till we know what they did say! What was it, on the wireless, Mrs. Bland?"

"They said Sir William was dead . . . and they understood he was murdered!"

Wharton nodded funereally. "I'm afraid it's only too true, Mrs. Bland."

She paused in the middle of a dab with the handkerchief.

"You see," Wharton went on, "we were just making inquiries of your husband here—about Sir William's movements last night—"

Her eyes opened wide. "He was killed last night!"

"Yes . . . probably about nine o'clock."

"Nine o'clock!" She looked round, staring with a horror that, in spite of all the good-will in the world, Travers felt to be simulated. "Then while we were here, he was killed! . . . Wasn't it dreadful! You were playing chess—and he . . ." She dabbed furiously with the handkerchief.

Wharton got to his feet. "Now, Mrs. Bland, don't you go thinking about things like that!"

Bland rose, too. "You run away now, dear. . . . This is a man's job." He raised her from the chair and led her towards the door. The handkerchief dabbed and there was the sound of quiet sobbing. Travers, more self-conscious than ever, relieved his feelings by polishing his glasses. Sanders sat there impassively. Wharton fluttered to the door, then fluttered back again.

"Well, Mr. Bland, I don't think we'll keep you any longer to-night." The word was gently accentuated, with no uncertain promise of a resumption in the morning. "You definitely assure us you had no idea where Sir William was going?"

Bland spoke impressively. It was impossible not to believe him. "Mr. Wharton, I assure you I had no idea where he was going. I was the most surprised man in the world to hear he had even gone out. When I heard this morning that he'd been away all night, you could have knocked me down with a feather."

"Mr. Bland will perhaps pardon the question," put in Travers, "and he will also recognize that whatever we talk about will be treated with the most implicit confidence. Tell us, Mr. Bland. Sir William was engaged in financial operations of a rather important nature?"

Bland regarded him steadily, then all at once he smiled.

"Are you Mr. *Ludovic* Travers?"

"That's right."

"Of course! Unpardonable of me! . . . You're a director of Durangos?"

Travers admitted it.

"What I mean," said Bland, still smiling, "is that if Durangos don't know, then who does?"

Travers smiled, too. He rather liked the look of Bland, and his manner, though how he was besotted enough to endure that wife of his he couldn't imagine.

"We'll take that as read, shall we? The point is this. Had negotiations proceeded far enough to make it worth anybody's while to get Sir William out of the way?"

"But surely! . . . I mean to say, this isn't America! . . . if people do that sort of thing in America."

"Possibly it isn't!" said Travers dryly. "For all that, if I'd known a week ago that Sir William was to be dead yesterday, I could have made quite a good thing out of the information. Tell me frankly. Was Sir William about to tread on anybody's toes—or had he done it already?"

Bland shook his head. "I hate to be unromantic —but nothing of the sort!"

"Just one other thing," said Travers. "Were negotiations in such a state that Sir William might suddenly have decided to go off personally to— well, see a client or discuss a point?"

Bland shook his head again as he turned to Wharton.

"I've already answered that question when I assured Mr. Wharton I had no idea where Sir William might have gone. May I elaborate it, once and for all? I tell you, beyond any possibility of error, that I didn't know he'd gone out. There was nobody on earth I expected him to go and see. And as far as I myself am concerned—because we've got to come to that question sooner or later, gentlemen—I was in this house with my wife and Mr. Cross from six o'clock till eleven, as I told you. What's more, you have my free consent to see Mr. Cross, who'll corroborate that evidence."

Bland's voice became rather indignant towards the end of that statement. Travers took it upon himself to pour oil on the waters. He turned to Wharton.

"That's very good of Mr. Bland. And most comprehensive." He smiled over at the watchful face of the secretary. "If all witnesses were as concise as you, Mr. Bland, Mr. Wharton here might lose his job! . . . Oh! and pardon this question. Sir William wasn't the sort of man who'd be likely to-—er— have a liaison?"

Bland laughed. "Lord, no!"

"And he was perfectly sober?"

That really amused him. "Sober! My dear fellow! There wasn't a more bigoted teetotaller in existence! He wouldn't even let the cook use sherry!"

Travers drew back and left the stage to Wharton. Wharton didn't seem to know what to do with it. The blank wall he'd run up against had definitely queered his pitch. He fidgeted with his hat, hunched his shoulders, supposed they'd better be going. In the morning, if Mr. Bland would suggest a suitable time . . .

"But it's impossible!" Bland's eyes opened in consternation. "My dear sir, you don't realize! . . . Mr. Travers! will you explain to Mr. Wharton!" He was most agitated. "You don't realize the issues involved!"

"I think perhaps I do," began Wharton.

"Anything you like to-night," went on Bland. "I'm absolutely at your disposal. But don't you see? There's nobody but myself who can handle things!"

Wharton nodded. "Anything you can think of, Mr. Travers?"

"I don't think there is. Unless, of course, who were Sir William's solicitors?"

"Brotherston, Hall and Brotherston," said Bland, like a shot.

Wharton added the dear old formula. "Any enemies? Any threatening letters?"

Bland shook his head.

It was on the tip of Wharton's tongue to ask if Sir William had been a secretive sort of person; likely to keep things to himself. The thought prompted a more important question.

"One thing I've rather wondered. Why did Sir William live down here in that extraordinarily unpretentious way? I mean, living at Combe Cottage when he might have had a country house."

Bland frowned slightly. "The question's really the answer. He was just that sort. . . . He hated publicity and he liked comfort; stodgy, middle-class comfort. A day's fishing and a square meal when he got home, that was his idea of perfect felicity!"

"Surprising!" The exclamation came from Sanders. Bland looked at the speaker, but failed to place him.

"Possibly!—but perfectly true. Sir William was just as happy in his hobbies as in his work."

"Most men are!" said Wharton heartily. "Mr. Tim Griffiths—or Sir Timothy, I should say—got on well with his uncle?"

Bland closed up at once. "Why not?"

"Hm!" said Wharton. "As you say, why not?" He glanced over at the grandfather clock. "If any-thing should turn up, we can rely on you to let us have it?"

"Most certainly!"

"And you'll keep us aware of your movements?"

"Here—or Eaton Square will find me."

"Capital!" Wharton still hesitated. "I suppose you know the people round here, and the district, pretty well?"

"The people—I'm afraid not at all; the district— very well indeed. We've been here now, off and on, for some years. Still, you couldn't call it holidaymaking!"

"Quite!" said Wharton. There was still a certain hesitancy in his manner. "What I was going to suggest was this." He looked round at Travers. “Perhaps in your absence Mrs. Bland might lend hand to Mr. Travers here. He was coming down this way for a short holiday, so I got him to bring me down with him. I’m not staying here myself.”

“What sort of a hand?” asked Bland.

“Well . . . if she could give him the lie of the land—so to speak; give him confidential information about—er—people and so on. Purely a suggestion, of course,” and he looked hopefully.

“I’m sure Mrs. Bland will do anything she can.” He spoke perfectly seriously. “After all, women have their own methods of getting information!”

Wharton chuckled. “They have, indeed!” He held out his hand. “Good night, Mr. Bland! We’re extremely grateful to you. Say good night to Mrs. Bland for us!” And he shepherded his small flock out to the front door.

“What about you, Mr. Sanders?” he asked, when Travers had restarted the engine. “Mulberton suit you?”

“Yes . . . if I’m not trespassing.”

“Nonsense!” Wharton urged him in and took a back seat with him. Travers ran in reverse as far as the fork, then took the same road back. Except for a light in one of the bedrooms, Combe Cottage was in darkness. Wharton talked away.

“You people have any more ideas before you left town?”

“If they did,” said Sanders, “they came after I left. Then they’d be in the six-thirty.”

“You mean to say you haven’t seen your own story!”

Sanders spoke with what sounded like studied indifference. “How could I? . . . And cooks don’t enjoy their own meals.”

“You’re right there!” said Wharton. “What’s the program now? Get some sort of a story off?”

“If I can. . . . Get the bare bones through and leave them to work it up.”

“That’s the idea! Red-hot news! That’s what you people call it, isn’t it?”

Sanders grunted something.

“Staying on here?” Wharton went on cheerfully. “A day or two. . . . Not that it’ll be much good. I’m only a reporter, Mr.

Wharton; not a detective. All I get now will be what you people care to hand out."

"You never know!" said Wharton hopefully. Then he leaned across and whispered, "Take my tip! Stick to Mr. Travers! He's more soft-hearted than I am!"

....

At the police station Sanders mumbled his thanks and hurried off.

"Where's he going?" asked Travers.

"To get a car to rush him to Taunton.... He'll probably get a trunk-call through from there."

"Never saw such an icicle of a chap!" said Travers. "He was absolutely uncouth most of the evening. Now he's almost human."

"Force of influence!" said Wharton flippantly. "You go along now and fix up your room. Don't wait for me!" Travers was in time to see him disappear through the door. For the moment he felt the tiniest degree annoyed; then he smiled. Wharton's methods were at the same time so devious and so naive that it was impossible to be annoyed with him and keep one's sense of proportion. Half an hour later, when he came back, Wharton found Travers had taken him at his word and had already had a meal. The General was courteous to an alarming degree.

"You're quite sure you didn't mind my telling Bland about your staying down here?"

"Quite!" said Travers. "The only thing is, George, that it'd have been rather awkward for you, when you announced so suddenly the engagement between myself and Scotland Yard, if I'd refused to have the woman.... What's the parcel?"

"Ah!" said Wharton, and passed it over. "A pair of the inspector's pyjamas. And a new tooth-brush. The local barber's coming to shave you at eight-thirty!"

Travers laughed, then pulled out his pipe. "Mind if I smoke?"

Wharton looked at him. "That's better! Do you know, you always worry me when you start talking all dignified!" He sat down before the plate and cold joint. "Let's compare notes. Tell me everything you noticed."

"Well," said Travers slowly, "if we begin at the right place, there's that remark I heard on the telephone before we went up to Combe Cottage. Griffiths was in the room with Daniels—"

"Or Daniels was in the room with Griffiths. There's a difference, you know."

"I know there is. But when a master tells a man not to talk so loudly and not to be a bloody fool, it shows my point of view rather than yours. Tell me! Didn't you get that impression up there? Didn't you think there was some sort of understanding between Griffiths and that butler person? Don't you think Daniels took distinct liberties?"

"Perhaps he did. . . . You didn't like him?"

"A soft-footed, slimy sort of person! I didn't like his eyes, George."

"They won't hang him for that!" observed Wharton between bites.

"And, of course, *Griffiths knew his uncle was dead.*"

Wharton stopped chewing. "Ah! Now you're coming to it! You mean he'd been drinking quite a lot."

"Quite! If he'd known the old man was coming home, he'd never have dared to get in such a state. From what Bland told us, I should say he never tolerated drink of any sort in the house."

"Hm!" said Wharton. "There's a fallacy there. Let me put it this way. I'll believe Griffiths knew his uncle was dead if you can prove to me two things—that he stood in sufficient fear of his uncle to respect implicitly his views about drink; and—much the same thing—that he hadn't had a drink at Combe Cottage since he'd been down there."

"But surely!" protested Travers. "Didn't I tell you that he hadn't a bean except what his uncle might dole him out?"

Wharton cut him short. "It's no use saying 'surely.' If it's a question of a man's neck, we've got to find out! There's got to be no possibility of doubt!" He leaned over impressively. "That's one of the things *you* can do. Get the Bland woman to gossip!"

"Quite!" said Travers thoughtfully. "However, to go on with Griffiths. Why didn't he ring London to find if Sir William had gone there? Why was the whole thing confined locally, as it were?"

"Exactly! Of course there the dinner-suit might have influenced them. He wouldn't be likely to go anywhere very far—dressed like that. Still, there's something else for you. Ask Griffiths and hear what he says. Ask Daniels and compare. . . . And what was your opinion of the other place—Bland's?" Travers frowned. "You know when I went out to see to the lights of the car? Mrs. Bland was listening at the keyhole!"

It was rather indicative of the way those two understood each other, that Wharton asked for no details.

"Might have been natural curiosity. You must remember both her house and Combe Cottage had been in a state of tension all the day. . . . How did Bland strike you?"

"Bland?" said Travers ruminatively. "Hm! You see, I knew Bland already by name. He's pretty well known in financial circles. Pedersen and Gore passed him on to Sir William some years ago. He was one of their bright young men."

"Yes, but personally. . . . As a man."

"Frankly, I rather liked him. . . . Something a bit inaccessible about him somewhere, perhaps. . . . Fine presence, fine voice, obvious manners . . . some breeding . . . and a sense of humour. He's the sort of man I might get to hate very heartily . . . or I might get on with him very well indeed— and I don't say that about a lot of people, George. Pardon the blatancy!"

"Anything else?"

"You mean about Bland? . . . I don't know that there was. Everything that happened to-night was very different from what I expected. Still, that's nothing to do with it . . . I did think Bland rather too shrewd a fellow when he went on about three miles ahead of your very cautious enquiries, and boldly announced his own alibi." He laughed gently. "Which brings me to the very apposite remark—What point is there in discussing Bland when he couldn't possibly have been concerned in anything?"

"Hm!" said Wharton. "Something else you might do for us. See if the alibi's all he claims it to be. . . . And what about Mrs. Bland?"

"Now you've got me!" said Travers frankly. "A vulgarian. One of those hearts of gold perhaps, but common as they make 'em!"

Wharton nodded. "She thrust herself in. Why did she do that? Natural curiosity?"

Travers shook his head. "What should the wars do with these jigging fools?"

"What's that?"

"Sorry!" said Travers. "Merely a quotation. As you say, why should she thrust herself into men's business?"

Wharton grunted. "There's something else for you to find out. Have tea with her to-morrow; ring her up as soon as her husband's gone!"

"Good!" said Travers solemnly. "I will! . . . And will my evening be free, George? or shall I find out where the hamper came from, and who lent the rope . . . and who wrote the labels?"

Wharton refused to smile. "The inspector's seeing to that. He'll scour the district for the car and the hamper—though if you ask me, the car's in London. . . . One other thing you might do. Have a word with that woman who comes in daily to Combe Cottage." He pushed aside the plate, wiped his mouth prodigiously, then got to his feet. "And if an old hand might presume upon a little advice . . . lie a little more fluently! You're far too sensitive!"

Travers looked rather hurt at that. Wharton got into his coat and stoked up his pipe.

"Tell me! *Would* it be too much to ask if Palmer might . . ."

Travers hopped up like a shot.

"Take you back in the car? . . . Of course he will!"

A quarter of an hour later, Wharton was on the way back to town. Travers was realizing two things. Wharton hadn't divulged one single thing that he himself had noticed in those two visits of the evening—and he hadn't given any reason whatever for hurrying back to town.

CHAPTER VII
WHARTON IS BUSY

When Wharton left Mulberton that night, he had, however, no intention of proceeding beyond Taunton. From there he was proposing that Palmer should go on to town, collect up the necessary articles for Travers, and then call for him on the return journey. The interval he proposed filling in at Taunton. The reason was a phone message, received at Taunton and sent on to Mulberton, and waiting for him when he returned to the police station from Bland's cottage. It was from Norris.

> Reporter took ticket for Taunton only. Suggest he called there for enquiries. May know something of hamper.

At first glance, Wharton had been disposed to reject the implied advice—then he wondered. Sanders naturally left London hot-foot for Mulberton, and he travelled by rail. He could have booked right through. Then why had he booked only to Taunton? Perhaps because he had to change at Taunton in any case, and intended to re-book there.

A few moments' thought disposed of that theory. Sanders most certainly had *not* come from Taunton to Mulberton by rail. If he had, he should have been at Combe Cottage making inquiries a good hour before he actually did get there. And to be late was an absurdity. It cancelled out some of the advantages of the scoop. It meant that a fast-traveling competitor from London—say, by motor-bicycle—would overhaul him and get to Combe Cottage first, as Travers—an exceptional driver admittedly—had definitely done. Why, then, had Sanders wasted at least an hour in Taunton? Had he some idea of the place of dispatch of the hamper? Did he think Sir William had gone to Taunton the night he was killed? And was that why Sanders had been so taciturn all the evening—because he wished to use that taciturnity as a shield against questioning?

And Norris must also know something else, or he'd never have sent the message at all. It implied, for instance, that Taunton and the hamper had something in common. That was why Wharton, as soon as he reached Taunton police station, got a call through to town. But Norris wasn't in, and all the information he got was that news had come in about the hamper. Wharton replied with a "Hold the Fort!" injunction; put the Taunton police in possession of the facts, then hopped in again.

He slept most of the way. Palmer, a careful driver, drew in at New Scotland Yard at five in the morning. In five minutes Wharton was closeted with Norris and hearing all the news—and most interesting it was. Lord Zyon had offered a reward of £5,000 for information leading to a conviction, and the announcement had been made in the later editions of the *Evening Record*. The offer— part of a gesture of general abhorrence in view of the evening's meeting—had been proclaimed all over London by the *Record*'s splash bills. Then had been the broadcast description of the hamper—and results had been immediate. At 10.30, a taxi-driver had come to the Yard, and he was followed by a truck-driver half an hour later. "You'd like to see them personally?" asked Norris.

"Let's hear the statements first," Wharton told him.

"Very good, sir; we'll begin with the taxi-driver." Norris consulted the sheet. "William Clark, Paddington Station, 0435. Says he took a passenger at 11.25 for Covent Garden. Description's here. A porter—we haven't got him yet—brought the hamper on a barrow and the fare took it inside with him. The description of the hamper given by Clark tallies exactly, and there were cabbage leaves sticking out in front. We showed him the hamper, and he says it's the one, though he wouldn't swear to it. He reached Covent Garden at 11.45 and was stopped outside Dove's auction rooms. The fare paid up, and the last that Clark saw of him was him standing by the hamper on the pavement. No words passed but the ordinary. . . . You know where Dove's is, sir?"

"North side—by the Opera House."

"That's right, sir. . . . Now the truck-driver, Thomas Moon, of 299 Fulham Lane; jobbing contractor. He turns up every morning in the small hours, at Covent Garden, on the chance of there being a load for his ton Ford; has done it for years, and claims to be a well-known character. He did a couple of jobs and then came back a third time, purely on spec. As there was nothing doing, he thought he'd push off home. As he passed Barsteins'—you'll note that, sir!—a man held him up and asked if he were going home. I should say that Moon's name and address were in big letters on the side of the lorry. Moon said he was, and the man asked if he'd like to earn half a dollar. In the doorway of an empty shop was a hamper with cabbage leaves protruding. The pair of them shoved it inside the covered truck and the man got in with it. Moon said to him: 'Been picking up some bargains, mate?' and the man said he had, and his own van would be picking him and the hamper up near the Albert Memorial. Then Moon said he'd want more than half a dollar, as it'd be out of his way—and they agreed on 'three and a kick.' Moon says there weren't any labels on the hamper. Nothing happened except that the man stopped him alongside the Albert Hall and said that was near enough. . . . We've got full description of the man. We also showed him the hamper, and he says it's the spit of it."

"Know what happened *in* the Hall?"

"We've got everything, sir. The same man was seen inside the entrance that leads to the orchestra. He stopped one of Hyde and Powley's men—they're doing all the decorations—and handed over the hamper. He was the same man, only he had on a peaked cap. As the place was lousy with hats and coats at the time, he probably picked it up and used it. At any rate, the man he handed the hamper over to hadn't any idea it wasn't all right. The man said it was to go on the platform by Lord Zyon's orders. He also asked if he should lend a hand, but H. and P.'s man said he could manage. He wasn't asked to sign for it, and he put it on the platform as directed. There it stopped until it was sent for, which was practically at once. The rest you know, sir."

"You found the taxi-man who brought it to Park Terrace?"

Norris fumbled among the sheets. "Got his name and particulars here, sir."

"Never mind about that," said Wharton. "Can he swear that the hamper wasn't tampered with en route?"

"He had it on the seat beside him all the way. . . . You're wondering, sir, if the corpse was put in on the journey."

"Don't worry about what I'm wondering!" said Wharton. "What about the descriptions of the man?"

Norris handed over three typewritten sheets. "These are the individual descriptions, sir. I'd like you to have a look at them, if you don't mind." Wharton adjusted his antiquated glasses. When he'd read the second time, Norris handed over a fourth sheet.

"That's a description made up from all three. You agree, sir, it was the same man."

Height almost six foot; age forty-five; hair white at temples; wearing glasses of ordinary type; dark moustache of bow type, ends pointed; very protruding lower jaw; spoke as if he had lockjaw; thin facet sallow; waterproof buttoned to neck; grey trousers; black shoes.

"Seems all right," said Wharton.

"Some of it, of course, was what our own men got straight away, sir. What happened in the Hall, for instance; we got that first." Norris looked at him anxiously. "The thing is, sir, what amount of it is any use?"

Wharton had another look. "Hm! Tallish. Age, round about forty. Thin, sallow face. The rest's not worth tuppence!"

Norris gave a nod of relief. "That's what I thought, sir."

"Never mind," said Wharton. "Now we've made a start, we'll have a dozen people who saw him, before the week's out. . . . What about times?"

Norris exhibited yet another sheet. "Here we are, sir! Clark reached Covent Garden at 11.45. He checked it by his watch. Moon left Covent Garden at 12.15, because it was 12.20 when he saw St. Martin's clock. There were traffic hold-ups all the way to the Albert Hall, and he didn't get there till one. It was 1.15 when the hamper was put on the platform, and 1.20 when Lord Zyon rang to see if it was there."

"That leaves a gap of half an hour at Covent Garden," said Wharton. "What was happening?"

Norris smiled broadly. "For one thing, sir, the hamper was shifted across Covent Garden from one side to the other—Dove's to Barsteins'. I've got men at Covent Garden now, trying to trace anybody who moved it on a barrow. Then there's the matter of the telephoning."

"Telephoning!" said Wharton, always ready to find the flaw. "You're definitely assuming then that the man who rang up Major Heather was the man who was squatting there with the hamper!"

"Well, aren't you, sir?"

"I don't know that I am," said Wharton. "Still, it amounts to the same thing in the long run. If a confederate phoned, then we're merely looking for the confederate. . . . You're asking about telephone-boxes and so on?"

"That's right, sir!"

"Capital! And now what about that second gap? The quarter of an hour at the Albert Hall."

"Well, sir, he had to get the hamper inside. He had to keep out of the way till he got the labels tied on. He had to strip off the edges of the leaves so that Lord Zyon shouldn't be suspicious. He got the hat and then he had to wait for a suitable moment. . . . And a quarter of an hour isn't much!"

Wharton did some thinking aloud. "When the hamper was put in the taxi it stood on the seat. There wasn't room for it any other way. That was when one cabbage leaf protruded again—the one that made Lord Zyon so annoyed." He looked at Norris and made a discovery which Norris himself knew already. "So *that* explains the cabbage leaves! He intended to lay a blind trail, supposing the hamper were recognized at Paddington! Covent Garden—the one place in London that's thick with hampers! Nobody'd ever notice a hamper there!"

"But it was noticed, sir!"

"I know. But it shouldn't have been. The fault was his own for lashing it round so with rope. And he shouldn't have had a brand-new hamper. One of those dirty grey ones would have been less conspicuous. . . . Now what about that reporter? Why did you think it important?"

"That was because of Turner's report," said Norris. "He inquired at the barrier for a man of Sanders' description, with a ticket for Mulberton. There wasn't one, so he waited. Then, just as the train was starting—whistle blowing—Sanders came out of the refreshment-room and boarded the train. That meant he'd been there a quarter of an hour, and he also had a paper packet with him. When he got in the train was actually on the move or Turner'd have chased him; so he says to the ticket-man, 'That's the man I wanted!' 'Oh, him!' says the ticket-man. '*He* had a ticket for Taunton. You said Mulberton.' Turner asked if you could book through to Mulberton, and the man said of course you could." Norris pulled up suddenly there and looked the least bit sheepish. "To tell you the truth, sir, I gathered from that—and Turner did, too—that there was an actual coach that went right through. That made it seem a certainty to me that Sanders was stopping at Taunton. . . . then I thought it over and reckoned it was better to let you know than run the risk of us missing anything."

"Quite right!" said Wharton. Norris breathed again.

"Let me have a look at that report of Turner's," Wharton went on. He read it through for himself, then made a note in his book.

"Anything I've missed, sir?" asked Norris.

Wharton shook his head. "Don't think so. . . . Stenographer handy? If so, you might as well hear my side."

When all that business was over and Norris had got the hang of things, Wharton looked at his watch. Seven o'clock, and not much hope of anybody at Brotherston, Hall and Brotherston before nine. Of course one might ring up Sir Henry at his private address.

"What about some tea and a spot of breakfast?" he asked Norris. "And see if you can get a *Record*."

Over his meal he had a look at the paper. Sanders' report had got through; the barest bones, as he had hinted, and now covered with adipose tissue. The chief of the murder news seemed, however, congratulations on the scoop of its fellow journal and a further proclamation of Lord Zyon's reward. Wharton got out his pipe and waited for Norris.

"Now you've had time to think it over; anything that strikes you?" he asked.

Norris looked up from the report he'd been studying. "From what I gather, sir, we haven't got very much further. None of the men down there fit the case. Griffiths is a bloated muscley sort of chap, Daniels is square-faced and thick-set, and Bland is a different type altogether. And every mother's son of 'em was in Mulberton yesterday morning!"

"And what about a confederate?" asked Wharton. "I told you there was something fishy down there. Mr. Travers and I both noticed it."

"You and Mr. Travers were a little bit abnormal, sir," said Norris. "You were *looking* for things to see."

"Maybe!" said Wharton. "But that doesn't answer the question. Was there a confederate?"

"Bluntly, sir—I don't think it's feasible. A confederate means future blackmail—and your neck depending on another man's tongue. Only a fool would risk that—and we don't seem to be dealing with a fool."

"I think you're right," said Wharton. "Unless, of course, he was driven into a pretty tight corner." He shook his head. "We'd better keep to what we know. What *do* we know?" He put the question with disconcerting suddenness.

"Depends what you're assuming," said Norris guardedly. "Are you taking it that the man with the hamper was the one who killed him?"

"I think so."

"Very good, sir! Then we know he was a man of intelligence; sufficiently aware of facts and sufficiently cultured to be able to put that bluff across Lord Zyon and his secretary. He was absolutely callous—"

"A contradiction in terms, there!" interrupted Wharton. "If he was cultured, he ought to have been sensitive—and therefore he wasn't callous. But he certainly was cultured—in a way—and therefore he was abnormal. However—"

Wharton's philosophizing had been over Norris's head in any case.

"Well, sir; he was pretty callous to go about London with that hamper and what was inside it! And he was a man who knew London, and Covent Garden in particular. He knew where a hamper wouldn't be noticed, and where he'd be bound to get a vehicle to take the hamper to the Albert Hall. . . . But the best thing we know, sir, is that it's ten to one Sir William was killed down there. Somewhere near Taunton for preference."

"What have you done about that?"

"Seen Paddington, sir, and asked them to check up on all stops on that particular train. . . . We're almost bound to have that this morning."

"Good!" said Wharton. "That'll be something to get our teeth into. Anything from Menzies?"

"Only that death occurred after the evening meal—two hours approximately. That confirms the story you heard down there."

"Yes. . . . And it shows he didn't get very far after he left the house; if Menzies is right, that is—and we've never known him far wrong."

He had another look at the watch, then got to his feet.

"Think I'll get a shave. . . . If I'm wanted, I'm at Sir Henry Brotherston's, St. James's Square. If Menzies comes in, ask him to wait." Then he looked over at Norris and nodded. "You've done a lot of quick thinking since yesterday afternoon!" Norris left the room with his tail wagging.

. . . .

There was no difficulty in seeing Sir Henry before he left for Lincoln's Inn. He and Wharton had had dealings together before, and the lawyer was indeed Wharton's idea of the perfect witness—a book of facts, handsomely bound. Sir Henry was imposing and florid; standing four-square; pompous perhaps and cautious, but what he did say was authentic as Holy Writ.

This particular morning it was hard to say whether he or Wharton was the more anxious to see the other. Sir Henry was incredibly shocked; the murder, the slit throat, the hamper—all flung, as it were, in the teeth of that high finance and stratum of society that should have been sacrosanct; all this had upset him more forcibly than a public insult or a gross ingratitude. Wharton soon gathered that he was expecting to hear news from the innermost councils of Scotland Yard, and diplomatically supplied it.

"At least we've got his description, Sir Henry!" He found Norris' fourth sheet and handed it over. The lawyer had a look at it and was reassured. He nodded heavily.

"Won't be long before you have your hands on him. You're going to publish this all over the country?"

Wharton leaned across and breathed out the secret. "It's all a fake! It's what he *wanted* people to see!"

"But my dear sir! A man with a jaw like that! I mean, there can't be a hundred people in the country . . ."

"Just the cunning of him!" said Wharton. "Let me show you, Sir Henry. You're clean-shaved. Have a look at yourself in this glass! . . . Now deliberately thrust out your lower jaw till the top teeth settle behind the lower ones." He supervised the incongruous proceeding. "Now, sir; let me put these glasses on you. . . . Now look at yourself, and imagine in addition you've got a moustache! . . . Who'd know you? . . . Your hair's grey. This man's was dark. He probably whitened it, and the moustache, with wet chalk."

The lawyer agreed, as he handed back the glasses, that there might be a difference. The jaw effect was certainly an ageing one. But what about speech?

"The very thing!" said Wharton. "The lockjaw effect!" He tried it himself and went on talking. "There you are, sir! It doesn't make all that difference. And if he came, up from Somerset by train, he needn't have spent any time in the carriage—or very little." He waved his hands as if to say, "Away with all this foolery!" then his voice changed.

"Now, in the strictest confidence, Sir Henry! Who profits by his death?"

The lawyer made the usual facial preliminaries; talked round for a bit, then got nearer the point.

"Mind you, the estate won't be what people imagine! . . . Very much below a million. . . . Death duties, of course. . . . The position is also extremely complicated. . . . Sir William made a new will shortly before the arrival of his nephew back in England. . . . There's a body of trustees. . . . I may say I am one."

"Trustees for whom? The nephew?"

"Well, yes—the nephew. Sir William had a certain course of action he wished his nephew to pursue. He wished him to take up a business career—and he was going to give him a few months in which to think it over."

"I expect I'm a bit dense, Sir Henry," smiled Wharton. "Why did he make this will when he hadn't even seen the nephew in months?"

Sir Henry waved his hand. "Heart not all it should be. He might have gone at any time—and he knew it."

Wharton nodded knowingly. "I think I've got it. Sir William was waiting till his nephew had run through all his money. He'd probably spoken to him before and had been turned down. He knew his nephew was coming back to England dependent on him, and he therefore intended to approach him again. In the meanwhile, should anything happen to himself, you trustees had your instructions. You were to carry on as if Sir William were alive."

"Well—yes. That's roughly the position."

"And if the nephew definitely turned down his uncle's proposition, what did he get?"

"Fifty thousand pounds only."

"Only!" Wharton made a face. "And he is actually going to get that fifty thousand?"

"If he refuses to fulfil the terms already mentioned—yes! If he falls in with his uncle's wishes, then ultimately he gets—er—very much more."

"Exactly! And any other legacies?"

"Oh, yes! Certain charities profit immediately. The secretary—I don't know if you know him; Bland, his name is—gets ten thousand and Combe Cottage with contents."

"Bland knew it?"

Sir Henry shrugged his shoulders. "Probably— yes!"

"It's a lot of money!" said Wharton. "Any particular reason for a legacy as large as that?"

When Sir Henry had finally done hemming and hawing and Wharton had put two and two together, what seemed clear was this. Sir William was a very careful man. He was paying Bland less than Bland could get elsewhere; but with that peculiar procrastination that always accompanies parsimony, he had dangled before his secretary's eyes the ultimate reward.

"A sort of Jacob and Rachel business," was Wharton's comment. "And Bland knew he might go off at any time, which made it all the more interesting."

"Between ourselves," said Sir Henry, "it was reasons of health that made him dispose of his interests in the Associated Press."

"Hm! And then he found he couldn't keep out of things." He nodded philosophically. "And it wasn't that that killed him after all!"

The lawyer cleared his throat.

"Tell me, Wharton! What's the point of these inquiries? You can't for a moment imagine Sir Timothy—or Bland—capable of committing, or conniving at such a damnable outrage!"

Wharton gave a wry smile. "You mustn't pay any attention to my imagination, Sir Henry. It's warped. It's got to be!"

Before the other could ask the meaning of that final specimen of the circumlocution so dear to Wharton's heart, there was a tap at the door and a man-servant appeared.

"Pardon me, Sir Henry, but Mr. Wharton is wanted urgently on the phone."

That was why Wharton left with his information none too complete. What precisely, for instance, was that combine that Travers had hinted at and Bland had laughed off? And had Sir Henry been asked, quite likely he might have known where Bland acquired that extraordinary wife of his.

CHAPTER VIII
SENSATIONS FOLLOW

TRAVERS WAS in the middle of his breakfast when the waiter handed him a note from Groom—the local inspector. Would Mr. Travers come round to the station at the earliest possible moment? Travers gulped down his coffee and went off at the double.

The problem was an interesting one—which of two trails to follow first. The telephone message had come in a few minutes before, that a burnt-out car had been found in a field off a secluded lane a few miles away, just short of the village of Bantlebury. The second, an anonymous letter which had arrived by that morning's post, was equally promising.

I have heard on the wireless about the death of Sir William Griffiths. If the police want to know the sort of man he was they should inquire of the woman he meets who was seen with him on the night he was killed at Mortons Wood, and that was not the first time they was there. They ought to be shown up.

"What do you make of it, sir?" the inspector asked. Travers rather gathered from the look that accompanied the question, that Wharton had left behind him too flattering a description. Still, he had another glance at it. It bore no address and had no date other than the postmark of the same morning. The place of posting was Lampfield, a village a mile or so through Barlcombe.

"What time's the last post at Lampfield?" Travers asked.

"It doesn't matter about that," the other told him. "The last post's at seven, but Mulberton's the postal centre of the area. The post left Lampfield at eight this morning and came here. The post-office sent it straight across. It might have been posted any time between the second news last night and eight o'clock this morning."

The paper was white, lined, and coarse in texture; the sort of thing one might buy in a village shop. The envelope was the usual business type; the writing a scrawl—readable and no more.

"It's the wording that puzzles me," said Travers. "The first sentence is perfectly normal; the kind of thing you or I might have written. Then it becomes crude and malicious and vulgar. The errors are natural enough, and yet the whole thing doesn't look right."

The inspector had another look. "Whatever it is, sir, we'd better try it for prints. After that we can ask questions at the village shop. . . . And it wouldn't be a bad idea to go along and see if there's any truth in it."

Travers smiled. "Now that's what I call first-class deduction! Any chance of killing two birds with one stone?"

The inspector thought so. The police car was brought round, a couple of men taken aboard, and the inspector took the wheel. It was a great morning; the haze just clearing and the air deliciously cool. For Travers every inch of the road was interesting. The first stage was the route he had taken in the dark the previous night. There was the road along the river and the sharp turn to Wharton's precipice. But before they reached Combe Cottage the car halted, and Travers saw what he'd missed in the dark—a narrow lane that cut to the right to form a Y.

The four of them hopped out. Not only was the lane steep and narrow, but its surface was fretted with gullies from winters of rains. The metalling, too, was the original rock, or else the rain had so weathered it as to leave only the rock for a surface. On its left was the steep bank, and to the right—with merely a ruined hedge for protection—the land fell sheer to the valley. Everywhere were trees, rising from the sparse undergrowth of low shrubs and bushes.

"No point in going any farther," said Groom. "Those are Morton's Woods, Mr. Travers. Used to belong to a Colonel Morton. You two fellows move along up and see what you can see. We'll be back in half an hour."

"Where's the road go to?" Travers asked.

"It peters out up the top there," Groom told him. "There's a ruined cottage on the left. No one ever comes up here nowadays unless it's a courting couple."

The sight of Combe Cottage was far more interesting to Travers as they passed it; its trimness, its unsuspected size, its pleasant lawn and its spreading trees that rose from the side shrubbery and made a stretch of shade, and the flash of colour from the rose-beds—all so different from the squat, monotone building of the previous night. As for Bland's cottage, he merely got the sight of its roof as the car turned right towards Barlcombe.

They passed the church, with its vicarage alongside. "You know the vicar?" asked Travers.

"Mr. Cross?" Groom smiled. "Know him well, sir. If he'd been alive fifty years ago he'd have been one of these sporting parsons we read about."

"Good fellow, is he?"

"As a man, yes." Groom smiled again. "As a parson, he's a bit too unorthodox to please everybody."

A sharp turn to the right cut the conversation short. A mile along the road a policeman was seen standing, and Groom drew the car up. Again there was one of those narrow lanes, cutting away from the main road and winding uphill. A couple of hundred yards up that and two men were visible—a sergeant and a youngster in overalls.

"Where's the car?" asked Groom.

"Through here, sir!" The sergeant led the way through a gate, and further up the hill to where a wood sloped to meet them. In the angle of wood and hedge, was what had once been a car—still smouldering.

The sergeant nodded back to the youth in overalls. "I thought we'd better let you know about this, sir; though Mr. Flack here reckons it ain't the car Sir William drives."

Travers left them talking it over and moved round to the far side where the bank made a kind of platform, and the little wind there was blew smoke and fumes uphill. The heat was still considerable, though the smouldering wreck was little more than a chassis. Whether deliberate or accidental was scarcely debatable. The position in the field showed foresight and design. And the number-plates had been removed. So had magneto and carburettor. As for the engine number, the embossed figures on the cylinder-head had been stripped clean as if with a hard chisel.

The inspector's voice came over. "No doubt whatever about it being a Morris, is there?"

"The radiator might have been put on later," said Travers. "Still, the engine's all right. One of the first Morrises ever made." He smiled over at the young mechanic. "Rather before your time, I'm afraid!"

Groom motioned Travers aside. "What do you think about it? Any connection?"

"I doubt it," said Travers. "If it was the one used to carry the body in—and that's the wildest surmise—then why wasn't it burnt twenty-four hours ago?"

"Exactly! And what's it doing there at all?"

"There you've got me!" said Travers frankly. "I might go on theorizing all day and not be right. The whole thing is, why's it here in this field?"

"A fake insurance?"

"Who'd insure it? The whole bag of tricks wasn't worth a fiver. . . . If it was stolen, the best thing to do would have been to abandon it." He frowned. "Yet there's something very curious. Everything that was likely to carry a number was taken off; presumably so that it couldn't be traced."

"Why?"

"Lord knows! Still, you might get your people to inquire round the district for a very old Morris; especially if there's one missing."

Groom smiled ironically. "There's enough old Morrises in this district to stretch from here to Taunton. But you're sure it wasn't Sir William's car?"

"Perfectly," said Travers gravely. "Hardly a '26 Buxton; do you think so?"

Groom had a word with the sergeant and they pushed along back again.

"When do you think it was set fire to, sir?" asked Groom.

"Well, I'd say about two hours or so ago."

Groom nodded. "Just what I thought. It had to be set alight when it was daylight. If it had blazed away in the dark, it'd have been noticed. . . . And another thing. Whoever did the job must have known this district pretty well, or he wouldn't have known that lane at all, let alone getting the car into the field. . . . I told the sergeant to have a hunt round to find those missing parts. Whoever did it wouldn't have carried them very far, or else he'd have been seen."

As they turned at the corner there was still no sign of life at Bland's cottage. At Combe Cottage a gardener in shirt-sleeves was mowing the front lawn. Down the hill where the track cut back to Morton's Woods, a policeman was waiting.

"We've found the car, sir!"

"Have you, by Jove!" Travers was getting his first thrill. The inspector drew the car in and in a couple of jiffs the three of them were striding away up the hill. A couple of hundred yards and they came to a gateway, almost opposite the ruins of what had been a cottage, and there between the trees was a tiny clearing, overgrown with grass and weeds a foot high, in which wheel tracks could be plainly seen.

"Where's the car?" asked Groom.

"Down there, sir, in the undergrowth. You can't see it for the dip."

It was, in fact, that level stretch of clearing that hid the car from sight. After that twenty yards, the hill fell away sheer, and another twenty yards down lay the overturned car among the shrubs and stunted bushes.

Travers felt a sudden, curious uneasiness. What was worrying him he didn't feel like putting into words. And yet the idea must be ridiculous. Surely Wharton and Menzies knew what they were doing! Then he went hot and cold all over.

"Is the windscreen smashed?" he asked the policeman.

"Smashed to smithereens, sir—and blood all over the place."

He turned to Groom. "Do you mind if I get a message through to town? Got a piece of paper on you?"

Groom gave him his notebook. When he read what Travers wrote, his eyes opened.

"Keep this to yourself," he told the man. "Ask Sergeant Mills to rush it to Taunton, and get them to put it through. . . . Then come back here!"

Groom watched the man move off, then nudged Travers.

"Some truth in the letter after all! If he drew the car in at that gate after dark, he'd never have been seen. Only he did it once too often. He lost control—and down she went!"

Travers nodded. His thoughts he felt like keeping to himself—but one thing had to come out.

"If it was a woman, then who disposed of the body? She couldn't have done it."

"Her husband did it!"

"Yes—but where? Was the body taken up there and the car let down the hill? Or was it an accident?"

He let himself down carefully without waiting for an answer. There was no need to worry about footprints in that bone-dry, leafy sort of earth, with rocky outcrops everywhere. If a foot had slipped and made a groove, the breeze and the sun had dried it long ago to the general colour of the mould. But it was awkward moving round the car. One had to hold on by bushes or a tree trunk, and the best way to view it was from below.

The pair of them and the other policeman stood there looking at it for some time, then Travers spoke.

"There are two dents in the front bumper. One clean in the middle and the other on the edge. The one on the edge was the devil of a wallop. It's bent the bumper right back and that's why the wing is crumpled. . . . What tree did it hit?"

Groom spotted the tree at once—the bark bruised down low where the bumper hit it and higher where the wing crumpled.

"Yes, but why the two dents in the bumper?" asked Travers. "It didn't hit any other tree."

The policeman had a suggestion to make. "It come down that slope pretty fast, you know, sir. Why shouldn't it have hit the tree and then rebounded, and hit it again?"

"Might be so!" There he stopped. Scrambling down the slope was a man, steadying himself as they had done, by the bushes. Travers didn't recognize him for a moment, then saw it was Sanders.

"My God! The reporter!"

"Who, sir?" asked Groom quickly.

"A reporter!" whispered Travers, feeling rather helpless and somehow annoyed. What the rights of the press were, he didn't know; but he felt in his bones that nobody but the law should be where they were now. And where on earth had he sprung from?

The inspector gave a holler. "Hi there! What are you doing here?"

It was all very childish and absurd; the inspector trying to bluster, Sanders sliding the last couple of yards and then rubbing the earth off his trousers, the policeman holding by the wing of the car and glaring belligerently as if he wished to act as chucker-out, and Travers looking very uncomfortable. Sanders ran his eyes over the car before he spoke.

"What was it? An accident?"

"Never you mind what it was!" said Groom curtly. "You get back where you come from, and get back quick—if you don't want to get into trouble."

Sanders nodded coolly. "Sorry, inspector, but I've got my job to do the same as you have yours. . . . What harm can I possibly be doing?"

"Never you mind what harm you're doing. You get back to the road again!" Then he thought of something. "How'd *you* know there was anything down here?"

"I wasn't fifty yards behind the three of you," said Sanders. "Combe Cottage, I was bound for, till I saw you three hurrying up here." He smiled, but none too pleasantly. "Don't you think you'd better change your mind? I represent two of the biggest papers in London—the *Record* and the *Evening Record*. You wouldn't like me to say that the local inspector . . . well, I put it to you!" and he shrugged his shoulders.

"I think I'd go if I were you, Mr. Sanders," put in Travers quietly. "We're all going. Besides, there's nothing to see!"

"Nothing to see! . . . I suppose there isn't—except that the whole thing's a mare's nest."

"You mean . . . an accident?"

"Well, isn't it obvious? There's the car—screen smashed to hell. It's Sir William's car, or you wouldn't be here. And Sir William had a cut throat!"

Travers was vaguely hostile. That damnably superior attitude of Sanders was beginning to irritate him.

"I see—sort of 'men may have their throats about them when they drive, and some say glass has edges.'"

Sanders sneered. "Mr. Travers, there's no need to get annoyed. Your Nym and Bardolph stuff doesn't alter the case one iota. I've seen an accident like this—I'll never forget it—where a poor devil had his head sliced like a turnip."

Travers felt that he was making none too good a show, and got a grip on himself.

"As you say, it rather looks as if the whole thing was an accident—except that people don't get into hampers by accident. Let's hope it is."

Sanders nodded and turned with the others as if to go. "One lesson it teaches us . . . that when you've got money there's nothing like spending it!"

"And how do you make that out?" asked Groom. "He was driving a '26 car. If he'd had a new one it'd have had unsplinterable glass as standard!" Groom looked none too pleased with the retort. He gave the policeman his orders to stand by the car till relieved, then moved off up the slope with the others. They stood for a moment or two at the gate as if waiting to see who was going, and where, then as if by some common impulse moved off down the hill together.

"What are you doing now, Mr. Sanders?" asked Travers. "Sending this through?"

Sanders seemed in no way elated. "May do! . . . I suppose you gentlemen wouldn't care to tell me why it was that you were looking exactly where you—"

"You're scenting a mystery where there isn't any," smiled Travers. "I mean, the roads are all being hunted over. What more natural than to begin near his house?"

"Exactly!" His tone was perfectly dispassionate. "As you say, there was every reason to expect to find the car there. Sir William was known to have gone down the hill after leaving his house. What more natural than that he should have pulled the car up dead, and cut right back at an acute angle and gone up an unused road, only wide enough for one car, and ending nowhere? And what did he go for, gentlemen? Not to study the stars. He wouldn't see many up there. And he didn't take an overcoat." The corners of his mouth drooped to a sort of smile. "Perhaps he was thinking out some new financial manipulation. Perhaps not. But if you or I had gone up there, gentlemen, the world wouldn't have been so charitable. Some mighty unpleasant things might have been said!"

"Such as—?"

"Well, a vulgar rendezvous. Absurd, of course, to connect a man like Griffiths with a thing like that, but there we are."

"You don't seem to have a very good opinion of the dead gentleman!" said Groom angrily.

"I! My dear sir! none better. A great financier; an enthusiastic fisherman . . . and all sorts of other things if only we could remember them. . . . And yet he appears to have overlooked one thing."

"What's that?"

"The lady's husband . . . who owned a hamper."

Groom stopped dead. "Just a minute, sir! What are you hinting at? What do you know?"

Sanders looked at him as if he were some strange insect.

"What do I know? . . . I know the law of evidence, which permits me to keep my mouth shut if I don't want to open it! And I know by the way you've taken it, that the little feeler I threw out has a considerable deal of truth in it!"

He moved on. Groom glared, then followed. Travers was interested. Sanders had certainly drawn a bow at a venture and hit the mark. But it was the man Sanders that interested him. If every representative of the press were as deliberately uncouth and provocative as he, it was a wonder they ever got news at all. Was Sanders accustomed to be feted by the authorities wherever he went on the heels of crime? And was he piqued because he hadn't been made much of? But even that wouldn't quite explain the deliberate trailing of his coat-tails, his readiness to sneer and his disregard of those little courtesies that make the wheels go smoothly.

"I'd like to put a little proposition up to you, gentlemen," came Sanders' voice again. "I'm open to exchange a perfectly good piece of information—one that's going to my papers at once—for the answer to a direct question. What about it?"

"What's your question?" asked Travers.

"Why were you in that wood?"

Travers caught the inspector's eye, and smiled. "To be frank, because of an anonymous letter."

"Really!" This time it was Sanders who stopped. "Might I see it?"

"Perfectly truly, it isn't available at the moment. Later, we'd be delighted to let you see it."

"Might I ask what was in it? Just the general purport?"

"Well, shall we say—just scandal!"

Sanders nodded. "They all fall for it! The older the quicker! . . . Same old theme, Mr. Travers. *Cherchez la femme!*"

"And what's your information?" asked Groom. Sanders waved his hand at the car. "When we get to the police station, if you don't mind."

The three got in, Travers and Sanders behind. As soon as the car started, Sanders leaned over. "You saw that hamper at Lord Zyon's house?" Travers nodded.

"So did I. Do you remember the dimensions?"

"Can't say I do."

Sanders took a paper from his notebook and passed it over. "Make a copy. You're likely to want it in a few minutes. I took them down while you were out of the room." He nudged Travers quickly. "There! Look! . . . Did you notice that laundry? . . . There's an open shed there, with a pile of hampers; brand-new; the same size as that. I spotted it this morning and I measured one to see. Pass that on to the inspector when we get back. I want to get my stuff off."

"Thanks!" said Travers. "I will."

As soon as the car pulled up, the reporter hurried off. Groom got out to speak to him, but he'd gone. Travers passed on the message.

"Right!" said Groom. "We'll go round and have a look. I shan't be a minute."

Travers prowled up and down a good five minutes before the inspector came out of the station again. Taunton, he said, had reported that Superintendent Wharton had already left London on account of a message of their own, but the Mulberton communication had been put through. But that didn't account for the inspector looking so hot and bothered.

"What do you think, sir?" he asked, with a heavy attempt at irony. "Just shows the sort of thing you get trucked up with! One old fool says some one let his sow and pigs out the other night and he reported it and we haven't done anything! And an old woman says some one stole her linen line. She reported it two days ago and it hasn't turned up yet!"

Travers smiled. "Every soul has its own tragedy! What's happened to the pigs? Turn up again?"

"All except one. . . . Shouldn't be surprised if he counted them wrong."

Except for a cottage immediately adjoining its yard, the laundry was the last building on leaving the town. The open shed with its hampers was easily visible from the road, and under the same shelter stood a couple of delivery vans.

"You wait here a minute, sir," said Groom. "I'll fetch the manager."

Travers took a hamper down from the pile and checked the measurements. Colour, rigidity, pattern of weaving; as far as he could see it was the very spit of the one that had held the body. The trouble was, the manager didn't seem to know if one were missing or not. He knew he had two dozen, but how many were out he couldn't say. Give him a few moments and he'd look up the books.

"Pretty confiding lot, you people down here!" said Travers. "That butler at Combe Cottage went to bed and left a French window open!" He waved his hand round. "Nothing to stop anybody helping himself to enough stuff to start a laundry on his own!"

"Bless your soul, sir!" laughed Groom. "We're not troubled with burglars round here! I suppose I leave windows open nine times out of ten—in the summer." He stopped suddenly. "While we're waiting, what about seeing Mrs. Crump about her linen line?"

"She lives handy?"

"That cottage there. . . . Might as well go this way."

They went through a gap in the railings into the cottage garden, and down a gravel path to the back door. The woman herself came out just as they got there. Groom hailed her jocularly.

"Morning, Mrs. Crump! What's all this trouble about a linen line?"

"There it is, sir; right under your nose!" She pointed to the linen posts that stood one at each end of the gravel path. From the top of each hung a foot of rope. The length between seemed to have been cut off cleanly with a knife. Travers looked at Groom. Groom nodded.

"If you don't mind, Mrs. Crump, we'll undo these ends they left and take them away as evidence. You'll hear something about it very soon."

"You think it was him that took it?" he asked when they'd got back to the Yard again.

"I think it's more than likely," said Travers. "The rope on the hamper was something like this; I can't say more till we see it again. When he was in the shed, he'd see it—and he could walk straight in, as we did. And it's lonely enough down here. There wasn't much risk!"

"Then he must have come from the town!"

"Maybe! The thing is, once the murder was done he certainly knew where to lay his hands on the hamper. And that rather points to somebody with local knowledge." The manager called them into the office to prove his case by the books. Three hampers only were out. He'd had those new ones in a few days ago, the idea being that they should be used for the best customers. One hamper was definitely missing.

"Combe Cottage one of your patrons?" asked Travers.

"They are, sir." Then his eyes opened. "You don't think—"

"Never mind what we think!" said Groom sharply. "And don't you go thinking things either, if you don't want to get into trouble. . . . Have you a hamper at Combe Cottage or have you not?"

"No! we haven't one there. We were going to send one this week."

Groom took down the address of the firm who made the hampers, gave the manager yet another caution, then they moved off back to the police station. There Travers did some phoning.

First came Mrs. Bland. The usual politeness— how was she, and so on. Mrs. Bland gushed that she was very well, and would Mr. Travers care to come to dinner. Just a scratch meal—at seven o'clock. Travers said he'd be delighted.

Next came Combe Cottage, where he got Griffiths. Might he drop in for a few minutes? Griffiths was most effusive in his welcome, then swore about Combe Cottage and things in general. Travers, with his mind on the arrival of Wharton and the dinner with Mrs. Bland, suggested somewhere round about six-thirty. And so to lunch.

CHAPTER IX
WHARTON HAS AN IDEA

IT WAS WELL after lunch when Wharton arrived in Taunton, where the local police had Travers' message and a railway porter both waiting for him.

"You got the message through to the Yard?" he asked.

"Yes, sir; but you'd just gone. Inspector Norris said he'd see to it. Colonel Kenton and Doctor Menzies are on the road now."

"Good!" said Wharton. "Let's have a look at the porter."

A few words of the story and he decided things would be easier to follow on the spot. The sergeant agreed and the three of them adjourned to the railway station. The porter took up his position.

"Now then," said Wharton; "you were standing here at seven-thirty. You'd just shifted some stuff across the line and brought the barrow back. Now; where'd the man come from?"

"Through there, sir." He indicated a wicket-gate well beyond the end of the platform, and virtually outside the station bounds. Wharton had a look through it. Across the forty yards of open space a road could be seen, leading apparently to the town. "Where's that road go to?" he asked the sergeant. "It joins the station road again a little way along, sir. It makes a sort of island."

Wharton squinted round the corner. The gate was well clear of the booking-office approach and at that hour of the morning there'd be few people about. The porter went on with his story.

He was leaning on his barrow when a man hailed him; a man of fair height with a waterproof buttoned up to his chin. The morning in fact, at that hour, was a bit nippy. The first thing noticed was that the man was lame; his right leg bent over so that he walked on the side of his boot. He wore glasses, had a grey moustache, and his hair was grey at the temples. By him was a hamper from which cabbage leaves could be seen protruding. All he asked was whether the porter would keep an eye on the hamper for him and label it for Paddington. The porter, gathering that the farmer—for that's what he took him for—intended to take the hamper into the carriage with him, informed him that it was much too large for the rack or under the seat. What he'd do would be to label it and put it in the van of the express. The stranger thanked him and said he'd see him before the train left. Then he limped off through the gate again.

"Why did you take him for a farmer?" asked Wharton.

"He looked like one, sir. And he had an old chummy hat on, all pulled down. I thought he was going up to London for the day and was taking a present like. And he spoke like a Somerset man."

"And what happened then?"

"Well, sir, I labelled the hamper and put it in the van. I weighed it first and found it wasn't much over the hundred-weight, so I put it in. I didn't see him till I'd done that, then I walked along the train and he gave me a shilling."

The fact that the hamper should have paid carriage didn't concern Wharton in the least; and he set the porter's mind at rest by saying so. But what about where the man went to, after he left the hamper on the platform?

"That I don't know, sir," the man told him. "I know he went through that gate."

"And you didn't hear a car drive off?"

"No, sir, I didn't. You see, sir, we hear so many cars here that I shouldn't have noticed it if I had." That was the extent of the porter's information. The hamper they showed him was declared to be the same; fastenings, colour, size, everything; even to the weight. It was labelled in some name—he forgot what—as "Passenger to London." As for his description of the man, Wharton knew that was worth very little. The lameness was undoubtedly simulated, and even the news about the Somerset accent might be hopelessly wrong. The porter himself spoke more like a Londoner, and whether he was a judge of accent was extremely doubtful. Wharton dismissed him with a tip and his blessing.

"That hamper must have got here on a conveyance of some sort," he said to the sergeant. "And where did he go to? He could have got breakfast here, in the refreshment-room."

"He had a car, sir, and he went to garage it," was the sergeant's opinion.

It was Wharton's too. "That looks easy. All we've got to do is to find a garage where somebody of the description garaged a car at that particular time."

"It'd be quicker still, sir, if we could find somebody who saw it, then we'd know the make of car to ask for at the garage."

"That's true enough. Whom do you suggest asking?"

The sergeant suddenly had a brain wave.

"You might do worse, sir, than see the *Messenger*. It goes to press early this evening. If you could get them to put a notice on the front page, it'd be all over the town in an hour!"

Wharton hurried off at once. The *Weekly Messenger*, a publication more local than the daily of which it was a weekly summary, was just about to go to press. The editor was only too pleased to fall in with Wharton's suggestion—a heavy, black inset on the front page, with a reminder of Lord Zyon's £5,000 offer, and a request for two pieces of information. Then as a kind of return for favours received, Wharton radiated the light of his presence for a minute or two and gave a few facts that were not for publication. The editor was duly impressed. Indeed, as he was in the very act of leaving the room, Wharton added the sensational news that Sir William's car had been discovered. More, at the moment, he didn't know. He was just going down to investigate as soon as certain experts arrived from town.

The editor contributed some information of his own.

"Do you know, Mr. Wharton, we feel a special interest down here in this case! I don't mean because of Sir William or because it happened at Mulberton. . . . The reason is that it was one of our own men who's making his name over it."

Wharton didn't understand. The other waved a triumphant hand.

"Fred Sanders! Sanders of the *Record*! He started down here. He's a Taunton man!" Wharton closed the door again.

"Really now! I call that very interesting! . . . I suppose you lost sight of him for some years."

The other pooh-poohed that suggestion. Somerset men weren't like that—forgetting the rock whence they were hewn. But didn't the superintendent know about Sanders? How he'd lost his job over the *Mercury* amalgamation?

Wharton, having left town just before the issue of the midday *Record*, didn't know a word.

"He had a very bad time, poor fellow I . . . You know what hack work is, Mr. Wharton. Once or twice he sent us stuff down here, and I may say we were very glad to take it."

"Did he ever come down at all?"

"Once or twice. As a matter of fact I saw him the day Sir William was killed. He just dropped in for a chat." The editor was struck by a strange coincidence. "By the way, he told me he was going to see . . . or was it that he *had* seen?—Mr. Timothy Griffiths. He'd got an idea about getting a story out of him—about his expedition, you know." He clicked his tongue. "Of course! How foolish of me. He must have called in here on his way back from seeing Mr. Griffiths. He was on his way to town, otherwise he couldn't have been there the next morning when he was!"

The editor beamed over that piece of deduction. Wharton added that the world was a small place. He added, in addition, thanks and more thanks, then hurried back to the station. Kenton and Menzies had not turned up, but it wasn't about them that he was worrying—it was his trunk call to town. He got it—and he got Norris.

"Something urgent, Norris. Get taxis checked up to see if anybody took on a fare from the Albert Hall to the neighbourhood of Park Terrace, immediately after the hamper left the Hall."

"Very good, sir. Anything else?"

The tone was so patently inquisitive that Wharton smiled.

"Yes. . . . Have you heard anything about that reporter not being on the regular staff of the *Evening Record*?"

"Yes, sir! It came out in the noon edition to-day. He was a free-lance."

"Splendid! . . . You there? . . . Well, I want you to carry on a fresh investigation—in any way you like. Use your imagination." Even over the phone he couldn't resist a curtain.

"Very good, sir. . . . Imagine *what*, sir?"

Wharton glanced round, then breathed secretively.

"Imagine *Sanders* did it!"

He heard Norris' quick, "What! the reporter!"—gave a sharp, "That's right!" then hooked up the receiver.

. . . .

An hour later, Wharton, Menzies and Colonel Kenton were shaking hands with Travers in Mulberton police station.

"Now then," said Wharton breezily. "What's all this panic? Why drag Menzies from the joys of London—let alone the Colonel here?"

Travers smiled sheepishly. "To be perfectly frank, I rather did panic, as soon as the car was found. Still, you'll see for yourselves."

"See what?" persisted Wharton.

Travers looked even more sheepish. "Well, I suppose I was a bit of a fool. The doctor here will have to forgive me. . . . You see, when I knew the car had been found capsized with the wind-screen smashed and blood all over it, I . . . well, I wondered if the whole thing had been an accident!"

Menzies had a tremendous admiration for Travers, though Travers never suspected it. His grizzled, old face took on a dry sort of smile. "You did the right thing, Mr. Travers. Only, you see, we naturally thought of that. If a man's found with his throat cut, you don't necessarily look for a razor!"

Kenton, a tall, white-moustached sahib of a man, smiled too. "If it comes to that, you don't look for car accidents either!"

"Some of us do!" fired back Menzies. "Tell me, Colonel. You've seen a good many stiff 'uns after car accidents. Ever see a man or woman with a cut throat?"

"More than one."

"Good! Any other cuts or abrasions? I mean, if you examined carefully faces or skulls, did you see cuts from flying glass or contusions where the face or the skull struck?"

"I didn't do the looking—but undoubtedly they were there."

Menzies nodded triumphantly. "That's my point! Sir William's face was spotless. There wasn't a mark or a cut or a bruise. Why then should there be any idea of a car accident? Even when we knew he'd last been seen going off in a car, we didn't let it enter our heads."

"I'm sorry!" began Travers.

"Come along!" said Wharton impatiently. "No use arguing the point here. Let's go and see what there is to see," and he stumped off.

Travers caught him in time. Wharton's eyes opened at the news about hamper and rope. Menzies and the colonel pushed on ahead with a policeman as guide; the others, with Groom, spent a minute or two in the inspector's room, with the original hamper and rope on view. As for the hamper, there seemed no doubt whatever. Either it had come from the laundry or it had been made by the same firm that supplied the laundry. As the address of the firm was the Isle of Athelney, a phone call could easily check if and when hampers of that size and quality had been supplied anywhere in the district. The firm, as far as the laundry manager knew, had no agents, and the hampers could only be obtained direct.

The rope wasn't quite so certain. There were no severed ends, for instance, that made a perfect join with those odd feet left dangling from the linen posts. Still, they seemed to be weathered to the same colour and the strands were the same. Wharton noted them down for a microscopic examination.

"About that anonymous letter? Got it handy?"

Groom unlocked a drawer and produced it. Wharton sat contemplating it for a bit, then put it away in his pocket-book.

"I'll keep this if you don't mind. Dyerson'd like to compare it with the labels. . . . That burnt-out car you saw this morning, Mr. Travers? Had it got a rumble seat?"

"Quite a big one. Some of those early cars had them like that."

"It might have taken the hamper at a pinch?"

"I think so. In any case the inspector here has had the foresight to arrange for it to be brought along. Not that we were thinking about that. Still, we can prove your point. . . . But if that's the car that carried the body to Taunton, why wasn't it burnt yesterday and not to-day?"

"That's up to us to find out." He got up. "Anything else? If not we'll get along and see the other car."

As soon as he looked over the gate at Morton's Woods, Wharton made a wry face at the footmarks that had trampled down grass and weeds in the small clearing. Travers blushed as he followed a circuitous route in the General's tracks. Kenton had finished his first inspection and Menzies was having a look at the damaged wing.

"What about it?" asked Wharton.

"The petrol was on," Kenton told him. "It was driven to the edge there, then slipped into neutral and let go."

"Anything unusual?"

"Yes," said Kenton. "The wing there, crumpled against the tree."

It was the one that Travers had already remarked on; the front near wing, crumpled up like a concertina.

"Did it strike the tree and rebound?"

"Don't see how it could," Kenton told him. "It hit the tree and it overturned. Why did you ask?"

"Because of the mark in the *middle* of the bumper. How'd that get there if the car didn't rebound and hit the tree twice?"

Kenton smiled enigmatically. "That's what's unusual!"

Travers collapsed. Wharton, with the aplomb of the half-informed, stepped into the breach.

"If it's unusual, what do you suggest?"

"Give us time," said Kenton imperturbably. "Wait till we get her moved, then well talk some more."

"What about lights?"

Kenton turned the switch. Two lights went on.

"I'd say there weren't any lights on when she was let loose down here. The battery would have exhausted."

Menzies, who had stepped aside while Kenton tinkered with the lights, leaned well down into the car and retrieved the foot-mat. He pointed to the matted fibre where the blood had congealed.

"Lusty old boy! What's the Bard say? 'Didn't think the old man had so much blood in him.'" He laid the mat aside, then began examining the broken glass that lay heaped up against the under door.

"Just a moment, doc!" Kenton called out. "Don't touch that glass, if you don't mind." He changed his mind. "No! I'll tell you what we'll do. Get it all out and see what there is. Everybody lend a hand, and mind you don't tread any in."

That was easy enough once the hood had been drawn back. In five minutes the car was clear of all but the smallest splinters, the ground had been searched round the tree and even the bushes had been shaken and explored. Kenton looked round.

"Now we'll get her up. How many are we? Two at the gate and five here; that's seven. I think she'll cant this way."

With an improvised wedge or two and a rail for lever, they got the car on its wheels with hand-brake hard on. Once more the ground was searched for glass, then a rug was produced from the back of the car and the pile of broken glass deposited. Kenton explained his scheme.

"It'd be too much to put the jig-saw puzzle together. What I'd like you to do is assemble the pieces to a kind of rectangle so that we can measure the area against the holes in the screen."

Travers saw it in a flash. The car had been run to the edge of the slope and then the brake taken off. The car, gathering impetus, had torn down the incline and gone full tilt into the tree. The end of the bumper had bent, then with the slight recoil the wing had crumpled and the car had slowly toppled over. But that first striking of the tree could never have bent the *middle* of the bumper. What more natural, then, than to suppose that the dent in the middle of the bumper had been caused by a previous accident—and since the car had presumably been in order when Daniels brought it round, by an accident that very same evening!

That must be the basis of Kenton's scheme. There had been two collisions. And if two collisions, why shouldn't the glass have been broken at the first one? If it had, then the broken pieces had been carefully gathered up before the car was brought along to Morton's Woods. If there were any missing, Kenton's test would show it, and prove at the same time that there really had been a previous accident.

And with regard to that first collision, the car must have struck the obstacle with considerable force or the middle of the bumper could never have been dented so badly. But the shock had not put the car out of action, since it had been brought along up that steep hill to where the second accident had occurred. That seemed to be in Kenton's mind too, for he was flooding the carburettor. Then he adjusted the controls. A quick jerk at the starting handle and the engine was purring away. Next he lifted the bonnet and listened; shut her off, restarted her and listened again. Then he left her ticking over quietly.

"Good job it was an open car," said Wharton, surveying the mosaic of glass. "If it'd been a saloon you'd have had a bushel of this stuff to sort out."

Kenton ran his rule over it. Travers followed him to the shattered screen. Wharton's rectangle of glass represented about two-thirds of the area that was missing. Kenton checked it again, then explained his theory.

"What are you going to do about it?" asked Wharton.

"First of all," said Kenton, "we'll run her in reverse up the slope again and out to the road. Then we'll have a hunt round for more glass. There might be some in those weeds and rubbish."

Kenton took the wheel with four of them pushing and two manipulating the improvised blocks. When finally they'd got her out on the road again, they lined up at the bottom of the slope and searched the track again. Not a single piece of glass was found.

"That seems pretty conclusive," said Wharton. "The point is, Where did the original accident occur? It must have been in a side road or somebody would have noticed it and reported it when inquiries were being made."

"Not necessarily—if you'll pardon me," said Kenton. "We have to remember the collision wasn't a serious one. It might have happened and the car been driven off again in a matter of seconds."

"You're forgetting the time taken to pick up all the glass!" said Wharton.

"Yes . . . perhaps I am." He shook his head. "Do you know, I don't see why that first collision should have smashed the screen at all—unless a projection hit it."

"You mean, the bumper hit a tree and a projecting branch hit the screen?"

"Well, something along those lines. Mind you, those bumpers aren't a lot of good. They're quite a cheap set and were put on specially. They weren't standard on that particular make of car that year."

"If that reporter fellow were here," said Groom feelingly, "he'd be giving us another lecture on the folly of being economical!"

"What's that about the reporter?" Wharton asked.

The inspector unburdened his soul. Wharton was graciously pleased to disagree.

"Well, I don't know that he's far wrong. However"—he looked round for Kenton—"what do you say, Colonel? Start at Combe Cottage and try the roads for what he might have hit?"

Kenton agreed and Groom set things going at once. Travers glanced at his watch and saw that if he wanted to get back to the town and then up to Combe Cottage in time, he'd have to hurry. Still, Wharton was going back and so was Menzies. Kenton proposed hanging on a bit longer. The brakes were tested and Travers volunteered to drive the damaged car. Menzies got in alongside.

"You can see things better like this," he explained. "You, for instance, at the wheel. If you hit the bank now, and shot forward, where'd you hit the screen? Not dead in line with the wheel, where that main breakage is. You'd hit the wheel first, then skid. If you hit the screen after that, it'd be about here—opposite where I'm sitting."

"You mean the breaking of the screen was a fake?"

"That's not my line," said Menzies. "But it's sound common sense." He produced a sliver of glass from his pocket and chuckled. "Here's one piece Wharton didn't put in his damn puzzle! See the blood on it? See the thickness? The double edge?" He put it back in his pocket. "The throat wasn't cut with that! It was cut with a single edge —sharp as a razor. Much stiller than a razor, of course."

"Why?"

"A razor edge would be bound to turn, no matter how tight it's held. You try holding a razor tightly and see what sort of a hand you make of it!" He shook his head with what looked like considerable satisfaction. "No! it was drawn across the throat—swish!—like that! And it wasn't a razor."

Travers winced—and changed the subject.

The car was drawn into the police garage and locked up. Travers fidgeted round, then said he'd have to be pushing off.

"Oh, yes!" said Wharton. "You're going visiting." He fell into step as far as the hotel door. "One little thing I'd like you to remember specially when you see Griffiths. Find out if he ever ran up against that reporter before. Even if he'd ever had a letter from him."

"What—Sanders?"

"That's right!" Wharton spoke so off-handedly that he overdid it. Travers suddenly saw a great light.

CHAPTER X
TRAVERS—AND DELILAH

As Travers opened the gate of Combe Cottage, something suddenly struck him as peculiar. Why hadn't Tim Griffiths gone to London? One would have thought that as soon as his uncle was dead, he'd have sprinted hot-foot to the lawyers to see what was coming to him—and to get his fingers well into it. If Travers' judgment was correct, Griffiths should have spoken to Wharton about the matter the previous night; at the least he should have rung up himself that morning and suggested that there was surely no need to rusticate any longer! Wharton had neither laid an embargo nor hinted at it. The Tim Griffiths, therefore, who was continuing to stagnate in Mulberton, had yet another side that might repay research.

Daniels, the self-styled butler, showed Travers in. His manner was slightly fussy; why, was soon apparent.

"Is there any truth, sir, in the tale the gardener brought just now? He says the car—Sir William's car—has been found, sir!"

"Yes," said Travers, strolling on towards the door through which apparently he was meant to go. Daniels put down hat and rain-coat hastily and followed on his heels. He opened the door and announced Travers and the news in the same voice.

"Mr. Travers, Sir Timothy . . . and it's true, sir!" Griffiths, clad properly and seemingly in his soberest mind, held out his hand. Travers had never seen him so subdued.

"Glad to see you, Travers. . . . What's this about the car?"

As he told as much of the story as he thought Wharton would sanction, Travers was again brought face to face with that curious problem of master and man. There was nothing in the demeanour of Daniels that was other than respectful; indeed it was his obvious knowledge of his job, his manner of speech and his smooth deference that made so conspicuous the fact that he was remaining in the room without an invitation. He merely stood there, head slightly bowed, listening to what Travers spoke—not to him but as pointedly as possible to his master. It was only when the story was over and there was nothing else to be learned that he gave a quick nod and made as if to withdraw.

"Oh! just a minute!" said Griffiths. "Of course you'll stay to dinner? Such as there is."

"My dear fellow, I'd be delighted! Unfortunately—or fortunately!—Mrs. Bland asked me first. I'm due there at seven."

Daniels bowed again and departed.

"Mrs. Bland asked you, did she?" said Griffiths. "Do you know her at all? I mean, is she a friend of yours?"

Travers explained away the circumstances.

"I just wanted to know," went on Griffiths, "to save dropping any bricks. Really, you know, you're in for a most appalling time! She's a terrible woman!"

Travers smiled. "Oh, I don't know! A bit on the surface, shall we say."

"My God I she's awful! Do you know where Bland picked her up? She was a chorus girl!"

"Girl! She must be forty."

"They have 'em older than that!" said Griffiths. "Ten years ago he married her and he's stuck it out. After he married her—perhaps I should say, when my uncle took him on—he kept her well out of the old man's way. Then he told him to bring his wife down here with him. You see Bland always mucked in here, so the old man had some rooms got ready. She came. The old boy stood it for a week, then he bought that cottage the Blands occupy now and told Bland in so many words to take his wife to hell out of it. My God! she hated the old boy like sin." Travers smiled discreetly. "Well, I don't think I should have liked it very much myself! What did Bland think of it?"

"Bland? . . . Can't say. He's one of those deep devils. And he knew which side his bread was buttered on. . . . By the way, she was round here this morning, nosing about."

"For what?" asked Travers quickly.

Griffiths prevaricated. "Oh! just to see what she *could* see, now the old man's gone. All gush and girlishness! Damned impertinence I call it—as things are."

Travers nodded. What he was waiting for was the opening to put his question. By an extraordinary stroke of luck it was Griffiths himself who broached that subject.

"Something I wanted to ask you," he said. "Who was the fellow with you and Wharton last night?"

"Oh, that chap!" said Travers airily. "He was a reporter. Rather important person, we gathered. Represents the *Record*. Those fellows can be remarkably useful, you know, when you want any publicity for a case."

"I've got it!" said Griffiths. "Was his name Saunders or Sanders, or something like that?"

"That's right! Why? Do you know him?"

"The curious thing is I ought to have known him, if you know what I mean. I thought I knew him last night. I said to myself when you'd gone, 'I've seen that chap somewhere or other!' What put me off was his having no moustache."

"Had a moustache, had he?"

"Well, he had when I saw him last. In Taunton it was, one day last week. I was just drawing in to the curb, outside the Royal, when this chap comes along in a little car and hits my wing. He hopped out and apologized and all that; then he said, 'Aren't you So-and-So?' and I said I was; and the long and short of it was he asked if I could give him a yarn or two for a story. Just shows you what damn liars those fellows are! He told me he'd lost his job and was on the rocks."

"Why didn't he sell his car?"

"Car! My God! you ought to have seen it. Collection of old iron! I'll bet it was among the first half dozen Morrises turned out."

Travers made some fatuous remark and the conversation switched to other subjects, and all the while in the air was the feeling that Griffiths was fencing for an opening. What it was Travers didn't know, till the question came.

"You're absolutely certain it was an accident?"

"I put it to you," said Travers. "The smashed screen and the blood and . . . well, it's pretty horrible to talk about."

Griffiths closed his eyes for a moment as if with a sudden spasm of neuralgia. When he spoke again he didn't seem quite at ease.

"And who did that damn business with the hamper?"

"Ah!" said Travers. "That's what the police are here to find out. A lunatic seems the best suggestion —unless of course . . ." he broke off tantalizingly.

"Unless what?"

"Too absurd really! It was suggested that the car was taken up there for an assignation with a woman; that her husband went to catch them, saw the smashed car—and *voila*!"

The smile that had dawned on Griffiths' face died away. "I wouldn't have thought it, mind you, but you never know. Just the sort of thing—er—old men of that age . . ."

Travers helped him out in his groping. "Any woman likely? . . . Strictly between ourselves, might that row with Mrs. Bland have been a put-up business, for instance?"

"You never know," said Griffiths frowning. Then his face cleared. "Of course I've been away. What's been going on I shouldn't know."

"Exactly! Still, if anything turns up I'll let you know." He waved away the thanks. "How's the film going? Trade show yet?"

"I say! Didn't you have a ticket? It's to-day. Of course I couldn't get away."

"It must have missed me," said Travers. "But why didn't you go up? Not necessarily to the trade show—but to town?"

"But I didn't think I'd be. . . . I mean it was—"

"Nonsense! Go up to town. Get out of this atmosphere for a bit. You've heard from Sir Henry?"

Griffiths looked like a man whose doctor has told him there's nothing to worry about.

"Oh, yes! I heard this morning. You really think I might?"

"Of course I do!" said Travers heartily. "Not only that, there'll be things you *ought* to see to, unless you want Sir Henry to have you in leading strings. There's a pretty big career in front of you, young feller, if you set your mind to it."

On his face Travers could see the quick envisagement of the new prospects; the innate conceit of the man reacting to the new situation.

"I think you can take it as official," Travers went on. "Naturally the police want nothing from you but assistance, and Daniels can do that. Wire Sir Henry and go to town to-morrow. Where's the funeral?"

"In town." He squared his shoulders, then grinned cheerfully. "Do you know, I think I will. I'll go up to-morrow, first thing in the morning. . . . Now, what about a spot, to celebrate?"

"Bit soon for me," said Travers. "Still, the merest spot—and plenty of soda."

Griffiths raised his glass. "Well, lots of fun!" Perhaps he caught the sudden look that passed across the other's face. "And a peaceful bed for the old boy. He wasn't a bad old scout—in his way." Travers drank gravely and put down his glass. His face puckered to that whimsical smile of his.

"And you're not a bad scout—in a way! There's only one person who rather upsets things."

The other looked up quickly. "Who's that?"

"Yourself!" When he came to think of it afterwards in cold blood he wondered how he'd had the nerve to do it, but for five good minutes he told Tim Griffiths more home truths than he'd heard for some time. It was amazing, too, the way Griffiths took it; in some ways he didn't seem the same man. If he wasn't at the penitent form he was remarkably near it.

"You're quite right, Travers. . . . I suppose I have been a bit of a swine . . . in some ways." He shook his head, then squared his shoulders again. "Once all this business is over, you're going to see the difference. I'm cutting all this out. I'm going to settle down."

"I know you are!" smiled Travers. "You'll forgive me—er—talking to you like a father."

"Forgive you!" He shook his head again. "You're an extraordinarily good fellow, Travers. Everybody says so—"

"Nonsense!" Travers positively blushed, then breezed his way out of it. "You go up to town tomorrow and have a change of scenery." He glanced at his watch. "Well, I think I'll be pushing along."

"Don't be in a hurry!" Griffiths hesitated in a curious manner. He made as if to say something. Travers could see him working up to it, screwing up his resolution and hunting for words—and wondered what the confidence would be.

It didn't come. "I wonder . . ." began Griffiths diffidently; then there was a tap at the door and Daniels appeared. "Pardon, sir, but I thought you rang."

"Then you thought wrong," said Griffiths curtly. Daniels bowed meekly and disappeared.

Travers hung on for a minute or two after the man had gone, but whatever sudden impulse it had been that had moved Tim Griffiths to open his heart, had gone too. He sensed that only too well. What intrigued him more, as he strolled along towards Bland's cottage, was the aptness of the butler's entry.

Had the case been provable, and a taker available, Travers would have laid ten to one on there being something more than chance in the moment of interruption. Had there been more listening at keyholes?

He smiled at the audacity of his own deductions—then frowned. And he was still thinking it over when he reached the cottage gate.

. . . .

"You really *must* see our little nest!" Mrs. Bland had kittenishly remarked as soon as he arrived. The cottage was rather large for that, as Travers, with a simulated archness, informed her. The main room was quite a big place, running from front to back, and looking even more spacious by daylight than it had done the night before. By a French window it opened on a kind of loggia, whose roof was supported by wooden posts covered with untidy ramblers, and the garden—nearly all lawn—stretched away up the hill.

"That chimney there—just visible!" said Travers. "It can't be Combe Cottage, surely!"

"Oh, yes!" she assured him. "Though it's much further off than it looks!"

Back in the living-room again, she opened a door to the right which showed a smaller room. From it another French window led to the loggia.

"You must look in here! This is my hubby's study!"

Travers winced at the description, looked as directed and saw nothing but a room a man might occupy* Absently he was hoping that Wharton would not forget their agreement; that no later than 8.30 he was to be called up on the phone, to return to Mulberton on urgent business.

"We'd better stay in here now," announced his hostess. "And we'll have a drink. That'll give Gertie a chance to get dinner on. And I know what you men are!"

"Perhaps you're right!" said Travers. He hollered 'when' as directed, took a lot of soda, waited till her tot was ready, then clinked glasses in what was meant to be the accepted style. A bit more chatter, then:

"Oh! you must hear our wireless! We keep it in the kitchen, you know. So handy for the maid."

She disappeared into the kitchen. Travers sat resignedly over his drink and cigarette. Only fifteen minutes gone—and it seemed an hour. It was an awful pity, somehow, about Mrs. Bland. She meant so well. Pretty too, in a way; rather like a Testout rose about to drop. Damn fascinating woman when she was younger—to the right man, that is, and at the right moment. Pity, too, she'd gone to all that fuss about that red gown. So unnecessary, and made her look plumper and more blowzy than she was.

The door from the kitchen opened and she appeared, holding a loud-speaker.

"Sorry I've left you so long! Where shall we have it? Here, I think." She set it down and surveyed it. "Do you dance?"

"Abominably!" said Travers. "Worse perhaps than that!"

She laughed. "I don't believe it! . . . Just a minute now!" and out she flew again to the kitchen. There was silence for a minute, then with a suddenness that made him start, the loud-speaker blared. Mrs. Bland came back full of beams, rubbing her hands.

"Now then, you frivolous man! We'll see if you're a dark horse!"

"But really!" protested Travers as the chairs were whisked back to make a space. The protest was smothered as she manoeuvered him into position. . . . A minute, and the dance flopped. Travers flopped too, and smiled weakly.

"Well, I warned you!" The announcer's voice cut him short.

"You're not half bad!" she told him. "If I had five minutes with you, you'd be first-class."

The band began again. Travers sparred for time.

"Where's the program coming from?"

"From the Midland. It's a special dance program." She looked at him roguishly. "Don't tell me you're highbrow!"

He smiled modestly. "Well, I have my moments. Er—quite a good set you have."

"It is a good set. Works by electricity, you know. You just plug in and tune in. The other night we had the most marvellous thing! *Bolero!* Do you know it?"

"Ravel's *Bolero*?"

"That's it! It was on from London, and Mr. Cross—he's the Vicar of Barlcombe; such a nice man!—well, he was playing chess with my husband and he said he'd like to hear it. Of course we knew it was on—in the *Radio Times*. Perfectly wonderful! Do you know it?"

"Oh, yes!" By hook or crook he meant to keep that conversation going, even if it meant bellowing through that infernal music. "All drum taps and things. Works up to a tremendous climax."

She nodded. "Makes you go all goosey! And wasn't it awful!" Her eyes opened wide with the horror of the recollection. "Us sitting here and listening to that and all the while that dreadful person—whoever it was—" She shuddered expressively and waved her hand in the direction of Combe Cottage. Then she jumped up quickly. "Don't let's talk about it! . . . Another foxtrot! Come on! Like you did the last."

The very last second brought reprieve. The music stopped and before the adenoidal member of the band could announce the next item, the maid popped her head inside the door to say that dinner was ready.

The meal was quite good and the maid a thoroughly efficient body. She too came down to Mulberton from the villa in Golders Green, whenever Mrs. Bland came down. Travers talked all that over as the hands of the grandfather clock slowly moved round. Then, gravelled for lack of matter, he admired the clock—a clumsy affair with an exaggerated breadth of base that gave it a dumpy look.

"Quite a charming clock you have there!"

"Yes! isn't it sweet! And it keeps the most marvellous time! My hubby says it doesn't vary a minute a month!"

Travers was duly impressed and clocks lasted out the blancmange and fruit. Then over coffee and cigarette he worked out a more subtle move.

"I suppose you go to plenty of shows in town?"

She laughed. "I'm always going! You see, I'd be so much alone—in the afternoons especially."

"You like the theatre?"

"Oh, yes!" She looked him clean in the eye. "You see, it's in my blood. . . . I used to be connected with the stage myself. All our family were!"

"Really!" said Travers. "I'd no idea I was being entertained so charmingly by so"—he smiled delightfully—"so important a person!"

Her smile was alluring. "You're laughing at me!"

He protested. "My dear Mrs. Bland!"

The look this time was of rather a saucy nature. "You know you could be rather attractive if you liked! Like my husband. You ought to get about and see things. Have a good time while you've got the chance."

Travers smiled warily. "How do you know I don't?"

That amused her immensely. "You men are all alike!" The thought probably inspired the refilling of his glass. Travers, in his new role of dark horse, made no protest. The clock hands showed 8.25.

"When's Mr. Bland coming back?"

Her interpretation of that innocent remark was extremely disconcerting. She balanced her chin on her hand and looked at him with what was undoubtedly meant to be provocation.

"Why do you ask that?"

"Well," said Travers lamely, "I—er—just wondered!"

She leaned closer. "You know, you and I could get on quite well together . . . couldn't we?"

"Yes," said Travers slowly. "Perhaps we could." He hopped up to fetch an ashtray. "By the way, how do you get on with Griffiths? Sir Timothy, that is."

"Him! . . . Oh, he's all right. Thinks too much of himself, that's all."

"Yes," said Travers. "Perhaps you're right. . . . Did he get on all right with his uncle?"

Her voice lowered. "They had a terrible row. . . . I oughtn't to tell you!"

"Why not?"

She hesitated, then blurted it out—as he felt she had all the time intended. Griffiths had had words with his uncle the very evening he was killed. They'd called each other the most dreadful things. The old man had a vile temper. Tim had told him to go to hell and the old man had said if he left the house he'd never set foot in it again. All about money, it had been, and some girl or other Sir William had put his foot down about.

"Don't you go saying anything!" was the end of it. "I'm not supposed to know anything about this."

Travers promptly promised secrecy. The clock had gone the half hour. What the devil was Wharton doing! If she began making eyes again. . . .

"Oh! I've got some news for you!" He told her all about the car. And what did she think about the theory that Sir William might have been carrying on with some woman?

She appeared to think it pretty feasible. "You never can tell with crafty ones like that. Just the same as anybody else, aren't they? You don't tell me!"

Travers nodded sagely. Then, in the study, the telephone bell rang. In a couple of minutes he was expressing his desolation. Just his luck that his man should suddenly have arrived from town, with news of something urgent that simply must be attended to. Still there might be another chance, perhaps—if—er—

"How long are you staying?" she asked mysteriously.

"Only a day or two—unfortunately. Nothing to keep me here now."

He was moving over to the door and she followed. Some perversity; some itch to be clever, to prove to himself what a shrewd fellow he was, must have prompted him to the foolishness. He lowered his head to her ear.

"That reminds me. You didn't tell me when Mr. Bland would be back!"

She must have put out her left hand and switched off the light. Then her arms were round his neck and he found himself in an embrace that was luxuriously passionate. Her lips pressed on his and her face felt like fire. She whispered in his ear:

"Not till the day after to-morrow!"

Travers, face fiery red, gently released himself. His voice sounded ridiculous. Thank God! the room was dark.

"Tea to-morrow. . . . May I come?"

His hand reached for the door knob and as her hands felt for him again, he opened the door.

. . . .

As he walked back to Mulberton, he found it difficult to analyze either emotions or impressions. That horrible affair of those few minutes ago, would keep obtruding itself like an obsession. For all his aversions, he was probably full-blooded enough. Given the right woman—and every other propitious circumstance—all sorts of things might happen. But this was appalling! That woman with her gush and her slang and her suburban vulgarity. . . . For the tenth time he went hot and cold all over. Blast the woman!—and Wharton too. Why didn't he do his damned inquiries himself?

And what had he learned? He shook his head. Only too easy to jump to conclusions and let the wish father the thought. But perfectly unbiased and unprejudiced, what might be deduced? That for some reason of her own, she wished to have him—well, on her side. To learn or conceal? That he didn't know. And she'd been anxious he should dance—or was it that he should hear that damn wireless set? And she'd shown him the rooms—and prevaricated about her connection with the stage—and she'd been bursting to tell him about that quarrel.

Then a thought—a startling one. Had Bland left her there with implicit instructions? Was she—using her own methods and armoury—working to a schedule he'd laid down? And had the riddle of the case been spread out before him that evening, if he could only have pieced it together?

And yet that was absurd. Bland had a cast-iron alibi. So presumably had his wife. And yet it wasn't absurd. There'd been something in the air that evening; something that she'd tried to convey to him; something that he'd been meant to see—and to remember. Perhaps Wharton might make something of it from a detailed account. Travers blushed. Not too detailed. . . . And of course there was all that other news—about Sanders.

THE FIRST SHORT-CUT

CHAPTER XI
THE MAN WHO WAS MAD

MYSTERY WAS in the air when Travers got to the police station. A constable headed him off at the door.

"Mr. Wharton wants to see you, sir. This way, sir!"

Travers followed round to the back and through a side door. In a small waiting-room were Wharton and Kenton. The former seemed rather agitated.

"I thought you were never coming! What's been happening?"

Travers blushed involuntarily. "Don't court-martial me, George! Why didn't you ring up at eight-thirty?"

"Because I wasn't here." Wharton spoke crisply. "Get any news about Sanders?"

"Heaps! . . . Why?"

"Never mind why. There're big things on . . . if you've got the right stuff."

"Well, Griffiths saw Sanders in Taunton last week and Sanders spoke to him. Sanders had a moustache, and an antiquated car—an old Morris."

The other two looked at each other.

"Had Sanders an appointment up there—at Combe Cottage—for that night?"

Travers shook his head. "Nothing doing, George l"

"What about it, Colonel? Good enough, do you think?"

"You're the master," said Kenton. "If I were you, I'd do it. If we should happen to be all wrong, there'll be no harm done."

Wharton nodded. "Sorry there's no time to explain, Mr. Travers. Sanders is in there now—telephoning. We persuaded him to use the station phone instead of going to Taunton. You'll come in with us. Play up to any cues. Be perfectly natural and don't look surprised at what's said. Look as if you knew everything. . . . We're going to try a short-cut. If it works out right, we'll save days. If it don't, we shan't lose very much."

Travers nodded. What it was all about he wasn't too sure. Wharton pulled out his notebook and began scribbling. Kenton fiddled with his moustache, then moved nervously over to the door. Travers took out his case, got a cigarette going, then wondered if it were any use throwing out feelers. Then Groom popped his head inside the door.

"All right! He's just finishing!"

"Come along!" said Wharton, and started off. They followed him into the yard and round to the main entrance.

"Talk!" whispered Wharton, and began it himself. "Now my idea is this. If you go into it carefully . . ." he continued with ample gestures to expand this imaginary theory till they were in the room, then broke off dramatically.

"Why! Here *is* Mr. Sanders!"

He gave the reporter no time to protest or even wonder, but took his arm affectionately. "The very person we wanted! Don't you think so, Mr. Travers?"

"I'm sure Mr. Sanders will do what he can," said Travers fatuously. The inspector fell in behind them and closed the door of the inner room. Wharton moved across in the direction of the bay window, his voice still effusively brisk.

"Let's sit down and see what we can make of it. Take a seat, Mr. Sanders. Make yourselves comfortable, gentlemen!" and he pulled out his pipe.

The air in that room was stifling hot, though the window was open at the bottom and the blind had flapped as they came in. In the far corner, clean away from their own party, a plain-clothes constable sat writing earnestly; not a local man by the look of him; there was something too smart and efficient about him. Travers took a seat by the door, Groom alongside him. Kenton was halfway to Wharton, who was by the wall. By luck or management Sanders was the other tip of the crescent, so that the five sat looking at each other. Sanders, in his chair by the table at the bow window, was perhaps the most impassive of the lot. He sat with crossed legs, waiting to see what it was all about; face a cold mask and eyes expressionless as ever.

Wharton was in his element. Had the situation been other than it was; had perhaps that hamper and rope not been on the window table, staring them all in the face; Travers for one might have seen the humour of it. As it was he felt his heart begin to race at an alarming rate. In the air was some peculiar disquiet which Wharton's false geniality made all the more tense.

"The time has come when we can afford to indulge in theories." He looked round. If his eyes rested longest on Sanders, Travers didn't know. It might have been imagination. "What your theories are, gentlemen, I'm not perhaps competent to judge. My own theories may seem just as improbable to you as yours will to me. However; if you listen I'll give you the outlines. Afterwards you can criticize." He smiled benevolently. "The meeting will become a debating society!"

"Sounds promising!" said Kenton.

Wharton adjusted his glasses, then had a look at him over the top of them.

"Well, perhaps it will be. . . . We'll start off not too far back; the evening of September the fifth in fact—and we start with hypotheses which are, frankly, nothing but hypotheses. We'll make use of them to open the case.

"For instance: we'll assume that by means of a telephone call or a note or any other device, Sir William Griffiths was induced to leave his house and proceed to a certain place by car. He may have assumed the call came from a certain woman with whom he was having an affair. He may have assumed it to be from the man who sent it; in any case, he left the house hurriedly in his car.

"A further hypothesis. Two hundred yards from his house, the car was hailed by his murderer. Possibly Sir William knew him and feared him and swerved to avoid him. Possibly he stopped and admitted him. Possibly the murderer mounted the running board and attacked him. In any case, the car swerved violently and crashed into a tree—a tree set clear of the bank. The slope was steep—one in five—and the bumper hit the tree full centre. This evening we found the tree and the mark of the collision. The bark of the tree was badly bruised and the murderer had disguised the scar by colouring it with earth. He made a good job of it. If we hadn't been looking for it we shouldn't have discovered it.

"To resume with the hypothesis. Sir William may have had his throat cut before the car crashed. He may have been knocked out by the collision and then the murderer may have cut his throat. But it wasn't an accident. Half a dozen things'll prove that. The blood on the wind-screen may have been—indeed almost certainly was—put there. The breaking of the screen wasn't an accident. There was nothing to break it, except the jar, and that would have cracked it—not smashed it. No! the screen was deliberately smashed to give the impression of death by accident. Then perhaps, when the murderer saw his victim's face, or his puny little body; when something surged up in him—some temporary madness, shall we say?—he had an idea.

"Mind you, he had to work in a hurry. His own car was handy; how handy we don't at the moment know. He tried the damaged car and the engine ran all right. He reversed it, let it run down the slope, then turned it into the narrow lane. He took the body out as soon as he got inside the gate, then he let it crash down to where we found it. Then he went for the hamper which he'd seen. He also helped himself to some linen line. Possibly he went for them in his car, or he may have gone on foot across country. Then he put the body in, lashed the hamper roughly, put it in the rumble and set off for—London, shall we say?

"On the road the car may have broken down. Or he may have decided to go no further than Taunton. Certainly he spent the night in the open or sleeping in the car in some side road. Before light he had the idea of the cabbage leaves and he rearranged the packing of the hamper. At a little shop on the outskirts of Taunton he bought some labels and a bottle of ink. I should imagine his fountain pen had run dry. Then he took the hamper to the station, and garaged his car at an unpretentious little garage, where, incidentally, by the reversing of his collar and waistcoat, he posed as a non-conformist parson! Then he took the train for London, with the hamper safely in the van."

Wharton paused. He relighted his pipe with extreme deliberation.

"Now, Mr. Sanders. Perhaps you wouldn't mind going on from there!"

"I!"

"You! . . . Do you object to notes being taken?" He nodded over to the far corner.

Sanders stared as if he were trying to mesmerize him. Wharton never batted an eyelid. Travers, heart racing away, held his breath and waited for the spring. Then Sanders smiled—or his lip curled.

"I'm a reporter—not a policeman. Get on with your theories!"

Wharton shook his head. "At the moment you're neither. You're a man—asked to make a statement. Do you wish to make one or do you not?"

"Statement! You and your comic tricks!" He laughed. "Mr. Superintendent Wharton—the clown of the C.I.D.! Haven't I watched you before—posing and posturing? Do you think you were fooling *me*!" He spat the words out. "You and your 'Mr. Sanders' here and 'Mr. Sanders' there! You're not a detective. You're a pantaloon!"

Wharton was outwardly unruffled. "Never mind about me! I may be all that—and some more! . . . You admit it then, so far?"

"Who's talking?" said Sanders curtly. "You get on with it. I'll say what I have to say—when the time comes."

"As you wish," said Wharton imperturbably. "You remarked just now, with some justification, that I was a dud detective. I might retort that you were a dud criminal. First of all you had that tremendous coincidence; that you were on the spot when the hamper arrived at Lord Zyon's house. Fine journalistic enterprise, I admit, to get in the house yourself; all the same I venture to think you'd have managed to get your story—and your scoop—anyway. That interested me at once. Then one of my men reported that you spent a long time in the refreshment room at Paddington. If you were sent to Lord Zyon's house as you said you were, you should have had ample time beforehand for a meal. If, on the other hand, you spent the night doing certain things, and arrived at Paddington at a certain time, then you'd certainly be hungry. Then, instead of coming straight here—as the same enterprising journalist should have done—you halted at Taunton. You lost an hour there. Why? Because you had to get the car out of the garage. You used it to get somewhere near Mulberton, then you walked the rest of the way. The same night you used it again, to get to Taunton. In the early hours of the following morning—this morning, that is—you destroyed the car and then came on to Morton's Woods. You went to the tree where the car struck and you picked up any pieces of broken glass you'd missed and threw them over the hedge with the rest. You also sent an anonymous letter so that the police should find the car. You were watching, and you joined Mr. Travers and the others. You then announced the discovery of the hamper. Doubtless, if we hadn't done it, you'd have discovered where the rope came from. You proposed proceeding from notoriety to notoriety. What your next move would have been, I don't know."

"Then I'll tell you!" broke in Sanders. It was staggering the way he was taking it all; mouth set firm, an occasional sneer, eyes level and not a trace of concern. "My next step would have been a reference to a piece of cheap advertisement of your own—and a piece of grossly bad taste; the reference you made at a certain dinner, that if a man wanted a thrill he'd get it out of being suspected of murder!"

"You were going to confess, then?" asked Kenton.

"Confess! I'd nothing to confess! I didn't commit a murder!"

"Who did then?"

"The man you gave that advice to! . . . Tim Griffiths! He was the man who knew all about that murder!"

Wharton concealed his incredulity. "How do you know? See him?"

"Never mind how I know. That's my affair." He looked round at the four of them. "You'd like my version of what happened? I'm quite prepared to tell you—entirely without prejudice. And I'll write my name at the bottom."

"Carry on!" said Wharton. "As you say, entirely without prejudice."

Sanders shifted his chair the foot or so that separated him from the table which occupied the bow of the window, and sat with arms resting on it, leaning over towards the men whose eyes were fastened on him. He spoke quietly; with a sort of grim repression that was terrifying in its fascination. He made no gestures; his only movement was a forward thrust of the head as if he wanted them to see the things he spoke about.

"I was born here, in Mulberton. I lived with an aunt, a Mrs. Long, in that cottage next to the laundry. I remember that laundry being built. I also remember William Griffiths, as he was then. He had Combe Cottage even in those days. When I left the school I worked there for over a year—as the gardener's boy.

"Then my aunt got me a job in Taunton. In my spare time I began writing things for the *Messenger*. Then I got my nose in there—and I thought I was wonderful. My aunt died and I lived in Taunton, doing quite well in a small way. I meant to get on. Every hour and every penny I could scrape up, I spent on books and trying to learn things—the things that matter. Then Walters—the editor— gave me a chance in town. He knew Griffiths and recommended me. I went to town, and I made good. I got married and we lived in a flat off Victoria Street. My wife gave birth to a child—a daughter. It died. After that she was an invalid. I saw she had all the things she wanted. I lived up to what I earned—and beyond it.

"Then they told us the *Mercury* was going." He smiled ironically. "They say no man ever believes he'll die. Everybody else, perhaps—but not himself. I didn't worry. I'd sweated blood for the *Mercury*. I'd given them more than I took. The *Mercury* wouldn't let me down. . . . But it did. It staggered me. I wouldn't believe it. When I knew it was true I went to see Griffiths himself. His secretary asked me to leave a chit. I did. Two days later I called to see what had happened. I got a reply—'Sir William Griffiths regrets . . .'

"I hawked my services to every paper in town. I did hackwork. I got into debt. I sold up this and that. The suit of clothes you see me in is the only one I've got. . . . I swallowed my pride and did things occasionally for the *Messenger*, though I wouldn't let them know how things really were. When Lord Zyon took over the *Record* I called on him. A secretary saw me—as usual. The reply was the usual. When I saw that secretary in the house that afternoon, he didn't even remember my name!

"We left the flat and took a room in Chapel Street, Pimlico. . . . Then my wife died. . . . I don't want your sympathy—nor does she." He leaned forward. "I don't lie. I don't exaggerate. But as sure as they say there's a God in heaven, I know the man who killed her! . . . After that things didn't matter so much. I sold what I had and I buried her. . . . Then I went on as before."

He paused for a moment to wipe the perspiration from his face. Travers suddenly realized that his own collar was soaking wet and a trickle of moisture was running down his cheek. Sanders leaned forward again.

"A week ago I saw Tim Griffiths in Taunton. I'd run down there to see Walters . . . in my car! An old friend—I'll let you have his name and address if you want it—gave me that car. He bought it at auction for a fiver, and then tinkered it up himself. I promised to pay him for it—sometime. That was the first day I'd used it. He thought it might be useful, running about where anything turned up. Still, I saw Tim Griffiths and I got something out of him. I wrote it up and sent it to the *Outdoor Magazine.* I got a ten-pound note for it and half of that went to pay for the car. Most of the rest was booked too.

"Then I had an idea. Why not see Griffiths and find out if he'd ever thought of writing up that expedition of his? Why not propose that I should do it for him? . . . Sounds cool to you perhaps, but it sounded pretty good to me. I came down from town specially that morning. The car went wrong at Frome and that made me late. I called on Walters, then I pushed on again. I tried to make up time by taking a short cut, but after all those years I'd forgotten the way. That was really how I struck the place where I burnt the car. Then it went phut again. By the time I got to Mulberton it was nine o'clock."

His eyes fell for a moment. In the room you could have heard a pin drop.

"I don't ask you to believe what I'm telling you." He shook his head. "I'm merely going to tell you what happened. If you have the sense I think you have, you'll know it's true.

"It was nine o'clock as I came through Mulberton town. I pulled up outside that cottage by the laundry; sentimental reasons if you like—also a nut had come out of the wing support and the car was rattling. I looked in at the laundry yard to see if there was a piece of rope handy. I found a bit of stout string in that shed where the hampers were. I thought to myself, 'Fine chance for a man to walk off with the lot!' Then I tied up the wing and pushed on. When I got to the turn I wouldn't risk the car up that hill, so I drew in at the side by a gate and walked on up the hill. . . . *Then I saw the car!*"

He moistened his lips and looked round as if for a drink. Nobody stirred. He felt for his handkerchief and wiped his face and his mouth, and his hand was shaking like a leaf.

"It was in the shadow, against that tree where you found it. The lights were out. I don't know now why I did it, but I went round to the bank and opened the door. I couldn't see anything. Then I felt for the light switch and pressed the starter instead. When the engine started I must have jumped back a yard. Then I found the switch that flooded the dashboard . . . Then I saw the body and the smashed wind-screen. The body was on the floor of the car, face down. . . . I turned it over . . . then I saw who it was."

He lowered his eyes again and seemed to be thinking something over. When he looked up again his eyes had a new light in them.

"I won't tell you all I thought because you wouldn't understand. What I saw was the man who'd made thousands, some of it by the sweat of men like me, who'd been kicked into the gutter for the sake of a little financial manipulation. I thought of the little flat I used to have. . . . I thought of—all sorts of things. Then I saw that fat swine Zyon—the man who'd seen me in the gutter and put his foot on me. I thought of his Work-for-All League; the cynical, hellish, bloody impudence of it. He—the fat bastard—playing with the bodies and souls of men like me, to increase his circulation!"

He had half risen to his feet and his voice was a shriek. As he saw the glare in his eyes, Travers made as if to rise too. Wharton went over quickly. "Steady on, Sanders! Take it steady!"

The other smashed his hand aside. "Take your hands off me!" He stood for a minute, breathing hard, eyes on the table; then wiped his forehead with his hand and sat down again. Wharton backed to his seat. Sanders curled his lips to a sneer as he leaned forward again.

"Shocks you, doesn't it? Vulgar display! . . . Awful bad form! Well, you'll hear some more. I did it—not as you said I did, but I did it. If things had gone right I'd have seen that hamper opened at the Albert Hall. As it was . . . things turned out as they did. I knew it was a gamble. I knew it was a hundred to one against getting away with it, but I took the risk. As soon as you, Wharton, and Travers there, had me into Combe Cottage that night, I knew it was all up. I let you go on playing with me. You see, I thought perhaps I was wrong—that you didn't suspect after all. As soon as you got me in this room to-night, I knew better."

"That all?" asked Wharton quietly.

"Yes . . . for the present."

It was Kenton who was the ultimate cause of what happened. Afterwards he said he couldn't help speaking. The irony of the whole thing struck him so overwhelmingly.

"My God! you've been a fool! . . . Don't you see what you've done—if you've done nothing else? You set out to get a scoop and you've made yourself the laughing-stock of Fleet Street!"

Sanders let his eyes rest on him, then passed him over as if he hadn't been there.

"You any proof that you found the car as you described it?" asked Wharton.

"Perhaps I have—in my own time."

Wharton lost some of his indifference. "Your time's too late! . . . Proof, I said. Proof definite —here and now!"

Sanders seemed to be faced with a problem which he'd never visualized. The sneer faded, became a puzzled look, then a frown. Then he sneered again.

"You don't bluff me, Wharton! It's my time— not yours!"

"Have it your own way!" said Wharton contemptuously. He got to his feet and approached the table. Sanders rose too and backed away. Wharton paused. "That depends on you. Are you talking or are you not?"

"That's my business. You can't hold me, Wharton—and you know it. You can't get a word out of me if I choose to keep my mouth shut."

"You know a lot!" said Wharton. "Shall I tell you why you can't prove that cock-and-bull story about Griffiths committing the murder? And about finding the car against that tree? Because it isn't true. I put it to you that *you did that murder*! . . . That gets you, doesn't it?"

Travers' hand felt for the back of the chair. For a moment he thought Sanders was going to spring. Wharton thought otherwise. This time it was he who did the sneering.

"Shall I tell you what you're going to be? You're going to be a hold-on—till the case is water-tight. You think I can't hold you! Why, you poor fool! By your own admission you removed a body. When you did that you committed a felony. The body had clothes on it and money in its pockets. You took—"

"Don't talk such bilge to me!" His voice was a drawling sort of snarl. "Felony be damned. It's up to you to prove that the clothes were taken with felonious intent!"

"I say we'll hold you!" Wharton's voice cut like a whip. "You are charged—now. You! Frederick Sanders, with the willful murder of William Griffiths on the night of September the fifth." He went on monotonously with the official caution. "Do you wish to say anything in answer to the charge? You are not obliged to say anything unless you wish to do so, but whatever you say will be taken down—"

Travers didn't quite see what happened then. For one thing Wharton was in the line of view. Then Groom made a flying leap forward. But Sanders appeared to have moved first. In a flash he had whipped up the window and was gone. Everything was confused. There was a sort of scuffle outside. Inside was the rush to the window and everybody talking at once. Wharton looked out into the darkness, then looked in again. His face was comically bewildered.

"What's happened? . . . Has he let him go?" Out sprinted Groom and Kenton.

"What's the matter?" asked Travers. "Who's let him go?"

Wharton nodded back. "We had a man out there ready in case he bolted."

Then Wharton bolted himself—for the phone; and fired his orders at the sergeant.

"Get Taunton quick! Give 'em a description! Tell 'em to keep a look-out!"

"Description of what, sir?"

"Oh, my God!" said Wharton, and snatched off the phone himself.

....

For Travers the next hour or so was a nightmare. Groom disappeared altogether and Wharton spent most of his time hovering near the telephone. What the police could do, Travers couldn't for the life of him imagine. Finding a trouser button in the Sahara wouldn't be much more difficult than looking for a single man in country so thinly populated and so densely wooded as that; and the whole of Exmoor right on one's doorstep—so to speak. Moreover, there were things about the handling of Sanders that he didn't in the least understand.

"Why did you force things like that?" he asked Wharton when a chance presented itself.

"To save time. Didn't I tell you it was a shortcut? And wasn't it?"

"It was!" said Travers. "The best thing in short-cuts I've ever seen. What I meant particularly was, when he accused Griffiths. He told his tale, then you proceeded to rile him!"

Wharton nodded. "You didn't see him as close as I did. That was the only way to make him speak —to save his own skin! You believed him? That yarn about finding the car?"

Travers smiled ironically. "I did—and so did you!"

"Who said so? . . . And why did you believe him?"

Travers polished his glasses nervously. "I wish you wouldn't cross-examine me like that, George! . . . I don't know why I believed him, except perhaps that he rang true. He didn't exaggerate. He didn't slobber . . . and he didn't hesitate."

"But he was mad!"

"*Mad*'s a very relative term. He'd been brooding for months. Like some other self-made people, he wasn't far from the fringes of egomania. And he's been abnormal ever since he saw that body in the car."

"He's mad!" insisted Wharton. "Stark mad. Didn't you notice his eyes the first time you saw him? He's dangerous!"

"In more ways than one," said Travers grimly. "As he is now, you can't prove him right or wrong. If we don't get him, we've got to start all over again. If we do get him, we've still to prove a case —that is if he keeps his mouth shut, and he certainly will!"

"No use looking for trouble," said Wharton. "Wait till we get him, then we'll see."

He was looking tired and worried; with precious little sleep for the last day or two and with the prospect of still less. Travers' heart smote him.

"Sorry, George! . . . Of course it will be all right! I'm just being awkward."

Wharton looked at him. "Not awkward; say, argumentative. . . . You know what the time is? Best part of one. Get away to bed! You can't do any good here. If there's anything important I'll knock you up."

Travers expostulated. Wharton hustled him off. When he came back he opened out to the sergeant.

"One of the best in the world! Plenty of money; not a bit of side, and a damn sight more brains than you or I will ever have."

The sergeant raised his eyebrows.

"Really, sir! . . . Then why's he a policeman?" Wharton looked at him, grunted . . . and filled his pipe for the twentieth time.

CHAPTER XII
WHARTON BEGINS AGAIN

AT ABOUT HALF-PAST five in the morning, Wharton, asleep in a chair in the waiting-room, was roused by the sergeant on duty.

"You're wanted, sir; down at the station!"

Wharton scrambled up and stretched himself.

"What's up? Have they got him?"

"I don't know, sir. The inspector wants you urgent."

The only means of locomotion seemed to be the sergeant's bicycle and he set off. The morning was breaking clear and the air was keen along the river and the tree-covered road. In the station a freight train was waiting, and in the recess in front of the booking-office door a group of men were standing, looking at something on the ground. Wharton cleared his throat and the group opened out to show what was on the dark sheet.

Sanders, if it were Sanders, lay on a tarpaulin. Even Wharton, who had seen death in horrible shapes, flinched for a moment and turned his head away. Another quick look and he drew the tarpaulin over again.

"Who knows anything about it?" he asked Groom.

The fireman and driver were both there. All the fireman knew was that as the train went under Barlcombe Bridge, he was looking out for the home signal; then, all at once, quicker than he could speak or act, he saw something which might have been man or animal, clean under the engine. He gasped to the driver and the train was pulled up; then they saw . . . that there! The driver corroborated to the extent of what he knew and was adding details of what had happened to the body, when Wharton cut him short.

"Was he lying on the line, or what was he doing?"

"That I don't know, sir," the fireman told him. "It looked to me as if he didn't know we was coming. He sort of stumbled like."

Wharton nodded. "We're much obliged to you. Both of you will be wanted for the inquest. Got their names and addresses, inspector?"

The inspector had. The train moved off for Barnstaple before Wharton made another move.

"You'll see to all this, inspector. I don't want my hands tied. What about his pockets?"

They hunted them through. But for strictly personal articles everything seemed to have been destroyed—except a wad of paper, tied round with string and addressed to Rodman of the *Evening Record*. Wharton made no bones about untying it; then he put on his glasses and had a preliminary look.

They were in pencil, on pages torn from a notebook. By the time he'd gone over them once he could gather only vaguely what it all meant. Then, Groom and his men moving off with the body, he sat down in comfort, got his pipe going and tried another reading.

Out of the shrieks and ravings and incoherencies he now got some idea of what had been in the demented man's mind. All the festering introspection of months had come to one hysterical head. Some of it he had heard a few hours before. There were curses on those who trafficked in souls and bodies; rhapsodic prophecies of a press which should be un-desecrated by financial swindlers; talk about his wife, whom Rodman must have known; then more tortuous rhapsodies about the life to come and the mystery of death. There was something horrible about it, like overhearing the conversation of a lunatic whom one had once known as a friend; ravings repeated over and over again as if they beat on the brain. Rodman, he wrote, was to have everything. Then the long scrawl ended with sentences that had appeared before half a dozen times, heavily underlined. *"I didn't do it, Rodman. Don't let them tell you I did it!"*

Wharton still sat there over his pipe, wrestling with that reiterated statement. What hadn't he done? All that horrible business with the hamper had certainly been his, and the removal of the car to where it had been found. What else? The murder? Wharton thought definitely not. Like Travers he had been impressed as Sanders told his story. More than once he had boasted that he could smell a liar a mile off—and Sanders had spoken too quietly, too *sanely*, to be lying. What then of the screed intended for Rodman? The inquest would certainly find Sanders mad. Why, then, believe him when he protested he hadn't done the murder? But then again, why should a man lie when he lifts his foot to step into eternity?

By the time he had finished his second pipe, Wharton thought he could explain the paradox. Sanders' reason had gone—but not quite. What that repeated protestation showed was that all through the letter he was clinging on to sanity. As the idea hammered away at his brain—that at all costs he must let Rodman know he didn't do the murder—so he wrote it down, over and over again.

Even then as he cycled slowly back, Wharton knew that was only half the problem. Had Sanders written that anonymous letter, or had he not? If he had not—and there seemed little connection between the writing and that of the screed—then the question of an unknown woman still remained. And even if Sanders *had* written the letter, there was still the possibility that there was some truth in it.

And what of Sanders' charge against Tim Griffiths? That opened such mazes that a man might wander for hours and not find a way out. Why should Sanders turn his hand against the man who'd done him a favour, and who was expected to do him a bigger one? Was it because he was the nephew of his uncle? Was it spite or was there any truth in the accusation? Was he merely trying to lay a false trail so as to get yet another sensation out of that ridiculous remark he—Wharton—had made at the dinner?

But truth or no truth, Wharton began suddenly to recall the things that he and Travers had noticed—the remark Griffiths had made to his man over the phone, Griffiths' drinking, the unusual presence of the man in the room, and—if Travers' deductions were correct—that listening at keyholes the previous night. And trying to find in them some new significance, Wharton found he had overshot the police-station.

....

Travers said little. For one thing he had no way of expressing what he felt. The death of Sanders had shocked and distressed him, and in some vague way he felt himself responsible. Something might have been done if only he'd had the sense to think of it. The grotesque business of the hamper seemed just then very remote and inconsequent. As for the importance of the dismissal of Sanders as a live factor, that he couldn't for the moment quite appreciate.

"What you were saying last night, George; that hypothesis of yours that Sir William had been lured away by a phone call or a message; had it any basis in fact?"

"Not a ha'p'orth!" said Wharton frankly. "It was all bluff. It had to be!"

Travers nodded. "Well, it was a good bluff, George. There's only one good bluff—the one that comes off! . . . Still, as you asked for my opinion, I'd say it's half and half. We haven't got to begin all over again . . . and we have!"

"You mean?"

"I think Sanders told the truth. I can't prove it, and perhaps it never will be proved. All I know is in my mind I'm certain—certain as that I'm at this breakfast-table and you're over there—that Sanders found the car up against the tree, and that he was amazed when he found it."

"I think you're right," said Wharton. "How could Sanders have lured him away? There wasn't a phone message, so the local exchange guarantees. Sanders didn't get to Mulberton till dark, so he couldn't have delivered a note. And there wasn't a private letter for Sir William that morning."

"Did Sanders write the anonymous letter—about Morton's Woods?"

"I don't know. I'm sending the screed and the letter and the labels to Dyerson this morning. He'll know! . . . And talking of women, do you mind telling me again what happened last night? I don't think I was sufficiently placid to hang on to it all."

Travers went over it in full detail. He was grateful that Wharton's face had never the suspicion of a smile.

"That woman's merely trying to please. . . . Bit sex-ridden perhaps. . . . And you're going to tea to-day?"

"Well," said Travers diffidently, "I suppose I'd better."

"Of course you'd better!" From somewhere or other Wharton summoned an alarming enthusiasm. "Get hold of her. Phone her up now! Carry on for all you're worth! Get all the news about Griffiths. Turn her inside out!"

Travers fumbled for his pipe, then fidgeted with his pouch. "The bother is, George, not what to do, but what *not* to do!

. . . Besides, unless I'm wrong, it's myself who's supposed to be turned inside out."

"Spread yourself! Get round her!" The ample gesture indicated the extent. "Tell her you don't think her husband understands her!"

"Quite!" said Travers dryly. "And what are you doing yourself?"

"Going over the car again with Kenton. Then I may call on Daniels."

"Where's Menzies?"

"He went back last night. The formal inquest's to-day."

Travers hesitated. "I've got an idea. I don't know how it'll strike you. . . . You ring up Combe Cottage, as soon as you know the train's gone, and ask for Griffiths. Daniels will say he's gone. Then ask Daniels to come along here, because you and Kenton want to consult him about the car, as you understand he used to drive it. As soon as he leaves I'll go up there and see the two women and the gardener and get all the gossip. If you want to question Daniels, you can still do it here."

. . . .

Travers' elongated form paid for dressing. The grey suit which Palmer had brought down from town, the grey hat and the subtly contrasting tie, gave him the air of a somebody. Add the new Bentley and the effect was irresistible. The gardener touched his cap as he opened the gate, and the stoutish woman who came to the door looked for the moment like ducking to a curtsy.

"Sir Timothy in?"

"I'm afraid he isn't, sir. He went back to London this morning."

"Daniels about?"

"Well, no, sir. . . . He's just been sent for, sir."

Travers simulated a certain exasperation and found himself in the lounge-hall. Though he was amazingly ignorant of the fact, he had a way with him. That mournful smile could be wonderfully appealing, and the grave courtesy with which he surrounded himself was indeed so natural that it was impossible to be stiff in his company.

"You'll be the housekeeper," he told her. "Do sit down, won't you?" He smiled, then prattled on. "I was here the other night, and last night, seeing Sir Timothy. Terrible business this, about Sir William!"

She was hardly at home with him at the moment.

"You been with Sir William long?"

"Ever since the war, sir."

"I say, that's capital!" He launched into a panegyric of domestic service, and those servants who knew a good place and kept it.

"What's your name—if you don't mind my asking?"

"Rigg, sir. Mrs. Rigg."

"Of course! You knew it was all an accident, Mrs. Rigg?"

"Daniels was saying so last night, sir."

"Yes." He shook his head solemnly. "You come down here often?"

She smiled. "Well, it was like this, sir. Cook and a footman used to come, and then one year they was both ill, so I came, and Mrs. Struthers came in as usual to help, and Sir William he liked everything so much that he said he'd have nobody else about the place except us."

"Splendid! And what about the car, Mrs. Rigg? Didn't Sir William have a better one in town?"

"Oh, yes, sir! There's a bigger one up there— and a chauffeur. You see, it's like this, sir. When we come down here for this long holiday, all the town servants have their holidays; except what have to be there. The chauffeur goes on his holiday, so Daniels and I came down from town in the other car with the luggage and Sir William came down by train."

"A very sensible arrangement! I expect you rather like it down here. . . . Sir William a good master?"

"He was, sir."

Travers smiled knowingly. "But he had a temper!"

"My word he did, sir! . . . Though he's dead and gone—poor gentleman."

"Sir Timothy found his uncle a little trying at times?"

"Well, you see, sir, he's been away."

"Quite so!" He wondered how he could lead up to the quarrel of the one important night, and decided not to risk it.

"When Sir William went out that night, you saw him go?"

"I heard him, sir . . . and little did I think he was going to his death—as they say."

He nodded sympathetically. "Where were you exactly?"

"In the kitchen, sir. I heard the bell go for Daniels, then I heard Mr. Timothy say something to his uncle—when the door opened that was—and then Daniels came back and said he had to get the car."

"And you were worried about Sir William not coming back that night?"

"I didn't know anything about it, sir. I just went off to bed about nine, the same as I always do. You see, sir, I have to get up in the morning!"

"I expect you do," said Travers apologetically. "You're an important person, Mrs. Rigg!"

"Oh! I don't know about that, sir." She smiled all the same, obviously pleased; then her tone changed. "I don't mind telling you, sir, that I knew something was going to happen! Next morning I said to Mrs. Struthers, 'Mark my words,' I said. 'Something's going to happen!'"

"Why did you think that?"

"Because of the clock being smashed, sir! It's as bad as a mirror!"

"The clock smashed!"

"Yes, sir—the clock! Next morning Mrs. Struthers was dusting and she told me the clock wasn't there, so I asked Daniels what had happened to it, and he said Mr. Timothy had accidentally knocked it over and broken the face, and he was taking it into Mulberton to have it mended. That's when I knew something was going to happen!"

"And where's the clock now?"

"Back again, sir. It came back only this morning from the shop."

"That's very interesting!" said Travers. "I wonder what sort of a hand they made of it. I've got something I'd like to have mended myself. . . . Would you mind if I had a look at it?"

The drawing-room was light, spacious and airy; full of chintz and coziness, and its French window opening out on the gravel drive and the lawn. On the mantelpiece stood the clock; a French, gilt affair in the shape of a globe supported by two cupids. A careful scrutiny showed that the hands had been straightened and the face had been touched up with white enamel—presumably to conceal the marks where the broken glass had scratched it. Travers lifted it up.

"Must have been a pretty hard knock to capsize a thing like that!"

Mrs. Rigg hesitated. She almost spoke, then thought better of it. Travers looked at her encouragingly.

"Don't you think so?"

"Well, between ourselves, sir, I did think so." She hesitated again, then blurted it all out. "What I thought, sir, was it was knocked down during the quarrel the master and Mr. Timothy had. Terrible it was! Just before dinner. Shouting they were"—she stopped suddenly. "Of course you're not supposed to know that, sir."

"That's all right!" said Travers. "I did hear something about it, as a matter of fact. There were one or two quarrels like that, weren't there, after Mr. Timothy got here?"

"Not so bad as that, sir!"

"Curious!" said Travers reminiscently. "What on earth should they want to quarrel for? What was it all about? I mean—you as an old servant to the family . . . and so on?"

"Well, sir, in town they were saying Sir William wasn't going to let Mr. Timothy have any money after he spent his own. They say he warned him beforehand, and Mr. Timothy asked him whose money it was!"

"And what was the big quarrel about the other night? That, too?"

That she didn't know. She had heard the voices and shouting—Sir William's shrill falsetto and the other's blurting sort of bass. Daniels told her there'd been a fine old row, but what about he hadn't said. Also Mr. Timothy had gone to his bedroom and refused to come down to dinner. Daniels had been sent up to tell him that Sir William would like to see him again. Then he'd come down, and as far as Rigg knew, the dinner had proceeded in peace. *Next morning Daniels had advised her not to say anything about that quarrel.*

Travers was beginning to imagine all sorts of things. He had let her talk without comment, not so much because he feared to make her suspicious as that he was wrestling with an extraordinary idea. Back in the lounge again he gave his most seductive smile as he fingered the case that held the Treasury notes.

"Quite right of you not to talk! Take my advice, Mrs. Rigg, and say nothing—not even that you've been talking to me. People are very uncharitable. Do you know, there are even people who'd say—if they knew Sir Timothy had quarrelled with his uncle—that he'd had something to do with killing him!" He saw her face flush and her eyes open. "You and I know better, and that's why we must keep our tongues quiet. . . . A small present, Mrs. Rigg, for your kindness."

Before she could thank him he seemed to see for the first time that collection of curios on the lounge wall.

"How very interesting! . . . Most unusual! I suppose Sir Timothy brought them back with him."

As he ran his eye over those wicked-looking knives and daggers, he prattled away like a spinster at a christening. He fingered the handles and gave a pretended shudder. On one there was the faintest mark where the finger had rubbed. He nodded benignantly as he turned away.

"Most interesting! . . . Going to be a hot day, Mrs. Rigg. . . . I wonder if you'd mind fetching me a glass of very cold water from the kitchen!"

As soon as she left the room he nipped back to the wall. The knife went into his breast pocket; through the lining till the blade rested alongside his ribs. The rest of the knives he spread out to cover the bare space. Then he went over to the door.

The water he drank to the last drop, then from the door admired the roses. When the door finally closed on him he got no further than the drive, where the gardener was hoeing weeds out of the gravel. Travers admired the roses again, said he loved gardens, said he thought the view was wonderful—then asked where the garage was.

Had any of the gardener's conversation been vital, Travers would have been in a bad way. The broad dialect was too much for him. The main theme seemed to be something about onions. He had claimed to the flower-show committee that there were three kinds of onions, and they'd offered prizes for two. As far as he could gather, Travers himself was being asked to settle this particular point.

The garage—well back of the house—affording no opportunity for side-tracking, he was confining him-self to an occasional "Quite!" when something really interesting presented itself. That part of the kitchen garden at which he was looking seemed to have been swept by huge locusts.

"Hallo! What on earth's been happening here?" The gardener was off at once on another track. The gentleman might well ask what had been happening. The other night—that was the night Sir William had met with his accident—somebody went and let out the sow and pigs.

"Oh, it was you!" Travers exclaimed involuntarily, then explained where he'd heard of that remarkable happening.

The other resumed. He was sure he'd shut the sty. He always did. He led the way over to the corner of the orchard and demonstrated how it was done. Sheer devilry it was! All that bed of young cauliflower and the marrows and Lord knows what else ruined. And the police had done nothing! One of the suckers had gone altogether—lost, or killed by one of "they voxes."

Travers wondered if foxes ate pigs, even the most infantile of suckers, but said nothing. Also that knife was feeling most uncomfortable against his ribs. In spite of that Travers had to see the orchard and the ditch, overgrown with weeds and brambles, where two of the pigs had been found. Then, more than suspecting that if the ditch were cleared the missing pig would be there too, he managed to lure the gardener back again. A last question and the pigs were dismissed.

"Why do you keep pigs here?"

That was soon explained. Pigs made manure—and the best manure there was. That sty made Sir William independent of the local farmers. Travers nodded as if he understood all the economics of the situation, passed over half a crown—and departed, with the knowledge that the last half-hour had been thoroughly, if amusingly, wasted.

......

It was not till lunch-time that Wharton appeared. What he'd been doing he didn't say, and Travers didn't ask him—but he seemed in quite a good humour. All he did impart was that Kenton had gone back to town again. Then he asked Travers for his story. His remarks were none too commendatory.

"Not much more than we knew before. . . . What's the particular thing about the knife?"

"This. If his throat was cut up there, in the house, it might have been done with a stout knife like this. Whoever did it would have washed the blood off, and that'd have been done with strong soda water. Soda keeps on crystallizing out. If you wash down a piece of furniture with soda solution, there'll be a film of soda on it for days afterwards, no matter how often you wipe it off."

Wharton had a look at the handle through his glass. There was certainly something there, on the bone handle. And it looked as if there was something between the handle and the blade. What he'd do would be to get it to town.

"That'll settle it! . . . Anything else happen?" More with the idea of leg-pulling than anything else, Travers related the affair of the dead pig—the week-old, pinkish innocent that had viewed the world once—and once too often.

"Damned old fool!" was Wharton's comment on that. "What about the woman—Mrs. Struthers? See her?"

"I didn't," said Travers bluntly. "And what's more, I'm damned if I'm going to! I doubt if she knows more than Rigg."

"Perhaps not," said Wharton placatingly. "However, what about a tankard? You've earned it."

"Thanks!" said Travers, with a wry smile. "If rewards went by merit, George, you'd be buying a barrel!"

CHAPTER XIII
WHARTON ENJOYS HIMSELF

WHAT WHARTON HAD actually been doing that morning was something after his own secretive heart. At the last moment he had changed his mind about staying with Kenton and Daniels. The colonel should keep the man there till such time as Travers could get his business done. A word, therefore, in Kenton's ear and Wharton set off in the car. There was, as he'd imagined, a way to Bland's cottage without going round and up that precipice of a hill—and he took it. A preliminary inquiry by phone had assured him that Mrs. Bland would be at home.

There were several reasons that had contributed to the alteration in Wharton's point of view. Sir William had been killed within a few moments of leaving his house. If Menzies were correct, it even looked as if he'd been killed before he left it, since the knife—or whatever had killed him—had been drawn across an unresisting throat. But the time was not yet ripe for more detailed inquiries concerning Tim Griffiths than those Travers was making at that very moment.

As for the Blands, there were several things that interested him. There was that question of an alibi which might as well be settled once and for all—and for both of them at the same time. If there had been a woman in the case, then Mrs. Bland—according to the description and experiences of Travers—was a not unlikely charmer, with the husband the *mari complaisant*. Admit that she was, as Travers had put it, a rose full blown, and the argument was still unaffected. Old men could be notoriously besotted, and in the eyes of old Griffiths she might have seemed as virginally enchanting as she probably was twenty years before. And as Travers had pointed out, all that business about pretending to hate the sight of her might have been to throw dust in people's eyes generally and her husband's in particular.

And if Sanders had really written the anonymous letter, there still remained the fact that Bland was among the interested parties. He stood to get ten thousand out of the old man's death, and that wasn't a sum to be sneezed at. And there might be other motives. Wharton was hazy about procedure generally, but at least he knew enough to be aware that over the haberdashery combine that Bland had been handling, there must be ample opportunities for graft. He might even have sold the pass in some way, and once Sir William had got an inkling of what had happened, then all over with Mr. Secretary Bland.

The maid showed him into the living-room, and in a few moments Mrs. Bland herself floated in. She had been at some pains to decorate herself, as he could see, and with the blinds drawn against the heat, the effect was quite good. Her manner was definitely quiet and refined. Wharton assumed his role of paternal adviser.

"Most sorry to bother you like this, Mrs. Bland, but something has turned up which I thought I ought to see you about. I expect it's a mare's nest—still, you know what things are!"

He noticed her getting rather anxious. "Of course you'll be able to explode the idea in a few seconds. That's really why I called to see you. . . . It's like this. We have a witness—what we're accustomed to call a *reliable* witness—who insists that he saw your husband the other night . . . the night Sir William was killed."

She was genuinely startled.

"Saw him! . . . When?"

Wharton had it all ready. The murder, as he placed it, would be between nine and a quarter to. It all depended on the accuracy of the evidence of Daniels and Griffiths.

"Well, about nine . . . or, say, a quarter to."

It was a curious thing, but Wharton was positive that wasn't the time she'd been expecting. He was even more certain that she was remarkably relieved. She laughed.

"But how absurd!"

"Exactly! . . . I remember Mr. Bland telling us the other night that he'd been here all the time." He gave a shrug of resignation. "Still, there we are! People start these tales and we have to inquire into them."

"It's a pity they've nothing better to do!"

Wharton gestured again. "You're right there, Mrs. Bland. . . . And now, purely officially—sort of once and for all. Mr. Bland was here in the house all that night?"

"Until eleven o'clock—yes. He walked with Mr. Cross as far as Barlcombe vicarage. I was still up when he got back."

Wharton pulled out his notebook. "If you don't mind, I'll take it down officially as I said. . . . Then we shan't have to worry you again. . . . September the fifth. What happened?"

She frowned. Every now and then she gave a little nod or a simper as things came back.

"Mr. Cross—he's the vicar of Barlcombe—came to play chess with my hubby. He's awfully good—Mr. Cross, that is. He got here at five o'clock and we had tea and talked. They didn't play any chess till Ted—that's my hubby—got back from Combe Cottage, where he always goes. That would be getting on for seven. Then they argued about a problem—I think that's what they call it; you know, they're published in the papers. Then they were going to make one up themselves. . . . Then, just before eight, we went into the study while the maid laid the cloth. Oh, yes! it was exactly ten to when we sat down to supper. You know, we call it supper because it was cold. I remember the clock striking after we sat down."

Wharton smiled ingratiatingly. "Wonderful memory you've got, Mrs. Bland!"

She explained effusively. "You see, when they play chess they nearly always go by the clock. It's the time they're allowed to take over the moves. . . . You know!"

Wharton did and he didn't. How it accounted for an accurate memory wasn't any too clear. Still, he nodded.

"And what happened then?"

"Then—well, I don't know who it was—I think it was me, really! We'll say it was me! I knew there was something I wanted to hear on the wireless. I'll show it to you if I can find the paper!"

She was up and away in the kitchen before he could say a word. She came back with the *Radio Times*—open at the place. Wharton read as directed.

SEPTEMBER 5TH
LONDON REGIONAL PROGRAM
B.B.C. Orchestra. Concert of Modern Music
8.15 *Bolero*, Ravel

There was much more to it than that, though that seemed what she wished him specially to see.

"Hm!" said Wharton. "Ravel's *Bolero*. I remember it. Gets on your nerves a bit."

"Oh! but it's wonderful! . . . How the drums keep tapping, and it sort of makes you want to jump out of your skin!"

"It is a bit weird. . . . And you heard it?"

"Oh, yes! Mr. Cross said he'd like to hear it, so Ted got it. You see, we keep our set in the kitchen for the maid really. We tune in with the ear-phones, and if we want the speaker out here or in the garden, we bring it out. . . . We were a minute or two late, but we got it; then we listened to it till it was all over. That was after half-past. . . . After that they played chess all the time till Mr. Cross left."

"And Mr. Bland was here all the time—except when he went to the kitchen to tune in?"

"That!" She laughed. "That didn't take half a minute!" Then she remembered something. "Oh, yes! Just when the music started Ted took advantage of it to write a letter in the study. I didn't know what he was doing, so I went after him. He said he was only scribbling a note . . . and he came out again in a minute."

"That'd be at eight-fifteen?"

"Yes . . . just about. The music went on ever so long after that."

Wharton closed his notebook and got to his feet. The whole movement was meant to be dramatic.

"All over, Mrs. Bland! . . . I'm merely wasting my time—and your own. When I see that busybody I'll send him away with a good-sized flea in his ear. . . . Good-by! . . . And we shan't have to bother you again."

She followed him to the gate, where they shook hands ceremoniously. At the fork roads, however, Wharton turned the car to the left to the unfamiliar road that led to Barlcombe. Under the lee of the church was the vicarage. At the door the maid said Mr. Cross was in, and took his official card. In half a minute he was being shown into the vicar's workroom, and the vicar himself was standing at the desk with a puckish smile on his face.

Wharton's eyes warmed to the man as soon as he clapped eyes on him. He was short—noticeably so—and in age about fifty. His hair was badger grey and a pair of black, twinkling eyes were laughing away in a chubby, cherubic face. His greeting seemed characteristic.

"Well, superintendent? You've come for me at last!"

Wharton was taken clean aback. He shook hands warily.

"Come for you, sir? I'm afraid I don't follow."

"Just my little joke. . . . Sit down, Mr. Wharton. . . . Cigarette? Rather have tobacco? Then try some of this."

He pulled out his own evil-looking briar and struck a match for Wharton. He had that trick of talking while holding a lighted match, which slowly drew nearer his fingers till it had to be discarded—the pipe still unlit. Before Wharton left the room the fireplace was littered with dead ends. Still, he got his own pipe going, then straightened his face. If anything he looked more puckish than before.

"My levity was perhaps uncalled for. I mean, this has been a deplorable business, Mr. Wharton."

For a few minutes they discussed the tragedy; then the vicar decided apparently that a sufficient tribute of repression had been paid to the deceased. He returned to his more natural mood.

"Seriously, you know, there's no reason why you shouldn't have suspected me! . . . if it had been a murder, that is."

"Really, sir! And why, may I ask?"

"A desperate affair! . . . Sir William objected to my having the rood screen cleaned. You see, some vandal of a predecessor of mine had had it painted and varnished. A century ago perhaps. Sir William made a fuss and he wouldn't subscribe."

"But you did it!"

"Oh, yes!" said Cross. "We did it all right! . . . Worse men than I have committed better murders for worse causes. . . . You'll have some beer?"

The question was so unexpected that Wharton very nearly said no. "Well, vicar . . . if you're going to have some—"

Cross was already pushing the bell. When the bottles and glasses came in, he took his tot like a good Christian. Wharton suddenly realized that he hadn't yet stated the reason for his own visit.

"Do you know, vicar, I haven't told you what I really called about this morning! . . . You must regard our conversation—on this particular point, that is—as implicitly confidential. I can rely on you for that?"

"I imagine so," said Cross coolly, and took a pull at the glass.

"It's this, sir. A witness whom we consider reasonably reliable insists that he saw Mr. Bland near Combe Cottage at about eight-thirty, the night Sir William was killed."

"Really! . . . And suppose he did?"

That tied Wharton in a knot. He, too, took a drink, then wiped his moustache carefully.

"What the police announce, and what actually happened, aren't necessarily the same thing—"

"Then it wasn't an accident?"

Wharton looked at him—then saw no reason not to speak.

"Assume if you like, sir, that it was anything. Murder if you like! . . . Whatever it was, we've still to question everybody connected with the dead man; certainly those likely to profit by his death. All alibis have to be gone into. It's a perfectly normal procedure, and only those with anything to conceal ever make any bones about it."

The vicar tactfully refilled Wharton's glass. "That, of course, puts a different complexion on things." He chuckled. "This is a most interesting moment for me. Do you know that few weeks go by that I don't read at least a couple of detective stories! For the first time—and, I hope, the last! —I'm up against the real thing!"

Wharton smiled, too. Somehow you couldn't help it when Cross was beaming away.

"A sort of personal interest, vicar!"

"The very thing! . . . Oh! just one question. A very blunt one. At what time was the—accident committed?"

Wharton grimaced. "Hm! . . . The accident. . . . Well, it might have taken place at nine o'clock . . . going by present information."

"I see. Not that it matters. The position merely struck me as an interesting one. Putting aside all question of what the crime is, and recognizing that you and I are having a friendly chat. . . . Assume that I'm a suspect. If I am, then my alibi is bound up that night with that of two other people—my good friend Bland and his wife. Four of us if you count the maid."

Wharton smiled plausibly.

"Very good, vicar! Let's assume, as you say. I'm here this morning to tell you that a fine old communion cup was stolen from your church last night between the hours of eight and ten. The cup was seen then. There were only two of you who had keys—you and Mr. Bland. We happen to know you're very hard up . . ."

"You're right there!" said Cross, and drained the bottle into his glass.

"And the Blands are hard up. One theory is that you faked a burglary. Another is that there was collusion between you and Bland . . . in which case, of course, if you tell the same tale and stick to it, you'll both get away with it, unless a reliable witness can shake any part of your story. . . . Purely imaginary, but you see what I'm getting at."

"Oh, rather!" The vicar chuckled away as he got up from his chair. With arms under his coat-tails he set his back to an imaginary fire and lolled against the mantelpiece.

"Merely a question of an alibi! Well, a parishioner of mine happened to see me go into Bland's house at five o'clock precisely. That shows I went there. Then I was in the company of either Bland and his wife—or Bland *or* his wife—till seven o'clock, when Bland got back from Combe Cottage. Then the three of us were together in the dining-room till just before eight . . . with exceptions."

"Such as?"

"Mrs. Bland once or twice paid a flying visit to the kitchen to see how things were coming along. You know what women are!"

Wharton nodded. "But about this five business. How do you know you got there at five?"

"Superintendent, you're a man after my own heart! . . . See that clock there? The church clock? Well, we have a man who sees to it weekly; puts it right by wireless, and so on. That clock keeps excellent time. It's famous for it. When I left here the time was almost five to. When I got to the Blands', their grandfather was striking five."

"What did your own watch say?"

"Don't carry one. Didn't I hear you say I was hard up?"

Wharton smiled. "Very good, vicar! Carry on!"

"The Blands' clock—perhaps you've seen it—is a wonderful timekeeper. I had it under my eye all the evening. Bland is good enough to ask me round to his place to play chess, whenever he's down and not too busy. We generally play to time moves. He's an old tournament player—so am I, for that matter. Still, we're getting away from the point. We went into the study at about a quarter to eight while the maid got things ready. At ten minutes to we sat down to the meal. At about a quarter past, we'd finished the main courses. I ought to say that I gobble my food like blazes—so does Bland. His wife is on a diet. . . . Where were we? Oh, yes! at the trimmings. Well, at about a quarter-past eight, or just before, somebody suggested—who, I don't know—probably one of those spontaneous affairs—suggested we should hear a rather novel piece of music that was being broadcast that night . . . Ravel's *Bolero*. A most amazing thing! . . . Still, perhaps you know it."

"I do, as a matter of fact."

"Well, Mrs. Bland was rather annoyed because she'd forgotten to tune in to it. We looked up the *Radio Times* to make sure, and found it was on at about eight-fifteen, so Bland nipped into the kitchen and tuned in. Then he brought the speaker in where we were. Then he apologized and went into the study, where he had a letter to write. That was one of the few times when I was alone."

He emphasized the statement so much that Wharton should have seen the irony. Apparently he didn't.

"Alone were you? How long for?"

"Well, say fifteen seconds! When Bland had been in the study a minute or so, Mrs. Bland was rather annoyed he was missing the music, so she went to call him. She asked him how long he was going to be. I could see her all the time, mind you, though she had her back to me. Bland said something—what it was I couldn't catch. Then she came back to her seat. Bland followed in another minute. He had the letter with him, and he put it on the mantelpiece so that he shouldn't forget it when he went out with me."

"The music was still on?"

"Oh, rather! Just working up nicely. I'd say it was about seventeen or eighteen minutes past eight when Bland came in again. The music went on till well after the half-past. As it was finishing, Mrs. Bland said it was getting on her nerves. I didn't mention the fact, but it was rather getting on mine. Bland laughed, but we heard it through, then switched off, and when the table was cleared we got down to chess."

"A game?"

"Not just then. Before the meal, Bland and I had done the problems in two of the Sunday papers. Afterwards we went into a problem he'd composed himself. We happened to find a flaw in it, then we put it right. Then we had a game—"

"What time was that?"

"Precisely five to nine when we started it. I sat where I always sat—facing the clock. We played till a quarter to eleven, and Bland and I left the house, so that I got back here at eleven exactly." He rubbed his hands. "What! are you answered yet? . . . Have some more beer!"

Wharton shot his hand over the glass.

"Not for me, vicar! Not that it isn't good beer —because it is!" But he took the pouch the other handed over, and they both stoked up again.

"Now, sir; about these three alibis. Give me a few seconds to change—as they used to say on the halls—and I shall have much pleasure in demolishing the whole three; yours to start with!"

"You will?"

"I'll certainly have a good try." He got out his notebook and made a few quick entries. "First of all, we'll say there was collusion between you and Bland. As this clock of his seems to be playing a big part, we'll say he altered the hands, and you altered the church clock to match."

The vicar nodded. "Pretty risky thing, you know, deliberately altering the hands of a public clock. Somebody would have seen it done. But it *couldn't* be done! When the time signal went on the wireless, the whole village would have noticed the discrepancy!"

Wharton laughed. "One to you, vicar! Well, we'll say Bland's clock was the one that was wrong. It was put on during the evening."

Cross shook his head. "That cock won't fight! . . . The clock was dead right when I got there, and it was dead right when I left. And I'll tell you something rather apposite. About a week ago I was playing chess with Bland, and I insisted that I must get home here at ten. Mrs. Bland played a trick on me; got her husband to attract my attention and then altered the hands of the clock . . . I spotted it straightaway."

"Your trick again!" said Wharton, with heavy jocularity. "Now another point. You say the *Bolero* music began on time, and it agreed with the published time, and it ended to time—that is, it agreed with the clock, which we've agreed to accept as correct. Now I put it to you. You weren't listening to the wireless at all! It was a gramophone pick-up!"

Cross roared. "Now I call that a good one!"

"Not at all!" said Wharton. "I'm perfectly serious. Why shouldn't it have been a gramophone?"

The vicar looked at him roguishly, then decided that he really was expecting to be taken seriously.

"In the first place, they haven't a gramophone."

"They might have had one for the occasion."

"True enough, but the maid would know that. We're putting her on your side. Also you see there's another difficulty. If you listen in a lot, as I do," he waved his hand vaguely as if to indicate that somewhere in the back regions was a set, "you'd know the difference between music direct from the orchestra and music from a record. And there's a much more important point. The *Bolero* lasted best part of twenty minutes. That means four sides and two records. That would have involved two gramophones and perfect synchronization when a side of a record ended."

"Oh, no!" smiled Wharton. "These ultra-modern gramophones change records and everything themselves. If there's a set of records of the *Bolero*, they'd have done the whole thing without a break."

"You ever heard one?"

"Can't say that I have."

"Well, you'll find there's the rattle of the disks as the records are changed—and there's a break. No, superintendent! You'll have to give in."

"It certainly looks like it," admitted Wharton. "However, just one last shot at you—then I'm done. Bland wasn't in the study at all. He wouldn't have had time to *write* a letter. He might have *scribbled* something. I say he didn't do either. He had that letter all ready. Actually he was out of the house!"

"Don't you believe it. . . . I've knocked down that cokernut already. He wasn't away more than three or four minutes. Even that was broken up by Mrs. Bland speaking to him and him answering."

Wharton took his defeat like a man. Then he had to be introduced to Mrs. Cross, and see the screen and the clock, and by the time he got clear it was half-past twelve. A more amusing morning he'd never had. The vicar of Barlcombe filled to a nicety his idea of a village parson—tolerant, cheery and a man among men. Wharton promised indeed, very definitely, to come along and have tea some time, if his stay were prolonged; which he was careful to insist it wouldn't be. And if the vicar was in town, Wharton would show him a thing or two at the Yard. The two parted, in fact, like sworn brothers.

But because he was a methodical person, Wharton rounded the morning off by drawing the car under a tree and jotting things down while they were fresh in his mind. The combined statements of Mrs. Bland and the vicar coincided in every detail.

5.00 Cross arrives.
7.45 Study.
7.50 Sat down to meal.
8.15 Bland tunes in.
8.16 Music. Bland in study.
8.17 Mrs. Bland at study door.
8.18 Bland comes out.
8.50 Problem composed.
8.55 Chess begun.
10.50 Cross leaves.
11.00 Cross home again.

That meant one thing and one thing only. If Sir William was alive at 9 P.M. or even 8.45, then the Bland establishment was definitely out of it. They were out of it in any case, since Sir William must have been alive well after Bland returned to his own house. As for the story of a woman and an intrigue, Wharton assured himself it was merely the mare's nest he ought to have known it was.

And all that, of course, looked bad for Griffiths and Daniels. There was the faint chance that some intruder had been responsible for the murder, but it hardly seemed likely. In other words, Wharton was now deciding to hear what had happened to Travers during the morning; after that he proposed concentrating on the occupants of Combe Cottage. Griffiths, it was true, was absent, but for the purposes he intended, Daniels was a much more likely customer. Indeed, there was one scheme that might be put into operation at once. That was why his first act on arriving at the police station was to send a reliable plain-clothes man along to keep an eye on the butler.

....

An urgent message was waiting at the station. It was from Menzies, and Groom was obviously puzzled as to what it meant.

M for mamma, not M for man.

Wharton put the slip away in his bulging notebook, said he'd go into it after lunch, then hurried off to the post-office. He and the postmaster had had dealings together before. Had there been any call made from Combe Cottage since midday? There hadn't. But he had some news that cut across Wharton's optimism like a rain-cloud blown across an April sun. It was given because the postmaster was trying to be helpful. He had ideas of his own, and wished to clinch his association with the police.

"One call might interest you," he confided. "That Mrs. Bland was rung up about twelve-thirty by Mr. Cross, of Barlcombe."

"Very good of you," said Wharton. "But I'm afraid it's a bit wide of the mark."

And with that information still worrying away at the back of his mind, he pushed off in search of Travers.

CHAPTER XIV
MORE BLOOD

AN HOUR OR SO after lunch, Travers received an extraordinary surprise. He was sitting in his room at the hotel, deep in an easy chair, planning his course of conduct with the lady into whose arms fate and Wharton seemed to be hustling him, when the General himself appeared, in a mighty state of perturbation.

"Would you like to go back to town for a day or two?"

Travers stared at him. It was as if the condemned cell had opened and the warder had remarked: "What about a nice little eighteen holes this afternoon?" Then he wondered where the catch was, and took refuge in the facetious.

"If I say no, George, I shall have to go in any case. What's the idea? Scotland Yard getting jealous?"

Wharton drew up a chair.

"A message just came in from Norris. They've had an anonymous letter at the Yard. Have a look."

Travers polished his glasses.

If you want to know who killed Sir William Griffiths, go and see the new film, "The Unknown World" as soon as it comes out.

Travers made grunting noises. "The Unknown World. That'll be Pendry's film. . . . Tim Griffiths' film if you like. . . . You place any reliance on this sort of thing?"

"Of course we do! But look at it another way. Can we afford to disregard it?"

"Exactly!" said Travers lamely. "But just one other thing. The trade show was only a day or two ago, and the film hasn't been released yet. It shouldn't be too difficult within those limits to find who wrote the latter."

"Who attends a trade show?"

Travers opened his mouth, then closed it.

"Sorry! . . . Of course! . . . I mean, I see your point."

"That's just it," said Wharton. "I took the same optimistic view as you. I thought there'd be perhaps three or four whites on the expedition, and one of them would be the only possible man who'd know what was in the picture. Then I remembered your remark about the trade show. Scores of people there perhaps. Tell me now; is this nearer the mark? Somebody at that trade show saw something in the picture which to him, apparently, recalled Sir William Griffiths and his cut throat. Being an amateur sleuth and a bit of a busybody—he— or she—wrote that letter to us."

"Sounds feasible. . . . But another suggestion, for what it's worth. Mightn't that letter be a sort of red-herring? Was it written to lure you away from here? To get you to town?"

Wharton smiled. "Even if it is, the fact remains. Can we afford to disregard it? . . . And isn't it an argument why I should stop here and you should go to town!"

He put the copy of the letter back in his book. "Frankly, will you go to town and have a look at that film as soon as you can? Norris wouldn't see what you'll see. Also you know Colonel Pendry and everybody. You're in the swim. Find out what you think was seen. Still, you know what to do better than I do. . . . Any business of your own, of course, at the same time."

Travers hopped up. "A perfectly delightful makeweight, George! . . . What about you? Going to tea with Mrs. Bland?"

"Possibly!" Wharton kept a perfectly straight face. "You push off and I'll ring her up. See Norris first, in case he's got any ideas."

"Good enough! . . . Palmer's having a rather dizzy time of things. He's been whizzing between here and London for days."

"Never mind!" said Wharton. "I'll see the Murderers' Union and fix up the next one more handy. The smoke-room at the Odysseus. Free meals and beer."

....

Travers enjoyed that journey, in spite of the fact that there was no telling when he'd have to do it again. A most distracting business altogether, and murderers the most inconsiderate of people. For all that, it was good to be back in town again; good to drop in at Durango House and see how things were going; good to see Norris' honest-to-God face, even if he had nothing to contribute to the solving of the problem. He had had a busy time, getting together all those movements of Sanders, to clear that side of the case up. Travers told him all the latest, then used his phone to get hold of Silbermann's. There was nobody there. A couple of other shots and he ran Pendry to earth in time to arrange for dinner.

Pendry was in great fettle. The film was booking well, and already he was sounding Silbermann about a further try at Unknown Amazonia. When Travers broached the subject of the anonymous letter, he was flabbergasted.

"But wasn't it an accident? . . . I mean, the papers this morning?"

Travers smiled with all the mystery of the adept.

"Never mind about the papers, Steve! You wouldn't expect Scotland Yard to tell all they know. . . . Keep it dead under your hat, but listen to this!"

Pendry listened with all the absorption of one who hears of the mysterious doings of what are to him mysterious people. He was staggered.

"Perfectly incredible! . . . Who did it? Griffiths?"

Travers shook his head. "It's too hellish a thing to talk about in that way, Steve. One word to a soul and we're both well in the soup."

"That's all right!" Pendry assured him. "Don't you worry about me. And what is it you want to know?"

Travers explained. Was there anything in the film that struck Pendry as at all likely? Pendry thought for a bit, and said he wouldn't like to say, off-hand. And, of course, the film had been very heavily cut—a year and more's work put into an hour and a half. There was one thing perhaps. Still, Travers had better see the whole thing for himself.

"What about running it through?" Travers asked.

"When?"

"To-night? Time's a pretty important thing. Something else might roll up to-morrow."

"Damn it all!" said Pendry, "we can't do that. There won't be a soul round there except the night-watchman. Pity, too! Everything's round there; film and cut lengths. Still, there we are!"

Travers was far less resigned.

"What about getting hold of Silbermann?"

"That'd be a good idea," said Pendry. "Tell him you're acting officially. Pile it on a bit thick. Get him to come along himself."

"And what about an operator?"

"I'll do that. It won't be the first time."

It wasn't till half-past nine that they met Silbermann outside the new building in Wardour Street. Travers knew him reasonably well since Durangos had been behind that amalgamation with Imperial Pictures. With his topper and full rig-out, the managing director of New Imperials looked like a belated reveller in the empty display room. Travers had explained more fully what he'd said over the phone.

"All right! We'll run it through," said Silbermann, and moved off to the operating-room. "Very good publicity for the picture, Mr. Travers—or you think not?"

"I hope so," said Travers. "Where do I stay? Here?"

Silbermann explained that they wouldn't see much there. The best place was just outside the operating-room at the back of the tiny circle, under the portholes. If Mr. Travers saw anything, he must shout, and the film would be stopped.

Once he forgot that he was alone, Travers found nothing unreal in watching and listening to that film. There was not a penn'orth of difference between that show and any other. The canned music blared till the film itself began—preparations for leaving, on board ship, disembarkation, at the rail-head, and assembling and bargaining with coolies. The only thing that was unnatural was the tremendous concentration with which things had to be watched. The eyes daren't turn aside for a moment. Travers filled his pipe and stared through the lighted match. Things of trifling moment acquired an importance that was nerve-racking and altogether disturbing, and all the time he was wondering if the wood had been missed in the multiplicity of trees.

At last something came. The voice of the commentator—Malone's it actually was—began to describe the particular tribe the expedition had reached—squat, Mongolian people, nomads occupying the foothills and living in tents. It was now just after the spring rains, and their long-haired goats could be seen browsing. Then the head man of the tribe was seen—a scowling, cretinous-looking individual with slit, shifty eyes.

The commentator continued. The expedition was glad to reach this tribe. After that disaster to the provisions and the loss of the salt, they'd been on short rations for some days. Griffiths seemed to be specially admired by their women—picture of Griffiths entirely surrounded by hags—and in accordance with their idea of blood brotherhood, he was given by the chief the honour of killing the ceremonial goat. Not until then could the tribe fraternize freely.

Travers stared. The chief—obviously posed— presented the knife . . . the very spit, it seemed, of the one he had taken from the rack at Combe Cottage! The goat was seen dragged along by men; women and children running behind and raising a cloud of dust with their feet. Griffiths approached the goat . . . then the continuity was broken. The goat was seen dead, and by it squatted the chief with a bowl of blood. At the other side stood Griffiths. "Just a minute!" hollered Travers, and thumped the wall below the porthole. Pendry came out.

"Is it possible to let me see that scene in slow motion?" Travers asked.

Pendry smiled. "I thought you'd spot it! What's that about slow motion?"

Travers explained. Pendry shook his head.

"You can't show *any* sound film in slow motion. It's got to go through at ninety foot a minute." Travers clicked his tongue. "And what about the cut? You still got the length?"

"We've got every inch we took," said Pendry. "I'll run it through for you."

There were half a dozen false starts before he got the length he wanted. When it came, there was no need to wonder why it had been cut. One man held the goat by its long horns; another held the front legs, and a third the hind—all three grinning like devils. Griffiths, to do him credit, didn't cotton to the job. He appeared to shut his eyes and flinch away as he flashed the knife across the throat, and his back was turned as the blood spurted and the bowl was held to catch it. Even to Travers the scene was revolting, and he turned his head away. When he looked round again the length was run through.

"How's that?" asked Pendry.

"I don't think we shall want any more," Travers told him.

"Pretty ghastly, wasn't it?"

"It was! . . . What made you take it, Steve?"

"Well, in a way we wanted to please that gang. . . ." He hesitated.

Travers put the question bluntly. "Tell me straight out. Did Griffiths have anything to do with taking it? Did he insist?"

"Hm!" said Pendry. "He was keener than we were. Then when it came to the scratch, he didn't think so much of it."

Travers' face was extraordinarily serious as he looked at the pair of them. "Honestly now. Which was the real Griffiths? The one who wanted to cut the throat or the one who jibbed when the time came?"

Pendry looked down. He shook his head—then nodded.

"Griffiths would never have cut a throat in cold blood. No kind of a throat."

"Right I I'll take your word for it. . . . Now then; could you have some enlargements made for Scotland Yard? One of the knife, one of the actual contact and another of Griffiths turning his head away."

Pendry showed him a strip of the film. "The frames are pretty small, you know. When you get an enlargement, the definition won't be very good. , . . To-morrow do?"

"Splendidly! Very good of you, Steve—and of Mr. Silbermann."

Silbermann had been for some minutes in the throes of a pronouncement. Acknowledgment of Travers' thanks helped to loosen his tongue.

"Before we go any further, you realize the implication in all this?"

"I'm afraid I don't," said Travers.

"But surely!" expostulated Silbermann. "Are you preparing a case against Griffiths or are you not?"

"Frankly, we're not! We're investigating an anonymous letter. Don't believe the story-books, Mr. Silbermann. Innocent men don't get themselves hanged . . . and ruin films. If Griffiths is all right, he's nothing to fear. If he isn't, the law's the law, and it's bigger than you and I. . . . Just one thing, by the way. Do you know definitely who attended the trade show?"

"I think so."

"No gate-crashers?"

"Impossible! There were special tickets of invitation. If extra people came, they were accompanied."

"Good! And did a Mr. Bland come, by any chance? By invitation of Griffiths it'd be."

"Bland?" He thought back. "No! I don't know a Bland. Who is he? What's he like?" Travers described him. Silbermann was confident he hadn't been there.

"That's good enough for me!" said Travers. For all that, he wasn't any too sure. Bland had been in town at the time, and he'd been particularly vociferous when he'd thought Wharton was going to keep him down at Mulberton. True Bland had what Wharton considered a perfect alibi. Then Travers looked up to see Pendry grinning at him. "What are you shaking your head over?"

"Was I?" Travers pulled himself together. "The fact of the matter is, this job makes you so damned imaginative. Er—the trade show. What time was it?"

"Two o'clock," said Silbermann. "We filled 'em with lunch and then led 'em to it, as a fellow-director of mine used to say."

"And not a bad idea either."

The building was locked again behind the night watchman, and Silbermann's huge car drew up.

"Talking of filling 'em up," said Travers; "you two people come and have a spot of supper somewhere."

"Not for me," said Pendry. "I've got a job of work in the morning."

Silbermann thought the idea not a bad one, and Travers got in alongside. At Fragoli's, after a first-class snack and a half bottle, the film magnate was in a much better mood. He ventured on the latest anecdote. Travers countered with another, and the atmosphere became hilariously blue.

"Talking of honeymoons and all that," said Travers in one of the brief intervals, "haven't I soon got to be buying a wedding-present?"

The other stared.

"Sorry, of course, if I'm dropping a brick. Er— didn't some one tell me Miriam and Griffiths . . . ?"

Silbermann scowled and exposed his palms.

"Damn gossip! There isn't a word of truth in it! Miriam's in America. Been there for months."

"I say! I'm awfully sorry." Then he nodded knowingly, "It wouldn't have been a bad match, you know . . . as things are!"

"Why? Can't I give my daughter everything she wants? And she don't want him! I don't want him either."

Travers ventured on a prod in the waistcoat.

"A wise father that chooses his own son-in-law, what? . . . Now what about a final spot?"

. . . .

A call at the Yard to get a message through to Wharton, and then Travers wandered back to the familiar comfort of his own flat. As far as he could see, beyond the elimination of Sanders, the case had gone little farther. That Tim Griffiths should have cut his uncle's throat as he cut that goat's was too revolting a thing to contemplate. The man who flinched from blood at the last moment would never have screwed his courage to such a sticking point. And then there was Bland—the man with the perfect alibi; and Mrs. Bland—the woman who hated old Griffiths like that very devil; the woman who also had a perfect alibi; the woman who, in spite of what Wharton said, had nevertheless listened at keyholes. The woman who . . . there Travers blushed and left it.

The following morning something must still have been lingering in his mind, since the first thing he did on coming in to breakfast was to ring up Eaton Square. The butler it seemed to be who was answering.

"May I speak to Mr. Bland?"

"Sorry, sir! Mr. Bland won't be in before ten. . . . May I take a message, sir?"

Travers screwed his voice to a still higher falsetto.

"No, thanks! . . . By the way, I rang him up just after lunch the day before yesterday and you said he wasn't in."

"I'm afraid there was some mistake, sir. Mr. Bland was in, sir—all the afternoon. And all yesterday, sir. . . . What name is it, sir, please?"

"Most unfortunate!" said Travers quickly. "Tell him I'll see him some time to-day!" and he rang off.

So much for that. Bland hadn't been at the trade show, and therefore hadn't known what was in the film. The super-alibi remained inviolate and Wharton held the field. Even his theory as to who had written the letter seemed impregnable. Some visitor to the trade show must have been struck with the goat episode, and there the matter must end. It would be too much to go through Silbermann's list to find a person of the type required.

The morning passed and the afternoon. With the impatience of the amateur he was actually beginning to worry. Was Wharton side-tracking him?

Or was he too busy on some new discovery? By dinner he was almost aggrieved—then the telephone went. He hailed Wharton's voice with a joy that was unfeigned.

"Hallo! . . . Where are! you speaking from? . . . At eight o'clock sharp! . . . I'll be there." Then Wharton had hung up and Travers was left to scurry through his meal. Five minutes to the hour found him knocking at the door and hearing the General's "Come in!"

Wharton was looking serious.

"You perfectly free to-night?"

"Oh, rather! . . . What's on?"

"We're going round to see Tim Griffiths. The funeral's over and he knows where he stands. He may feel like talking and he may not. Personally I don't think he'll refuse—if he's asked in the right way!"

"Talk about what?"

"If you don't mind," said Wharton, "I won't tell you. When I spring a surprise I don't like to feel that half the audience is already in the know. It'll be much better if you sit there and look inscrutable. That'll keep him guessing."

"Anything new about Daniels?"

Wharton smiled at that attack on his flank. "Yes. Something quite interesting. Yesterday, when Daniels had gone back to Combe Cottage, I sent a man along there to see if what might reasonably happen did happen. Daniels left the house just after lunch and walked to Barlcombe post-office, where he sent a telegram—to Griffiths, Eaton Square, London. All it said was: 'Everything going well. Letter unnecessary.' What do you think of it?"

"Brief but voluble."

"That's what *I* think. He's got something to talk about, if only he's asked in the right way."

"Remember what I told you happened the evening I saw him? I'm dead sure he wanted to speak to me—and he would have done if that unknown quantity Daniels hadn't butted in."

Wharton looked at him over his glasses.

"You think he's so unknown? For instance, you say Griffiths couldn't have had the nerve to cut a throat. Why should *he* have done it when Daniels was there to do it for him?"

"You know something, George?"

"I don't," said Wharton. "I'm merely putting it to you." He went over to the glass; flicked his immaculate black coat with his handkerchief, then had a look at himself.

"Time we were moving. We shall have to bluff —and bluff big."

"Another short cut?"

"Another short cut!" repeated Wharton solemnly. "This time it won't be bungled. Two men are watching the house. Even if anything does go wrong, we've still got Daniels. If it comes off, we'll have the truth for the first time. . . . I took the liberty, by the by, of asking for the interview in your name."

It was Travers who took the lead at the door of the Eaton Square house.

"Sir Timothy at home?" he asked the footman. "I'll see, sir. . . . What name, sir?"

"Mr. Ludovic Travers—and a friend."

Travers still took the lead when the footman returned. He was first through the door with Wharton close on his heels. Griffiths, still in his morning black, came forward from the chair before the empty fireplace, where scattered newspapers showed how he'd been employing his time. At the sight of Wharton he had given a start, but now he kept his nerve.

"Glad to see you, Travers. . . . Hallo, Wharton! What are you doing here?"

Wharton seemed not to see the hand.

"Oh! just clearing up odds and ends. . . . This has been a melancholy day for you."

"Yes," said Griffiths. "Not the most cheerful I've ever spent. . . . Do sit down! . . . What'll you drink?"

Travers shook his head. "Not for me. Later on perhaps." Wharton followed suit. It was deliberate, perhaps, on his part, but for a few moments there was silence. Griffiths poured himself out a drink.

"Well now; what's it all about?"

"Sir Timothy!" The name was almost a command. Griffiths paused with the glass halfway to his mouth. "The time has come to talk. I'm not here to-night as a private individual. I'm here as the Superintendent of the C.I.D., who's had charge of the enquiry into the death of your uncle."

Strange to say, Griffiths seemed to show relief. He sipped the drink and set the glass down.

"Well . . . anything I can do?"

"Splendid!" said Wharton ironically. "What I'd prefer would be for you to make a statement."

"A statement? . . . What about?"

"How your uncle met his death on the evening of September the fifth."

Griffiths looked amazed.

"But I've already told you what I know!" Wharton nodded. "Ah, well! I see we've got to come to the point." He leaned forward. "Daniels has been talking! We've got his story and we want to see how it agrees with yours!"

"Daniels talking!" He gave a sort of snigger. "I don't know what you mean. . . . Where is Daniels?"

"At this moment at Scotland Yard."

Griffiths shot a look at him.

"What's he been saying?"

Wharton smiled wearily. "You'll hear that in good time. You think I'm bluffing? . . . Very well, I'll tell you something to interest you. As soon as I asked Daniels a question, he answered. He couldn't help himself!"

"What question?"

"Where he buried the pig!"

Griffiths stared at him, then his face flushed. For a moment Travers thought he was going to break down. His hand shook as he picked up the glass.

"All right! . . . I'll tell you. . . . And I'm damn glad!" He finished the drink, wiped his mouth, and sat there for a bit. Then he turned to Wharton.

"You were right! . . . You remember what you told me—that night at the Odysseus Club? . . . It's been hell! . . . All the time I thought you knew."

"Don't worry about that," said Wharton. "It was a damn silly thing to say in any case—even after a meal."

And he waited.

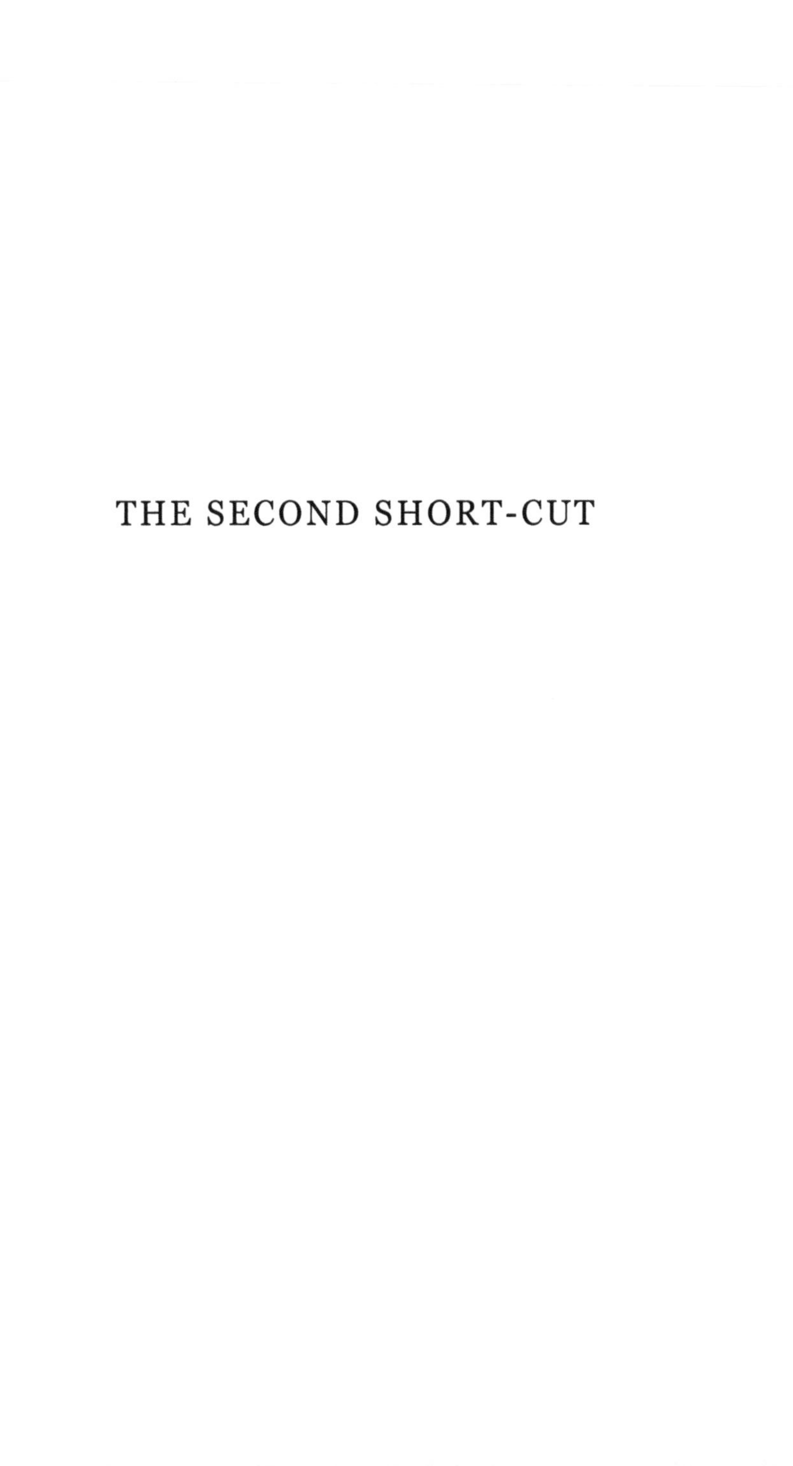

THE SECOND SHORT-CUT

CHAPTER XV
SEPTEMBER 5TH—AND BEFORE

THESE ARE THE stories told by Griffiths and Daniels—not in their actual words, but as Travers, at Wharton's request, summarized them for the use of the Assistant Commissioner. They are the stories as interpreted by Travers; gestures and looks turned into emotions, and things out of place or elicited by questions put into their proper order and context. It was Travers' commission to show the two men as they actually were, at certain vital times and under certain conditions. If the result is unconvincing, the fault is not his. The bald, disjointed stories as told and stammered and extorted, might have been more unconvincing still.

....

PROLOGUE

When Tim Griffiths went down to Combe Cottage at his uncle's request, two sides of him had to be in conflict. His natural conceit made him spread himself over the things he had recently done; the fact that he was to be dependent on his uncle for future supplies made him assume a deference which he was far from feeling.

It was a day or two before Sir William made a definite statement, and it was not difficult to recognize the psychological moment for which the old man had been waiting. There were big things in the air. Some months before, he had acquired a controlling interest in Montagu Brown—the largest high-class haberdashery business in town, with its branches in the West End and the better residential suburbs. The amalgamation with Hoods—its only rival in that class of trade—was virtually settled and all that remained was to put an extremely attractive proposition to two sets of shareholders. It was when he was certain that things would go as he wanted them, that Sir William decided to speak. His method of approach was typical.

"Well, young man! You've had your fling. You've lived your own life for five years. What now?"

Griffiths had temporized. Something would turn up perhaps. In any case he'd had a run for his money.

"Well, you should know!" the old man had said. "Ever thought of settling down?"

"To what?"

His uncle told him—to hard work: beginning at the foot of the ladder and working up; pretty quick stages perhaps, but working all the same. Say, three months in the mills, three in the warehouse and three in the headquarter branch of Montagu Brown. After that, the office of one of the buyers . . . then perhaps a turn at a desk. After that—well, it would all depend. Griffiths realized what at least a part of that program implied.

"My God! You mean sell shirts and things to people!"

The other said that was so. But there was another way to look at it. No man was qualified to act as director of a combine with millions of capital and thousands of employees who hadn't an inside knowledge of his firm's activities. Sir William himself had first made his money in haberdashery—newspapers had been his second love—and he'd been through it all himself. Then the old man got more kindly. Two years—three at the most—and there'd be big things waiting for the right man. He himself couldn't count on much longer. His heart wasn't all it should be. He'd rather hand over to one of his own name than to a stranger.

All the same he'd done no immediate pressing. "Think it over, my boy. Stay here as long as you like. Take a few days . . . a week if you like, and make up your mind then. If you decide before that —well and good."

Life at Mulberton hadn't been intolerable. The weather had been superb, and it was good to lounge in a chair under the trees or potter about in the car—a day at Minehead, another at Taunton, another at Exeter. There'd been a couple of tennis parties with some people he knew, and altogether the days had passed pleasantly. But for that decision worrying away at the back of his mind, they might have been idyllic—with some of the old man's money in his pocket and more to come.

Dinner, the one ceremonial of the day, was the irksome reminder. The old man, for all his hatred of shams and display, was a stickler for the proprieties of that meal. There would be he and his nephew confronting each other at opposite ends of the table; Sir William keeping his side of the bargain by making no reference to business; and the conversation therefore all bored and stilted, and on matters in which he himself could have had little interest. It was easy to gather that the greatest difficulty his nephew had was to conceal his contempt for the man on whom he was likely to depend in the future. Two men, of even greater importance in the tragedy, were forming a background during those few days. Daniels, the ever-ready, butler-cum-valet, was one. He was a go-between in the true line of descent from Pandarus; a fawner, a listener at keyholes who realized where his interests lay at the moment and realized even better where they were likely to lie in the future. With the possible heir, he had traded on both associations. He had assumed a familiarity which the other had been too indolent to check. He had deprecated Sir William's views on temperance. How, heaven knows, but he had seen that in the locked cupboard of the bedroom there had been a bottle and syphon—renewed when necessary. On that he had possibly traded, ingratiated himself, insinuated this and that, sympathized generally and even advised. Tim Griffiths, a loose talker like most egomaniacs, had confided in him.

"Do you know, Daniels, if I'd married the girl I should have been married to I shouldn't be here now, kow-towing to the old swine."

Bland had been different. He had flashed across the scene more rarely and more brilliantly. At first Griffiths—who before that visit had never really come into contact with him—had been inclined to accept him as a sort of menial. Then he had felt a dislike born of conscious inferiority: there was Bland; reticent, courteous, a thoroughbred, supremely competent, accepted by his uncle—even when the old man was most irritable or discourteous—as an equal and one to be relied on; Bland—perfectly courteous to himself in that man-of-the-world manner of his. Once or twice he had thought Bland had been sneering at him, but the irony was too elusive for his slower wits. Then there would be another Bland—friendly, solicitous, and, above all, sympathetically appreciative. Then Griffiths wondered how he could ever have disliked Bland or thought him hostile.

On one such occasion the two men had been sitting in the shade on the lawn, and Griffiths had been spreading himself in his old vein. Bland had been listening quietly; then all at once he'd looked up.

"Got any money at all?"

"Why?" Griffiths asked.

"Well, strictly between ourselves, I could put you in the way of making a good deal more. Put your hands on five thousand and I'll double it in three months. You know, Griffiths," he went on, "you and I could get on well together, if you don't mind my saying so!"

Griffiths too had felt a sudden rush of affection. For a day or two after that he'd thought of schemes to get hold of money. He'd even mentioned the matter to Bland again. The secretary had then been more retiring. He couldn't advise. Also the chance was rapidly disappearing. Perhaps . . . well, if Mr. Griffiths would care about raising money on his expectations from his uncle. Not that he'd suggest it. It might be done, of course—but not the kind of thing that he'd recommend. Perhaps at some future time. In any case, not a word or suggestion to Sir William, whose ideas were that to gamble in thousands was high finance, but to use your judgment over hundreds was—well, gambling!

"I know!" Tim Griffiths said. "The world's full of humbug. Take Silbermann for instance."

Bland listened to all that story, sympathized quietly, and hinted that he knew something already about that matter. One of these days, when he was more of a free agent, he might tell Griffiths something. Altogether there was a curious rapprochement; the pair of them getting thick as thieves. Daniels also seems to have been told all about it.

All this is a long-winded prelude, but it may account for Griffiths' state of mind when, after dinner on the evening of September the fourth, Sir William asked him point-blank what his intentions were. Then he attempted to bargain. He wouldn't mind this or that, but no selling things behind a counter for him. The old man then appears to have told him a few home truths. There was, in fact, a bit of a scene which culminated in a heart attack, though he wouldn't let Daniels call up the doctor. As for Mr. Timothy's threat of packing up and going away, Daniels was to report any signs at once of that taking effect.

Daniels reported all that to Griffiths. Griffiths was furious.

"Damned cantankerous old swine! He makes me that wild I could murder him!"

An absurd remark, which Daniels took rather too literally.

"There's no need for that, sir. He'll kill *himself* if he has another go or two like he had to-night!"

SEPTEMBER 5TH
(Before dinner)

Tim Griffiths got up very late the following morning; he took good care, in fact, not to make an appearance till his uncle had left the house. As he was reading the papers outside on the lawn, Bland drifted along and sat down beside him. Before five minutes had gone he was listening to the events of the previous night and a general restatement of all Griffiths' troubles. Bland's attitude was that of the older, more experienced man who gives advice where he has given affection.

"Do you really think," he said, "that Silbermann would forgive the pair of you, if you and Miriam got married in spite of everything?"

"I'm sure he would. He'd have to!"

"I'm none too sure of that," said Bland warily. "Of course she's the only child. . . . It'd be up to you to make good."

"Why shouldn't I make good?" demanded Griffiths. "The thing that worries me is why she threw me over. Everything was all right when I went away. The old man wasn't any too keen on it, but she was sure she could get him round."

Bland thought for a moment, then made up his mind.

"Look here! Can I rely on you not to let me down? If a word of this gets out, there's likely to be trouble for me. You'll give me your word never to mention my name?"

"Of course I will! . . . What is it?"

Bland lowered his voice. "It was Sir William who put the spoke in your wheel! He saw Silbermann personally. Silbermann thought you were a certainty for your uncle's money. Sir William disillusioned him. As you know, he had other ideas. Silbermann told Miriam to break it off and then packed her off to America."

Griffiths saw red. He'd tell his uncle what he thought of him. He'd see Silbermann . . .

"Don't be a fool!" said Bland. "Besides, you can't do that! Marry the girl and keep quiet; that's your policy."

"And let my uncle get away with it? I'll see him damned first!"

"If you must then—well, you must. Tell him what you think of him, but clear out afterwards. Slip across to America. Get off to-morrow. If she'll marry you, well and good. If she won't, you can always come back here again and eat humble pie. I know Sir William better than you. He'll come round all right."

When he'd gone, Griffiths consulted the sailing lists. On the following day was a boat that would suit him, and he could pick it up at Plymouth. Full of the idea, he mentioned it to Daniels, but giving no details.

"Don't be surprised if I clear out to-night or to-morrow morning. Not a word, but I think of going to America."

He swore Daniels to secrecy. Just before lunch he took out the car and went in to Exeter. There he went to a picture show, had tea at a hotel and was back at Combe Cottage at six. Before dinner he shirked the deliberate issue, but by an assumption of aggressive taciturnity goaded the old man into asking what was the matter. The question gave him the courage he needed. The scene was so violent that Daniels made his way into the room till Sir William cursed him out again. Griffiths said he'd be damned if he'd stay in the house a minute longer and went up to his room white with rage. After a few minutes, Sir William ordered dinner to be served. Then he sent Daniels upstairs to ask Mr. Timothy, with his compliments, if he might see him for a minute.

He came down, but only—as he frankly admitted—because he hadn't said all he wanted to say. To his amazement the old man apologized. Life was too precarious a thing for quarrelling. Some way out might be found. Timothy was the only relative he had in the world, and so on. He must have been a singularly impressive figure at that moment and there must have been some strange chord he touched on, since the nephew was not only taken clean aback, but found himself shaking hands with his uncle and owning up that the fault had been his as much as anybody's else's. *Daniels knew nothing of this reconciliation.* The dinner proceeded, both men very quiet and reserved.

SEPTEMBER 5TH
(After dinner)

After dinner, Sir William went as usual into the drawing-room and sat there reading the papers; French window wide open, as the evening was sultry. Tim Griffiths sat there too for a bit. He switched on the light when it got dusk—which was almost at once—wandered upstairs, wandered down again, then seeing his uncle was asleep in the chair, lighted a cigarette and stepped out to the lawn. As he did so he heard the sound of a train, then moved along to the gate. He stood leaning over this, smoking the cigarette and listening to the train as it gradually approached. He heard it pull into the station, heard it make the first puffs as it began to pull out again . . . then he heard something else—the high falsetto of his uncle's voice call, "Tim!"

As he went slowly back, he remembered it was a kind of indeterminate moonlight; all half-light and shadows and everywhere uncannily still. To his amazement, the light was out! He should have noticed that as he turned from the gate—but he didn't. A couple of steps inside the French window and he kicked against something; what it was he didn't know at the time, but he thought vaguely it was a cushion. At any rate he felt for the switch by the hall door and turned the light on. When he turned round he was almost paralyzed with horror.

The body lay there, throat cut from ear to ear the blood still oozing on the newspapers where it had fallen. One hand still clutched the sheet of paper he'd been reading. Behind the body lay the knife the blood settling round it to a pool.

His breath coming in quick gasps, he bent down and touched it—then found himself with it in his fingers. He stared again at

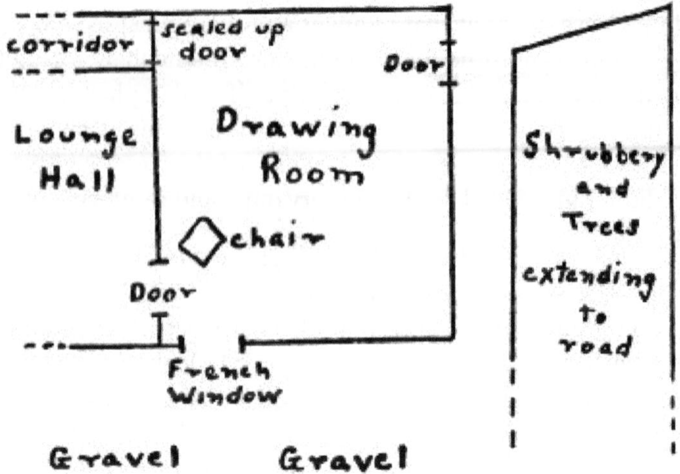

the body—then looked up. Daniels was standing in the door that led to the hall.

If anything the man was the more horrified of the two. He looked at the body; he looked at Griffiths. "So you did him in, sir—after all!"

"Did him in!" He dropped the knife. "You think?" . . . His voice became a shriek. "I wasn't here! *You* did it! *You* did it!"

Daniels kept his head. "Oh, no, sir! I wasn't here. I've just come from the kitchen . . . where he rang for me. And I heard that—when you knocked it down!"

He pointed to the clock. Griffiths noticed it for the first time, lying on the rug, face downwards.

"I didn't do it! I didn't!"

Daniels looked quickly into the hall, took out the key and locked the door. His attitude altered.

"You keep your mouth shut, sir! . . . Get away from that window and don't say a word!"

He watched while Griffiths backed away to the corner by the sealed-up door, then slipped across to the back door that led to the shrubbery, opened it, listened—then turned it with the same key. Then he switched out the light. The moonlight still showed the body where it lay by the door. Daniels nipped over, closed the window, bolted it and drew the curtain.

"Now then, sir? What about sending for the police!"

....

Five minutes later the recriminations were still going on. It must have been horrible—the body lying by the window; the voices in unnatural whispers that would persist in rising to threats or protestations, and then subsiding again. Both men knew they were in a trap. Griffiths swore that if necessary he'd say he actually saw Daniels in the room, turning off the light. Daniels could prove nothing. Let him bring Rigg along and prove where he was!

Daniels saw the strength of his own case in the evidence against the other. He had threatened murder, he had arranged secretly to slip off to America, then there'd been the quarrel, and he stood to profit by the old man's death—and he'd been caught in the act, the knife in his hand.

"You didn't see it!" insisted Griffiths. "You saw me pick it up!"

Daniels shook his head. "You're not going to put anything like that across me! There's only my word and yours—and who'll they believe?"

There was silence for a bit, then the idea came. Blackmail must have been in his mind all along; certainly from the time when he'd locked the doors and mentioned the police. Only then he hadn't seen the weakness of his own case.

"You leave it to me, sir. I can see a way out of this!"

He put the proposition up. Once he'd seen an accident where a woman had her head nearly severed from the body. They'd fake an accident like that. There'd be no risk. The local police would never know.

He slipped out of the room, locking it behind him; had a word with Rigg in the kitchen, then nipped up-stairs for a tot of whisky for Griffiths.

"Pull yourself together, sir! Keep your head and it'll be all right."

A quick rehearsal and it was all arranged. Daniels went to fetch the car—then he thought of something else. What about the blood to pour on the floor of the car and smear on the screen? By the time he had the car round he'd thought that out, but he said nothing to Griffiths. . . . Then they flashed on the light for a bit, gathered up the papers and had the body ready. The light was flicked out again and the body whisked out to the car. When Daniels finally left the room he had under his arm a china bowl from the side table.

The moon was now up and the gravel drive seemed white as paper. Daniels got the car going, but stopped again near the garage.

"What's the matter?" whispered Griffiths.

"Never you mind what's the matter. You stop here with the car."

Griffiths suspected a trap. He suspected it even more when Daniels was gone five minutes that seemed like hours. When Daniels came back he was holding something at arm's length.

"What've you been doing? What's that?"

"Get back in the house—and keep your mouth shut!" He set the bowl on the floor of the car and got in at the other side. "What the hell are you waiting for! Get back to the house!"

The car moved slowly on . . . out of the drive . . . round the bend . . . down the hill. A couple of hundred yards and the slope was steepest. Over to the left, once the car took the low bank, was a drop of twenty feet, and the impact would smash the rails like matchwood. He ran the headlights along —not a soul about. Then he stopped the engine and drew the car to a standstill. The bowl was set on the bank. A turn of the wheel, handbrake released, a shove—and the car was off. It gathered speed . . . he lost sight of it in the shadows . . . then he heard the impact. When he saw the car again, the near wheel had mounted the bank, bumper against the tree, but the car had not turned over.

When he got back, Griffiths was waiting for him —eyes staring.

"Everything all right?"

"It won't be if you start bawling. . . . You stay here!"

He went through to the drawing-room. If the body hadn't fallen on those papers there'd have been the devil of a job clearing things up. As it was it was easy enough. The clock was put on the table. He noticed the time by it—8.30. Then he came back to the lounge where Griffiths seized his arm.

"Why wasn't it suicide? Why shouldn't he have done it himself?"

Daniels sneered. "Wasn't he holding the paper? . . . And what should he want to kill himself for?"

Griffiths spoke with a curious intensity.

"Then I know who did it! . . . *Bland* did it!"

The other thought for a moment.

"By God, sir, you're right!" Then he looked like losing his nerve. "He'll be coming here! He'll know!"

There was a horrified silence for a moment—then panic. It was Daniels who got his nerve back first.

"I know. . . . You go to the gate, sir. Light a cigarette. If he says anything, say Sir William took the car and went off and he ain't back yet . . . I'll slip across the fields and see what he's doing."

He hauled Griffiths to his feet and got him going. The time by his watch was 9.05 . . . Then he streaked through the shrubbery path, over the fence and along the meadows where the hedges made a shadow. A hundred yards short of the cottage he stopped and got his breath, then nipped into the garden and approached the French window. If he were caught, he had his excuse all ready. But the voices he heard were coming from the far end of the room. A peep through the slit between the curtains showed Bland, his wife and Mr. Cross, of Barlcombe, talking away and pointing to something that lay on a table. The vicar seemed to be hilarious.

"I'll bet a fiver it's right! What about sending it up to the *Observer*?"

Daniels drew back again and made his way to Combe Cottage. He had taken less than five minutes to go and come. He coughed by the front porch and Griffiths came out.

"What was he doing?"

"He's got company. Mr. Cross was there. . . . And I've been thinking. If he'd have done it he'd have phoned up!"

"Afterwards, you mean?"

"That's right! To catch us out!"

Then Griffiths remembered. Bland had mentioned that Cross was coming for one of his chess evenings. . . . Then who had done it—if Daniels hadn't? And why had the old man called out if he hadn't seen Daniels with the knife in his hand and about to strike? And who else could have got that knife? Daniels had got it, as he came through the lounge! . . . But Daniels was looking at him. Perhaps he guessed what he was thinking.

"It's no use you starting that all over again. We're both in the same boat." He had another look at his watch. "At ten, we'd better get anxious. I'll go down to look for him, and find the car . . . then we'll call up the hospital. The police can come later."

Griffiths began to panic again. They'd know! Everybody'd know! What the devil did Daniels mean by getting him in such a mess! He'd ring up the police and make a clean sweep!

Daniels seized him by the collar and shook him like a rat.

"Keep your mouth shut, you bloody fool! . . . It's done, ain't it? . . . If they don't think it's an accident, why shouldn't it have been done down there? Haven't we got alibis? You can swear to me and I can swear to you!"

"All right! . . . Get me a drink!" He sank back in the chair and mopped his forehead. Daniels looked at him—then fetched a stiff tot. The light from under Rigg's door showed that she was not yet in bed. Griffiths took the drink at a go; then grew a bit surly. Daniels quietened him down.

"Tell you what, sir. You go up to bed. If the police or anybody ring up, then you know nothing about it, see? All we know is he went out."

Griffiths nodded, made as if to get up, then thought of something else.

"What was that you were carrying? Where'd you been?"

Daniels explained. What he didn't mention was that with the chance of a thundering good income for life, he'd been prepared to take risks, and take them ruthlessly. He'd opened the door of the sty and enticed the sow out. As the pigs came through, he'd clutched one by the snout, got it between his legs . . . then cut its throat with his pocket knife. He'd caught the blood—most of it. As soon as there was a chance he'd clear everything up. And he'd bury the pig and burn anything else in the incinerator.

He got Griffiths up to bed and saw that he had another tot. It would have taken best part of a bottle to get him under, with all that ghastly business keeping him awake. Indeed, Griffiths had another tot and yet another. Just after ten o'clock there was a tap at the door and Daniels entered— his face white as a sheet. When he went to find the car, it had gone! . . . Not over the bank, because he'd looked down there. It had gone! Been taken away! . . . And as he came in at the gate he was sure he saw a man following him.

It took the pair of them some moments to get over that panic. Somebody had found the car and had reported the accident to the hospital. They'd come and taken the car away. They'd be ringing up at any minute. As for the man whom Daniels had seen—he was probably some labourer going home to Barlcombe by a short-cut. Daniels instinctively drew back the blind and looked out. Then he shot back.

"He's there! . . . By the gate! . . . He's gone!" Griffiths clutched his arm.

"Who is it?"

"Shut up, you fool! . . . How should I know who it is? . . . Some tramp probably."

He remained there some time, peeping out, then drew the blind back. He poured himself the last tot, then from somewhere found up another bottle.

"You get back to bed and sleep it off. . . . I'll go down and wait. If nothing happens, I'll turn in." For the rest of the night he dozed by fits and starts in the lounge. At the first sign of dawn he got to work. . . . At nine o'clock he took Griffiths a cup of tea and found him sleeping like a log. There was a hasty conference. At his own suggestion Bland was rung up and in a few minutes the three of them were talking the strange disappearance over.

(The following morning, Travers, by special request of Wharton, saw Daniels. His statement was gone into and modified considerably. Then Travers composed the above summary.)

CHAPTER XVI
TRAVERS SETS A PROBLEM

WHEN GRIFFITHS HAD finished his share of the story, Wharton asked if he might phone, and as he rang up the Yard Griffiths watched him resignedly. That was what was convincing Travers. Since the confession had been made he seemed like another man—a man suddenly reprieved.

"Put me through to Inspector Norris!" came Wharton's voice. . . . "That you, Norris? You've got Daniels' statement? . . . Good! And listen! Check those times carefully with him, from eight-thirty onwards. . . . That's right! And send me a car along with a couple of relief men. . . . Yes, we'll be along straight away."

Griffiths looked at him as he came over again. "You're going to take me away?"

"Oh, no! We're going to do nothing that'll embarrass you in the slightest—except that you'll not leave this house till further orders. To-morrow you'll be asked to come to the Yard to make a statement." He looked down at him, trying to catch his eye and hold it. "Now . . . at this moment. You'll swear that what you've been telling us is true?"

Griffiths raised his hands dramatically.

"I'll swear it's true! Everything's true! I don't care what you do with me. Take me away now!" He stammered, at a loss for words. "I can't. . . . I've nothing to fear . . . it's all true!"

Wharton nodded. "Well, I hope for your sake it is. . . . But you're in a desperate corner. A single lie in your statement to-morrow; a single exaggeration even and it's God help you!" Wharton cut out the incipient protest. "You've been about the biggest thing in fools I've run up against. You've chucked away five years of your life and you've let your head get that swollen till it's like one of those figures you see at a carnival. The more you thought you were somebody of importance, the more you let Daniels—and others—play you for a sucker . . . and you hadn't the sense to see it." He glared. "Understand now? You're to stay here till we want you!"

Travers, who thought that Wharton had rather overdone it, felt a sudden pity for the man who seemed to have been as much fool as knave.

"Tell me, Tim," he said quietly. "Why was it you spoke so decently of Bland that night we saw you first?"

"I had to! . . . I had to show you it was an accident. If I'd hinted at Bland you'd have wondered why."

"I see. The weak point, as far as you're concerned, is why you ever lost your head so badly. Why was it, do you think?"

Griffiths shook his head. "You wouldn't understand. . . . I felt like being caught in a trap. . . . While I was sitting there I saw everything Bland had been doing—setting me against my uncle. . . . Then there was Daniels who said he'd swear anything against me . . . and it was . . . it wasn't as if it was daylight. I felt ill . . . as if I was going to be horribly sick." He buried his face in his hands.

"You may have your own grievances against Mr. Bland," said Wharton, "but you'd best keep them to yourself, unless you've got anything in the way of facts. Mr. Bland didn't do that murder—and I thought you said you knew it." He nodded to Travers and they rose.

"Keep a stiff upper lip, Tim!" Travers patted him on the shoulder. "You stick to us. As Mr. Wharton here has told you—don't let us down and we'll try to see you through. . . . And get a job of work. Ring up Sir Henry and tell him so. . . . Now you'd better pull yourself together. Come and see us out. You don't want your people imagining things."

"You're a good fellow, Travers!" Griffiths seized his hand.

Travers gently disengaged it. "I! Good Lord, no! . . . This is your best friend, if you take his advice."

....

It was after midnight by the time Wharton had posted his reliefs and the car was moving off.

"You don't trust him then?" asked Travers.

"He might lose his head," said Wharton. "Mind you, I think he's on the way to being a reformed character. He took all I had to tell him, and he took it like a man. All the same—"

Travers nodded to himself, frowned as he thought of Griffiths, then smiled as he thought of something else.

"When you entered that house to-night, George, what did you know?"

"Not a lot," said Wharton frankly. "I knew about the blood—"

"That it was pig's blood!"

Wharton looked at him. "You've been reading the novels. In our job there are three kinds of blood and no more. Menzies sent along word it was mammalian blood—but it wasn't human. That's all we know."

"What's the other kind?"

"That's Menzies' job," said Wharton. "Certain classes of mammals have the corpuscles oval. Some don't. *That's* the third kind, the oval ones. The round ones are, human and not human. The blood on that mat from the car was mammalian and not human."

Travers nodded. "Do you know, I always thought—"

"Of course you did!" said Wharton. "So did I. These story-book ideas are too fascinating to be untrue. I know that murder's a filthy thing and science can't make it otherwise."

"Yes," said Travers. ". . . I'm beginning to gather that . . . Daniels come up with you?"

"He did. I put a question to him down there and caught him out flagrantly, so I brought him along. Norris handled him while we were round there."

"What about the housekeeper?"

"We've sent her a wire in Griffiths' name to close the house and get back to town. He'll be told that to-morrow morning. When she's clear, Menzies and I and maybe one or two more will go over that drawing-room. Daniels'll go too."

"What do you expect to find?" asked Travers tentatively.

"Blood marks. Indications as to how he fell, whether he was standing or asleep when he fell. Confirmation of the statements, in other words."

"But he was standing! At least he must have been awake. He called out to Griffiths!"

"So he did!" said Wharton, as if the point had just occurred to him. Travers caught the sarcasm, then saw the reason.

"You mean it wasn't necessarily he who called out?"

"You've got it in one! How was the throat cut? What did it look like?"

Travers visualized that red gash across an old man's neck, and winced.

"You and Menzies said it was a clean cut. Exceptionally clean."

"It was! It was done in a flash. If he called out, then he was alarmed and the cut couldn't have been clean. . . . On the other hand, let's imagine a case. Daniels peeps in the drawing-room and sees the old man asleep—as he always was at that time. In a couple of jiffs he's back in the kitchen again and the housekeeper hasn't even known he was out. He listens. 'Sounded like the bell!' Off he goes; picks out the knife as he goes through, whips it across the old man's throat—knowing where Griffiths is—squeaks out, 'Tim!' and goes back to the kitchen again—to reappear in time to see Griffiths with the body."

"If Daniels did it, it must have been for a personal motive," said Travers. "Revenge, for instance. He intended to kill him and he intended to put it on Griffiths. *But he couldn't have had blackmail in his mind!*"

"Why not?"

"Well, how could he have known that Griffiths would fall in with his suggestion to fake a suicide or an accident? And he wasn't to know that the blood would fall on the newspapers. When the throat was cut, the blood should have gushed out all over the place. That would have taken a bit of concealing. Why, I've read that blood gushes out three or four feet!"

Wharton laughed grimly. "You've read! . . . Let me tell you something. I've gone into the question of cut-throat with Menzies dozens of times. I've heard what he always has to say, and I can reel it off like a parrot." He gave a sample. "Large arteries, when divided, cannot spout to any distance because the blood pressure is immediately lost. From *small* vessels it may go up to four feet. Still"—he waved his hand with large forgiveness—"you weren't to know that!"

The car drew up. Wharton brushed on ahead and Travers followed. Norris was in the room waiting for them. He gave the General a quick look, as if to see what had happened; then caught Travers' eye and winked.

"Got everything?" snapped Wharton.

"Everything, sir . . . at least, everything you asked for."

The three of them got down to Daniels' statement—a very lengthy document with differences that were only to be expected. Originally, for instance, he had claimed that Griffiths had urged him into camouflaging the murder. From that he'd been shifted to the plea that as an old servant he wanted to stand by a member of the family. From that he had finally been angled into an admission that if the death had been accepted as an accident, he wouldn't have been any the *worse* off financially.

"I kept the word blackmail out of it, as you see, sir," said Norris.

"Good! And what about the times?"

Norris produced a special sheet. Wharton selected a paper from the bulging notebook and the general statements were compared.

8.30 Train. "Tim!" Clock.
8.32 Daniels. "So you've done him in!"
8.37 Argument finished.
8.40 Car round.
8.46 Daniels returns with blood.
9.05 Daniels goes to Bland's house.
9.08 Cross. "I'll bet that's right, etc."
9.10 Daniels back.
10.05 Daniels sees man.

"What about the train?" asked Wharton.

"Gets in at 8.30, sir. It's the only one there ever is about that time. Also Daniels heard the train. He remarked to the housekeeper, 'Train's on time!' or words to that effect. He says she'll confirm that, and that he looked at his watch."

Wharton made some notes in his book.

"What about the clock?"

"Daniels says Sir William had a mania on clocks. Daniels says he kept his own watch correct so that he could keep the house clocks checked by it. The clock in the drawing-room he actually checked that afternoon, as he knew Sir William would be in there as usual that evening. And he says he took a special pride in the clocks because Sir William once complimented him on the way he kept them."

"And he claims his watch is a good timekeeper?"

"He says it is, sir. Apparently it *has* to be. Unfortunately there was a disaster. That night– owing to all the excitement and so on—he forgot to wind it up and the following morning it had stopped. He set it going again by the dining-room clock—which should have been correct—but he's not plumb sure it was right the previous night."

"I see." Wharton rubbed his chin for a bit. "Seems to me the watch was all right. Let's check his times, assuming the train was on time. Start at 8.30. Now then, two minutes for Griffiths to saunter back and for Daniels to find him with the knife."

"Near enough within seconds," said Travers.

"That makes 8.32. Then five minutes' argument. That enough?"

"You can do the devil of a lot of talking in five minutes, sir, if you make up your mind," said Norris.

"I agree," said Travers. "Also if Griffiths had had much longer to think in, he wouldn't have let himself be rushed into that false position."

"Right! 8.37 stands. Three minutes to get the car round. A hot night and she'd go off with a flick. All the same I think six minutes rather little for getting the body in and moving the car round by the garage."

The others disagreed.

"All right. 8.41 it is. Five minutes is correct for the sty. He'd have to work quick with the body out there and only Griffiths with it."

"He says he gripped the pig right up against its neck so the blood didn't splash—"

"The cold-blooded bastard!" said Wharton. "He'll remember that pig by the time I've done with him. Say the car moved off at 8.46. Then how long for the faking?"

"I went into that thoroughly, sir. He couldn't have been more than ten minutes. You'll be able to check when you get down there—"

"I know that. Say he was back in the house at 8.56. What'd he do next? Had a word with Griffiths, then went into the room again. How long in there?"

"Five minutes we worked it to, sir."

"We'll say seven in all. That makes 9.03 when he came out. Then they discussed Bland. Then Daniels started off to the house and he looked at his watch to see what time it was. It was 9.05!" Wharton looked round triumphantly. "Everything agrees! It fits like a glove!"

"Not only that, sir; he had an additional check. When he looked at his watch again after he'd got back, he found he'd been five minutes or so. That shows the watch was at least *going* then—and most likely going normally."

Travers was polishing his glasses and blinking away furiously.

"Tell me," he said, extremely diffidently. "Suppose you can't rely at all on Daniels' times as shown on his watch. Suppose you had to find out what time it was when Daniels was at Bland's house, and the only way to do it was to check the times Daniels took to do things—what, in fact, you've just been doing. What, in your opinion, is the largest possible margin of error?"

"Starting at 8.30, that is?"

"That's right. We've three things to prove that correct."

"Well, there isn't any margin of error, because we've proved everything to fit in. We claim that Daniels' watch was right!"

"I know. But supposing you have made an error. How far might you be out? You start at 8.30 and you add together the times Daniels took to do things, and you say the answer has been proved to be 9.05 or thereabouts. Might it have been 9.07 or shall we say 9.03? A margin of error of two minutes."

"Possible—but most improbable."

Travers nodded. "Let's be generous. Let's say *five* minutes for the margin of error. And now, in the most deadly earnest. You and Norris are both sure—positive—unalterably certain!—that when Daniels looked at his watch at 9.05 it couldn't have been more than five minutes wrong! If the watch were wrong—in other words—*it was right to within five minutes.*"

"Absolutely plumb certain!" said Wharton.

"Splendid! Now for the point. When Daniels looked at his watch it was one of three things. If it was right, the time was 9.05. If it was wrong, the time was either 9.00 or 9.10. You agree?"

Wharton nodded. Norris made some quick notes on his pad.

"Very well then; we'll move on for two minutes or so. When Daniels listened at Bland's house he heard Cross say, 'I'll bet you a fiver it's right!' That was in reference to the problem they'd been composing. If Daniels' watch was right, the time was then about 9.07. If it was wrong, the time was 9.02. We'll ignore the fact that the watch might have been slow, as that would only make my argument glaringly right! Pardon the vain repetition, but at 9.02—*at the earliest!*—Daniels heard and saw Cross and Bland rejoicing over a finished problem. *But Cross says that he is certain that problem was finished at 8.50.* Allow a small margin of error for him, and call it 8.52. . . . Now then; how could Daniels have heard at 8.52 a thing that happened when he was away faking the car?"

Wharton pulled a long face. Norris had another look at the time sheets.

"The argument's right enough. What's the solution?"

"That's more than I know," said Travers. "If you agree that Daniels' watch was right—and I think it was right—then the problem becomes even more mysterious. Somebody is making a false statement."

"You think Cross was wrong?"

"It certainly looks like it. Either he was bat-eyed and didn't see correctly—or he deliberately misstated!"

"Or the clock was wrong."

"Damn it, Norris!" snapped Wharton. "I tell you that clock was right! It's Cross who's wrong!" He hammered the table with such force that the papers jumped. "I'll go over every detail again with Cross. You get hold of Bland, Norris, and do the same with him. When we get down there I'll work out Daniels' times to a second."

"Bland still in town?" asked Travers.

"Yes. Mrs. Bland was on the same train that I came back by. The maid was with her." He got out his pipe, then took a look at the pair of them from over the top of his glasses. "The exasperating thing is, the whole story may be a pack of lies!" Norris shook his head. "Daniels told the truth, sir—at least, as near as . . . dammit! If I'm wrong, you can have the coat off me to-morrow!"

"I certainly shall!"

"And Griffiths was telling the truth," said Travers. "I can prove it in twenty ways. Every single thing we deduced or suspected before to-night has been corroborated by what we've heard to-night. Griffiths didn't even trouble to ask you what Daniels had said. He told his own tale and he didn't give a cuss. Afterwards he didn't wilt when you went for him like a bull-terrier. He didn't hesitate—"

"All right! All right!" Wharton waved his hand. "Have it your own way. We'll take it that we've tried a second long shot and all we've got out of it is the consolation that we've to begin all over again. The one certainty is that the second shortcut confirmed the first."

"How?"

"Sanders said Griffiths did it. Why did he say that? Because he was the man Daniels said he saw just after ten o'clock. Sanders must have been near the tree when Daniels went down to find the car. He watched him and followed him back to the house. Sanders knew that bit of ground as well as the back of his hand. It hadn't changed since he was a boy."

Travers glanced up at the clock. Gone two in the morning.

"Time we were in bed," said Wharton, but made no attempt to stir. He sat there going through all the motions and facial contortions of a man now exasperated, now perplexed, now hopeful.

"What I'll stick to is that Bland's out of it—and so's Cross, if he ever was in it. The whole three of the people listening to that piece of music at eight o'clock that night have an alibi that we'll never shake, though it's rotten as a diseased potato. You both say we've got to cut out Griffiths and Daniels . . . and that leaves, whom?"

"Just one little idea, sir," said Norris. "Before I go looking about for anybody else, there's something I'd like to satisfy myself about. I haven't seen the place, but I gather that Bland's cottage isn't a quarter of a mile away from where Sir William was killed."

"It isn't that!" said Wharton. "The road winds about, as Mr. Travers knows. It's like the hind leg of a jackass. Between the two houses it's exactly three hundred and twenty yards. I measured it on a large scale map."

"You can see the chimneys of Combe Cottage from Bland's garden," added Travers.

"That's my point, sir. I take it you could go on a bee-line without being seen?"

"It's pasture land, and it was dusk, and Daniels did it in an average of about a minute and a half."

"The very thing!" went on Norris imperturbably. "If Daniels did the return journey in three minutes, then anybody who was in a desperate hurry might have done the same and cut the throat into the bargain!" His voice instinctively lowered.

"Now, sir; putting it bluntly. Didn't either of these gentlemen go upstairs during the course of the evening? When you asked Mrs. Bland if anybody was out of the room, she naturally wouldn't have had the face to tell you that. And again; people don't quite consider that as being *out of the room*. Suppose then, as I said, that one of these gentlemen tipped the other the wink and went ostensibly upstairs. Three minutes—or four—wouldn't be much . . ."

"You're too late!" interrupted Wharton. "I asked Cross that, point-blank. He says he and Bland went up together just before dinner. It was that about being in the study that was the euphemism."

"Then I'm finished, sir," said Norris ruefully.

Wharton got up heavily. "We all are at the moment. The housekeeper's out of it by Daniels' evidence—"

"She's not the type," put in Travers.

"Exactly! That leaves that woman—Struthers—and the gardener." He made a note in his book, then treated himself to something resembling a grimace. "WANTED—somebody who knew the old man's habits; could imitate his voice; had the special knife all ready; had the pluck to cut quick and deep; knew the lie of the land for a quick getaway—and had a reason for doing it all." He peered over the top of his glasses. "*Not* Struthers, I think—or the gardener!"

Travers stood there nodding, then politely smothered a yawn.

"You'd better get along home," Wharton told him. "We're more than grateful to you, though you don't want us to tell you that. I shall be off in the morning as soon as you've finished with Daniels. If anything happens down there, I'll let you know."

As Travers turned to the door, Norris whispered in Wharton's ear. The General nodded.

"Oh! just one thing you might do for us. And there's not a man in London who can do it so well."

Travers had to laugh.

"Come, come, George! It's too late for that sort of thing!"

"But I mean it!" said Wharton indignantly. "The trouble with you is, you won't take yourself at your proper value!"

Travers smiled. "Life's too short. If we took ourselves seriously, the asylums wouldn't hold us. What is it you think I can do so—er—competently?"

"Inquire into Bland's financial affairs. See if he's been gambling—or double-crossing the old man."

Travers pursed his lips. "That last part's impossible. It'd take months in any case. If he's been speculating and got himself into a muddle?—yes, I might find out that. . . . But didn't I understand you that Bland was out of it?"

"Mustn't leave loose ends lying about!" said Wharton mysteriously. "Eliminate motive and he's still more out of it."

He hustled Travers from the room and Norris heard the good nights echoing down the corridor. The General was none too chirpy when he came back.

"Slow work, Norris! Slow work! . . . Push that bell for a pot of tea, will you? . . . Then we'll go into those times again."

CHAPTER XVII
CURIOUS CONDUCT OF A PARSON

MENZIES AND Detective-Sergeant Lewis, it was decided, should go down with Wharton. Daniels wasn't asked about it. What Wharton intended was a reconstruction of the events of the evening of September the fifth, with a checking of the times. Only when he was positive he had these to within a couple of minutes, did he intend to re-approach the Rev. Lionel Cross.

The first real call was at Mulberton railway station, where he found waiting for him the times of the train that Tim Griffiths had heard as he leaned over the gate. Actually the train had been one minute ahead of time. It had pulled into Mulberton at 8.29, and had therefore remained in the station three minutes instead of the usual two. It had left prompt to time. At that hour, therefore, Daniels' watch had been correct.

At the police station, Inspector Groom had nothing to report; still, he and Wharton had a talk over ways and means while the others went along to the hotel. At the tail-end of the short conference came something that made Wharton prick up his ears. "You knew Mrs. Bland had gone?"

"Oh, yes!" said Wharton. "She left by the same train as me."

"Mr. Cross was round there for tea the previous afternoon." Groom gave the information like one who talks without hope. "He was there till rather late."

"How'd you know?"

"One of the men here has got his eyes on their maid."

"Hm!" said Wharton. "Pity she's gone back! . . . And the vicar was there till late, was he? He'll be getting himself talked about if he isn't careful."

"Between ourselves," said Groom, "that wouldn't worry him a lot. I don't mean talking about her. What I mean is he's different from the ordinary run of parsons—not stiff and starchy; doesn't keep himself to himself. Not that I don't like him, because I do! I wouldn't mind if a few more parsons were like him."

Wharton nodded in agreement. "Has he been there long?"

"About five years. Before he came to Barlcombe he was a master at one of the big public schools—so they tell me. Sometimes he doesn't look much more than a schoolboy himself!"

So much for that. Half an hour later, which was at 8.00, the small party moved off in a closed car. Wharton and Groom were proposing to test the times taken between the two cottages; the other three men were left behind.

From the side door of the drawing-room the nearest way was by the path at the back of the shrubbery and then through a gate which opened on a meadow. One gathered that it had once been a paddock. The important thing, to which Wharton called attention, was that no window overlooked that route. As for the meadows themselves that clothed the slope like patchwork, their hedges were so overgrown with thorn and so riddled with gaps, that there was no difficulty in getting from one to the other. The line that Daniels had taken that night was easy to follow. The row of hedges led to the very boundary of Bland's garden, and the low railings were easy enough to climb. By the time the two men got there, it was dusk.

"You stay here," said Wharton. "I'll have first shot. Better synchronize the watches first."

He moved off from the loggia. The going uphill found out the weak spots and by the time he'd reached the door of Combe Cottage it was ninety-five seconds.

"Hm!" said Wharton. "Not bad for an old 'un!"

He took a few deep breaths to get his wind back to normal, allowed a minute for that and then moved off again. This time, once the short slope was breasted, he had merely to lift his legs and let the hill do the rest. The afterglow in the sky still gave sufficient light to see by, and the going was easy. Somewhere about halfway down he was pounding along, eyes on the ground at his feet more than ahead, when his eye caught sight of something approaching. A cow . . . too small . . . a man . . . the owner of the meadows! By the time these thoughts had flashed through his mind and his instinct had warned him to pull up, he and the stranger had practically collided. "Hell!" said Wharton to himself at the very last second—the experiment certainly ruined—then found himself looking at a face as startled as his own—that of the Rev. Lionel Cross!

"Hallo!" said Wharton between the puffs. "What are *you* doing here?"

Cross too seemed slightly out of breath.

"I was going to call . . . at the house there . . . I suppose somebody's . . . at home?"

"I'm afraid there isn't," said Wharton, none too genially—and wondered what else he could ask.

"And what are you doing?" said Cross.

"I? . . . Oh, taking a short-cut to catch up some people who've gone round by road." It all seemed very foolish and even grotesque, standing there in the half-light, talking at a man whose face wasn't discernible at more than a couple of feet.

"But this isn't a public road, is it?"

Cross cackled. "It isn't—but it's a short-cut!" He explained volubly how he'd been at Mulberton. On his way back he thought he'd like to call at Combe Cottage; just a friendly call on the new baronet. Unconventional time perhaps, but there you were.

"Well, it's no good going up now," said Wharton brusquely, "there's nobody there but a friend of mine . . . and I'll never catch up those people now." He held out his hand. "Queer sort of place to say good night! . . . You be in to-morrow? I'd rather like to have another word with you about those alibis."

He moved off slowly up the hill again, turned at the next gap but saw no sign of the vicar. Then he looked at his watch. Three minutes to go before that train was due! Back at Combe Cottage he burst in on the small group in the drawing-room.

"Doc! would you mind listening out there for that train? Lewis, you go and listen in the kitchen. Hurry up! It's due at any minute."

Once more he moved off down the hill, with an eye well ahead for a sign of the parson. As he mounted the fence of Bland's cottage he heard the train come roaring round the valley bend. His time to the loggia was fifty seconds.

"Was that you I heard talking up there a minute or so ago?" asked Groom.

"Yes. Did you see anybody go past the hedge there?"

"Didn't see or hear a soul," said Groom.

"Right!" He looked at his watch. "You try it out now. If you see anybody either way, don't stop, but let me know. . . . And don't forget! One minute's rest the other end."

He pulled out his pipe when the inspector had gone. Queer story that of Cross! Why was he coming along that back way? And if he wanted to call at Combe Cottage, why didn't he ring up first to see if anybody was there? Then, all at once Wharton thought he saw daylight—but a daylight that was more puzzling than Egyptian fog. Had Cross heard in Mulberton that the police were back? And that Daniels was back? And was it for a surreptitious word with Daniels that he was sneaking up that back way? And yet for the life of him Wharton couldn't fathom why. Something was going on somewhere; something peculiar and underhand, and in the middle of it seemed to be the figure of that damn parson! Had there been more than a jest—say, a puckish irony?—in those words he had used the first time he'd clapped eyes on him—"So you've come for me after all?"

There was a shadow at the end of the garden, and the inspector came trotting up. The time for the round trip was just under three minutes, but he was younger than Wharton, and had been a bit of an athlete in his younger days. He'd seen nobody, either way.

"Good enough!" said Wharton. "We'll get along back and find out how long it takes to cut each other's throats."

. . . .

It was about eleven the following morning when Wharton called again at Barlcombe Vicarage. The walk, the sun and the clear air had gradually removed from his mind the enveloping theories that had befogged it till the early hours. He now realized that the eccentricities of a man like Cross were best accepted as such. To use them as foundations on which to build a charge of murder was not deduction, but distortion.

Before he had been in the parson's study five minutes he was feeling rather foolish. Cross's manner was so free and open, so genuinely above-board, so unforced and natural, that only a lunatic could think him a Levite in whom was any guile. Wharton indeed was sorry that a certain obstinacy had rather petulantly made him decline the offer of a glass.

"Do you know, vicar," he said, "I think I'll join you after all. It's warmer than I thought."

"My dear fellow, please do!" He opened another bottle and put it handy. "Help yourself! . . . And how long are you staying *this* time?"

Wharton paused for the merest second in the act of filling the glass; wondering if the irony had existed merely in his own mind. Cross was regarding him blandly, his pink face dimpled with good fellowship.

"Well, to-morrow morning we'll be going back— for a certainty." He took a pull at the glass, then surveyed the vicar over the rim. "In the strictest of confidence . . . we know it wasn't an accident!" Cross made a face, then nodded. "Of course you rather announced that, you know!"

"How do you mean?"

"Well, correct me if I'm wrong. An official as important as yourself would never have come down here in the first place if you hadn't been pretty sure it wasn't an accident . . . and you certainly wouldn't have come down a second time if you weren't sure it was murder!"

"Hm! . . . And you had a shrewd idea that that little talk we had about alibis wasn't all it seemed to be?"

Cross smiled; a dimply, apologetic smile. "I wonder if you'll believe me! . . . When you came that morning I really and truly believed you'd come to see what I knew about it. I wasn't friendly with Sir William; I prefer to put it that way. He had said some unkind things about me. He called me a wine-bibber—or something like it—in a letter to the press when there was all that argument about our screen. He hinted that the whole conduct of rural clergy might reasonably be inquired into, and that some of us—myself that is—might find ourselves in queer street." He sighed. "He suggested some sort of ecclesiastical commission. All very alarming—and most amusing . . . at the time! Then this deplorable business happened and I began to see things in a different light."

Wharton took another pull.

"But Sir William didn't object to your playing chess with his secretary!"

Cross chuckled away. "He did once—and once only. I've beaten Bland only once at chess recently. Bland used to make no secret of the fact that I came round to his place, and the next morning Sir William would say, 'Well, did you beat the parson?' Bland usually was able to say yes; then the old chap would positively gloat. On the occasion when I beat Bland, he was most annoyed. I forget what he said. 'Why do you let that fellow make a convenience of you?'—or something like that. . . . Have some more beer!"

Wharton shook his head. "Not for me, vicar. I shall have to be getting along. But about those alibis. Would you mind if I went over them again?"

Cross hopped up quickly and assumed what was evidently his favourite position against the mantelpiece; looking like a latter-day Pickwick.

"Tell me one thing. If he was killed, when was he killed?"

"At eight-thirty to the minute!" said Wharton impressively. "That's beyond all question of doubt."

"And where?"

"Within less than a minute of where you were at the moment he was killed. That also isn't open to doubt."

"I see. Then all you want to know is where certain people were at eight-thirty?"

"Provided all the clocks were right—yes!"

Cross shook his head. "Then the three of us are no good to you. We're definitely out of it! . . . Take it from me that clock was right—and three people can prove it."

"Good enough!" said Wharton resignedly. "One last question and I'm finished with the three of you. What would you swear in a court of law that you were doing at 8.53?"

Cross frowned in thought. "I'd swear that Bland and I were rejoicing over having composed a chess problem—and a good one. Almost at once we sat down to play."

Wharton got up. "Well, you'll find me a man of my word. You'll hear no more about those alibis. . . . Now something far less exciting. You'll come along and have dinner with me at the hotel tonight?"

Cross looked genuinely grieved.

"Do you know, I'd do anything to be able to do that! But I've got to be away for a day or two. I'm going this afternoon. Tiverton to start with, then Exeter. . . . Perhaps when I come to town some time . . ."

. . . .

Wharton did several things during that short stay at Mulberton. What they were is of no particular consequence since they were all destined to prove time wasted. The day after he saw Cross, he set off back to town just after lunch. Lewis was driving the car and Menzies and Wharton sat behind. Then all at once, as the car was moving slowly along at the tail of the traffic entering Taunton, Wharton suddenly tapped on the window and made urgent signs for the car to be pulled in to the curb. Even when the car had come to a standstill he sat staring out of the window.

"What's up?" asked Menzies.

"That parson I was telling you about . . . Cross . . . Either I'm a Dutchman or he's just gone in that ironmonger's shop!"

"And why shouldn't he?"

"Why shouldn't he? . . . Because he told me only this time yesterday that he was going away for a bit—to Tiverton and Exeter."

The window was tapped again, and Lewis came round to hear what it was all about.

"He doesn't know *you*," said Wharton. "Follow him slowly up in the car and see where he goes. If he leaves the main road, stop the car and I'll take the wheel. Report back at the police station. We'll wait."

Cross it was, sure enough. He came out of the shop and without turning his head, moved off towards the town. Then he began to look about him, from one side of the road to the other. Finally, a couple of hundred yards on, he crossed the street and went into another ironmonger's shop.

There was no reason why Wharton should have been intrigued. Perhaps some facetious remark by Menzies aroused in him a certain natural obstinacy. He stopped the car and took the wheel.

"Follow him up and see what he does," he told Lewis. "Find out what he wants. Report as soon as you know."

It was an hour later when Lewis came back. Cross had gone into yet a third ironmonger's. And he'd been asking for something with which Lewis had no acquaintance. Neither had Wharton for that matter. Moreover, the General was repenting himself of the waste of time. He made no comment, but merely shipped his party aboard again and pushed on.

In the main street of Newbury, the sight of an ironmonger's shop brought the business again to Wharton's mind. He turned to Menzies.

"What's your opinion of parsons?"

"Parsons?" Menzies grunted. "Don't know. I've never cut any open."

"Oh, haven't you!" said Wharton. "Well, there's one I'd like to see cut open—brain end first. Figuratively speaking, of course."

CHAPTER XVIII
TRAVERS SEES DAYLIGHT

WHARTON'S CONFERENCE took place the following morning. All the gang were there—Travers included; with Rawson Pitt, the Assistant Commissioner, as nominal chairman. The dull, official atmosphere of the room was strangely enlivened by a cabinet gramophone that stood by the wall, with a couple of records on top.

At first the Assistant Commissioner had seemed most interested; he grew more and more depressed as time went on. And no wonder. Everything up to a point was perfectly plain-sailing. There were winds enough to swell a dozen sails—then the craft would strike on the same old sandbank and back out for another attempt to cross the harbour bar.

Take, for instance, Travers' contribution which had seemed pretty conclusive evidence against Bland.

"I thought I'd try Pederson and Gore," he told the conference. "He came from them originally, as I think you know. I mentioned the matter to Pederson—most diplomatically. He knew nothing. Then I tried another firm or two, one of whom gave me the tip to ask Pederson and Gore! That set me thinking. It's a not uncommon thing for one partner to be quite unaware of the transactions of his fellow-partner. So I went to Gore. He told me the whole thing, in very strict confidence.

"Some weeks ago, Bland—for whom he'd acted on previous occasions, and who'd done him more than one good turn—asked him to buy ten thousand Roofs—"

"Ten thousand what?" asked Wharton.

"Sorry! Rooifonteins. Mining shares. They were then quoted at thirty-seven shillings. He asked Gore casually—so casually, in fact, that Gore was very impressed—if he'd carry him. Gore, wishing to be equally casual—if you know what I mean—mean—said, of course, he would. On settling day they'd gone to thirty-three. Gore agreed to carry again; for another fortnight that is. Within a week—following on that disastrous de Beers' report—they'd gone to twenty-two. Gore got alarmed and rang Bland up. Bland told him not to panic. The very next day they began creeping up. Gore carried him the third time, then they dropped again, to twenty-three. Then he insisted on a settlement. . . . Bland *did* settle! but it was *after* Sir William's death. And he settled at that figure. In other words, he found seven thousand pounds!"

"Where'd he get it?" asked Wharton quickly.

"I don't know. I tell you the facts and leave you to draw the inferences. For instance, he saw Sir Henry Brotherston as soon as he got to town and asked for a confidential piece of information. What was he to get under the will?"

"I can't understand it," said Pitt. "Why was a man of Bland's ability such a fool?"

Travers made a wry face. "They all fall for it sooner or later. The bigger the man the bigger the fool. Somebody sold Bland a pup. He honestly believed in the tip—so perhaps did the bloke who gave it him. Now a really amazing thing is that immediately after Bland had settled, he told Gore to get him a thousand Branwick Combustion. They were then eleven and three: four days later, Bland sold for nineteen and six. Not bad going I think you'll admit." He looked round the circle and smiled suggestively. "If we wanted to be melodramatic, we might say that Sir William had his throat cut because Bland got the wrong tip first!"

"Bland didn't do it!" said Wharton. "The motive's there; I'll grant that. But it can't very well be called a motive till you've busted an alibi that can be sworn to by three people."

"While we're dealing with Bland," said Norris, "I'd like to mention that very interesting anonymous letter we had—about the film." He passed round a photographic copy. "Typed, as you see, on an Ensign; latest model. Paper that's sold by the Ensign people."

Pitt ran his eye hastily over his notes.

"You're suggesting that Bland wrote it?"

Norris smiled. "As Mr. Travers said, sir, I'm suggesting nothing. I'll tell you the facts and you can draw what inferences you like. That part where Griffiths cuts the goat's throat was never seen at the trade show; therefore the anonymous letter was sent by somebody in the know. Now Griffiths, when he got down to Mulberton, told his uncle and Bland all about the film. He mentioned that business about the goat, and Sir William was most indignant about showing a thing like that. Griffiths has given me and Mr. Travers a perfectly open account of what took place."

"The inference is that Bland overstepped the mark," said Wharton. "He wrote the letter to call attention to what didn't exist except in his own hand. Isn't that so?"

"That's right, sir."

"But at that time," went on Wharton, "nobody knew it was other than an accident. The hypothesis is a wild one, but let's assume that Bland committed the murder. Oughtn't he to have been overjoyed to find it accepted as an accident? Why queer his own pitch by suggesting murder?"

"Don't you believe it!" Menzies' voice was refreshingly abrupt. "We may throw dust in people's eyes, but some of them know how to blink! . . . Now take this man Bland, gentlemen. I don't know him, but I've heard a lot about him. I'd say that if he committed the murder, he'd want to know two things—how he stood and—if he were suspect— how his alibi stood. *He* knew it wasn't an accident. He knew—if he had any opinion of us at all—that *we'd* know it wasn't an accident. Therefore he'd want his alibi inquired into as soon as possible—"

"If I might say so," put in Travers, "he certainly mentioned his alibi to me and Wharton almost as soon as he saw us!"

"Exactly! And having satisfied himself that you were satisfied with his alibi, he naturally proceeded to make the position doubly sure by incriminating somebody else—*the man he'd tried to incriminate already when he called out 'Tim!' and rang the bell for Daniels!*" And having made that point, Menzies as abruptly left it.

"I quite agree," said Wharton calmly. "The argument's masterly. All I say is, bust the alibi of those people and we've got a case."

Norris cleared his throat. Even the action was apologetic, let alone the words that followed it.

"You're perfectly sure, sir, that nobody moved the hands of the clock?"

Wharton smiled patiently. "That isn't the point. I may or may not believe the hands of the clock were moved. The point is this—and it's the point of view of a jury! Cross will swear the hands were not moved. So will the other two. How can we prove anything to the contrary? What witness have we got? . . . And there's something else. In addition to those three witnesses who'll swear by the clock, there's a fourth witness—the wireless set! The music came from it—and it came from it dead on time!"

Travers' voice floated quietly across. "I see all that—about the wireless. There's also another witness, of course. I mean the maid. Maids have clocks in the kitchens; they have to. Also, very indefinitely I admit, I feel there ought to have been something abnormal happen to the maid that night. . . . If abnormal things were in the air, it seems to me the maid must have noticed something. The thing is, is it worth trying?"

"Of course it's worth trying!" barked Wharton, and made a note in his book. "We'll get hold of that maid. All the same, if Bland was clever enough to be in two places at once, he'd have had enough sense to foresee all that and make sure the maid didn't suspect anything!"

"One thing has struck me all through." Everybody turned to look at Kenton; a shrewd observer who rarely spoke unless he had something that was worth saying. "Naturally I speak as the man in the street. And, of course, you'll have noticed it already. . . . It's this. All this case seems nothing but *times*! I know it's a question of alibis; all the same, doesn't it strike you as really remarkable that everybody concerned—at Bland's house, for instance—*does* know the times! Griffiths and Daniels all know the times so well that they'll swear to them—"

"Daniels had to!" broke in Wharton. "While he was faking the accident he had to work to split seconds!"

"Well, I grant that. In itself it's explicable. Take it, however, in conjunction with Cross and the Blands. Mrs. Bland is really remarkable. I admit there's a certain—er—feminine inconsequence about her information, but the times she gave were infallible. If she were in a hole, she'd swear as hard as the others. Now what I want to ask is this!"—he got that out in the teeth of Wharton's interruption—"Take Cross and Bland. Who imposed his will on whom? Who drew the other's attention to the time and made sure he didn't forget it?"

"Bland, of course!" said Pitt. "It was his house. If anything was staged he must have staged it."

"In any case, Cross is out," said Norris. "There's no motive."

"I wouldn't be too sure!" said Wharton, who suddenly had an idea that was perfectly staggering. "Bland was out of his house that night—at Combe Cottage as usual. While he was away, why shouldn't his wife and the parson have fixed something up? That woman's a bit of a high-stepper. And no sooner did her husband go to town than the parson was round to tea—and he stayed pretty late! When I saw him about his alibi that morning, I hadn't been out of the house five minutes before he was ringing up Mrs. Bland!" He left them to examine that bombshell for a moment before resuming his usual role of pessimist. "Even if all that's correct, the one fact still remains. We've got to bust the alibi before there's anything doing."

"I must say," put in Travers, "that Colonel Kenton's point seems to me a very vital one. Putting aside the question of chess played with a time limit for moves, it does seem remarkable that three people should remember the times so well. But there's another point—the clock that was broken at Combe Cottage. *Why* was it broken?"

"To suggest an attack or struggle."

"But we've already been told there was no struggle! Wharton was telling us that it was proved in Combe Cottage itself that Daniels' story was absolutely correct. There was no other alteration of furniture to suggest a struggle. Sir William died in his chair! . . . What I put to this meeting is that the murderer entered by the back or shrubbery door, having made sure that Tim Griffiths was at the gate. He'd see the lighted cigarette, for instance, if he took a precautionary peep round the corner of the house, as he'd be bound to do. He entered then by that door. If he was Bland, his entry would have excited no comment supposing that Daniels had seen him or Sir William had suddenly woke up. But as things happened, everything was incredibly perfect. He had the knife with him, and having switched off the light he flashed it across the old man's throat. Then he called out to Griffiths, pushed the body over as he backed out, and then deliberately smashed the clock—*to show that the time was eight-thirty precisely*."

"It all comes to the same thing!" Wharton persisted wearily. "Eight-thirty is the vital moment. At eight-thirty and for minutes before it and for minutes after it, three people in Bland's cottage were listening to a piece of music; confirmed by the time it was broadcast, confirmed by a clock—and, if I may say so, confirmed by the events of a perfectly normal and explicable evening. I admit that when we get as far as eight-*fifty*, the times as given by Daniels don't agree with those given by Cross and the others. But what's it matter for the purposes of this argument? I still repeat. If you want this conference to be over in five minutes' time, then bust that alibi at eight-thirty."

"You heard the train from Bland's cottage, I think you said?" asked Pitt.

"I did, sir. And I heard it so loud that I'd have heard it if I'd been *inside* the cottage."

Travers made a sudden exclamation. "By jove! . . . Is that why the loud music was played?"

"You mean, to drown the noise of the eight-thirty train?"

"Exactly!" He looked round at the gramophone. "Mightn't we listen to the actual music, now?"

The A.C. himself took charge. The gramophone was wound up and the first record put on.

"I gather," said Travers, "that we're listening to an abbreviated version."

"I don't think so." He looked at the disks. "Two records and both sides; that's pretty long!" The whining, Moorish air began; below it the quick tapping of the drums. Travers thought of nights in Cairo and the nasal moaning from native cafes. The first side took four and a quarter minutes exactly, and the second the same. Towards the end of the third side the excitement really increased. As instrument after instrument joined in that weirdly fascinating tune, the drums beat more insistently; the music pulsed and throbbed till nerves began to fray. Travers tapped with his fingers and closed his eyes. By the time the last side was nearing its end, he was glad the music wasn't going on much longer. The maddening rhythm was enough to set shoulders twitching; the drums clamoured like the tom-toms of an African forest; frenzied and primitive.

"Thank God that's over!" said Menzies, and everybody laughed.

"Eighteen minutes exactly," said Travers. "If I remember rightly, it's timed for nineteen minutes on an orchestra. And now—what about it?"

Pitt looked round the circle. "I think we agree that that music would have drowned the noise of any train!"

"It'd have drowned Gabriel's horn!" said Menzies.

Wharton nodded away to himself like a toy mandarin, before he retired to the sandbank.

"Well, gentlemen; we'll assume all that. We'll say the music was played so that somebody shouldn't hear the sound of the train. That was at eight-thirty. The music was playing at eight-thirty. The clock said eight-thirty. *All you've done is to prove the clock was right!*" He smiled ironically. "And all that remains to do is to bust that alibi."

After that they began all over again. The case of Sanders was reviewed, passed and definitely finished with. Daniels and Griffiths took much longer before the weight of evidence and the special pleading of Wharton and Travers shelved them—at least temporarily. Then they got back to the same old topic. Pitt looked at the clock.

"Well, gentlemen, we've had four hours of it and we've got no further. . . . Is there any possibility of a new line of approach?"

"The only thing I can suggest," said Wharton, "is a variation of the same theme. We might try a massed attack on Cross—after we've heard what the maid has to say."

"But why Cross, when there's no motive?"

"It's up to us to find the motive," said Wharton. "Let me tell you a few more puzzling things about him; things that happened in the last day or two."

"A most interesting person!" was Pitt's comment when Wharton had finished.

"He is!" said Wharton bitterly. "That's why I'd like some opinions on him other than my own— what I called a massed attack. . . . By the way, there's one other peculiar happening that's got me beat. I told you he said he was going away for a bit. Well, as we went through Taunton yesterday, we saw him there; not where he said he was going, that is! He went into three successive ironmongers' shops—and he probably went into more. What do you think he wanted?"

A faint smile went round the meeting.

"Saucepans!" said Kenton flippantly.

Wharton was perfectly serious. "Oh, no! it wasn't saucepans! Take out Menzies and I'll give you an hour to guess in—and five pounds if you guess right."

"I'll buy it!" said Travers. "What was he asking for?"

Wharton paused impressively. "He asked at each one if they kept in stock iron or steel rod of about three-sixteenths of an inch diameter. If so he wanted a length of four feet. When they said they didn't keep it, he asked if anybody else had inquired for such a thing recently!"

"If anybody else had asked for it!"

"That's right! . . . Now, what's it mean?" Wharton permitted himself the merest suspicion of a smile. "Did he want something so trivial as a gadget for his ancient car? And why did he inquire what anybody else had done?"

Nobody had any ideas. Even Kenton couldn't suggest anything that looked in the least degree likely. Finally, after another half-hour, the meeting was adjourned for three days; Wharton in the meanwhile to explore the various avenues he'd suggested.

. . . .

It was nine in the morning when Travers arrived at Scotland Yard; it was two in the afternoon when he left it. During a leisurely lunch he sat pondering over the morning's problems, and the curious behaviour of Cross in particular. One solution there was, though he hadn't cared to suggest it. Indeed, if only one thing could be explained, a great deal more could be accounted for. The one snag was that iron or steel rod he'd been inquiring about. What was it for? A sort of rigid pull-through for a rifle? A long-handled toasting-fork?

From the restaurant, Travers moved on to the ironmongery department of one of the big stores. The best way to decide what a thing might be used for was to have it in front of you—to look at and then ponder over. But at the stores the assistant was positive they had nothing of the sort, and he saw no reason why stores should keep it. Then he made a suggestion. What he did have was stout, galvanized wire of the diameter required. Why not cut off the length and straighten it out? To give the colour of iron, the wire might be blackened.

Travers was delighted; ordered four feet and took it with him. Then, not being able to resist his collector's instincts, he went through to the antique department, carrying the package with him. He knew he was rather a fool. To look for bargains there was beyond the limits of sane optimism. Still, he had a look round. That refectory table was rather fine. Pity it had been so badly restored. His eye ran beyond it to the far wall. Then he stood for a good half minute in his tracks.

Five minutes later he was in a post-office handing over some telegraph forms.

"Tell me!" he said to the girl, with his very best smile, "is there any way I can be sure that this telegram reaches the other end without being misspelt?" She frowned over it.

Cross. Vicarage, Barlcombe, Somerset.

Urgent and confidential (Stop) Please travel Taunton night train (Stop) All expenses paid (Stop) Special official will meet you Paddington (Stop) Wharton requests your presence London immediately (Stop) Discussion whether tea may be pie, and so on (Stop) Reply paid to person and address indicated (Stop)

"You want all these 'stops' put in?"

"Oh, rather! . . . Sort of expense no object!" She thought it would be all right. At any rate, Travers paid up and departed. That is, he got as far as the door, then turned back again and went into the telephone booth. He rang up Scotland Yard. Wharton wasn't there, but Norris was.

"Sorry to trouble you, Norris, but do you happen to know precisely what the Rev. Lionel Cross was before he came to Barlcombe? Didn't I understand he was a schoolmaster?"

"Hold on a minute, sir," said Norris. . . . "Here we are, sir! Mathematical master at one of the big public schools—Fellborough, it's called."

Travers thanked him and hung up. A few yards along the pavement he found himself jauntily swinging that elongated parcel and tripping with the abandon of a ballet dancer. With a blush he pulled himself together.

THE THIRD PAYS FOR ALL

CHAPTER XIX
TRAVERS IS MYSTERIOUS

Travers had no extraordinary difficulty in arranging his evening; probably because to the initiated the program was a fairly blatant announcement of what the hospitality was really designed to cover. At 5 P.M. prompt, for instance, people were to be there—and there would be tea. Then was to come an unassigned interval till 7.30, after which dinner was the chief attraction. Then there was to be chess and music and chatter; and carriages—so to speak—at 11. *Strictly urgent and confidential* was, moreover, at the head of each letter of invitation.

Except for Menzies, who found himself unable to turn up, the gathering was the same as that which had formed the Scotland Yard Conference—with the addition of Chief-Constable Scott. Palmer showed the party into the small library room, then at five o'clock appeared at the door which led to the main room with a "Tea is served, gentlemen!" Travers was anchored to the hearth-rug, looking somewhat sheepish. With him was the little parson of Barlcombe, full of dimples, blushes and apologetics.

"I don't think most of you know Mr. Cross," said Travers. "But here he is! . . . Wharton you know. . . . This is Rawson Pitt, the Assistant Commissioner; the lad who's going to show you how chess should be played. This is Chief-Constable Scott—a quiet bird, but very wily. Colonel Kenton is a mathematician like yourself. Inspector Norris, so they tell me, plays a shrewd hand at poker." Wharton gave the vicar an enigmatical smile. "You're an elusive person, Mr. Cross! I called at your place yesterday and they told me they didn't know where exactly you were."

Cross tittered, then showed all his teeth in a smile. "Do you know, I'm afraid they didn't!"

Travers clapped them both on the shoulder.

"No bickering, you two! . . . Sit down everybody and let's have some tea. Palmer! bring the box!"

Palmer produced a cigar-box, sealed with brown paper; the top slit like a money-box.

"What's that for?" asked Wharton suspiciously.

"For shillings," said Travers. "The first fellow who says a word of shop—in goes his bob!"

"And who gets the bobs?"

"That," said Travers, "I'll leave to you. . . . If anybody has any objection, let him speak now or for ever hold his peace. Sorry, vicar!"

Cross, like the tea, went down extraordinarily well. Even Wharton thawed, then found himself once more under the spell of the most unorthodox and unclerical-looking parson he'd ever run across. The vicar himself seemed quite unaware that he was other than a rather humdrum individual suddenly thrust into the society of some really notable people. Before the meal was over everybody was chattering away, and the evening looked like being a colossal success.

"A fine clock you've got there!" said Scott, indicating the mahogany grandfather. "You didn't have that when I was here last."

"No!" said Travers. "It only came in yesterday." He hopped up and handed round the cigarettes. "Now come along to the kitchen, all of you. There's something I want to show you."

The kitchen opened directly off. Cross remained in the dining-room, but once the others were inside Travers closed the door behind him.

"Just an unusual request, if you don't mind humouring me. Would you all mind handing over your watches and giving them to Palmer. He'll put them in the safe." He poked his head round the door. "The time, by the way, as I dare say you've noticed, is about five-thirty-five."

He waited till the five watches had been removed, then pointed to the wireless set.

"Now you experts! What do you think of it?"

Everybody seemed to be an expert; at least, they all gathered round.

"A.C. or D.C.?" asked Norris.

"Don't know!" said Travers. "I'm the world's worst scientist—if that's what you blokes call yourselves. All I know is that you twiddle a knob and things happen."

"I notice you listen-in in your bedroom," said Wharton.

"If that were true it'd cost you a bob. . . . You mean the length of flex attached to the speaker?"

"That's right! What's it for then?"

"All the better to hear you with!" said Travers facetiously. "You notice the ear-phones? I do know that you can use them to tune in with when the speaker's in a room where you can't hear it." He clicked on the switch at the point, twiddled the knobs at the end of the set, set the front dial, and by that time the Children's Hour was coming through in full blast. Larry the Lamb was saying, "Yes, Mr. Ma-a-a-yor," and the Mayor of Toy Town was giving pontifical advice. Travers waved his hand. "There you are, gentlemen! Positively no deception!"—and clicked off again.

Back in the dining-room, Cross asked the company to excuse him for a few minutes. Palmer brought his hat and off he went.

"Where's he off to?" asked Wharton, suspicions again aroused.

Travers waved his hand at the chairs. "Make yourselves comfortable!" He waited till they'd all settled down before he answered Wharton's question.

"If you've all no objection, we'll talk shop for a bit." He took off his glasses and began the usual polish, blinking away as he watched the operation. "I'm in a rather awkward position. I don't want you fellows to think at any time between now and eleven o'clock that I'm—er—putting on too much side. All I want is that everybody should have a jolly evening. All the same, you know what you're here for . . . not that I mean I don't . . . I mean I shouldn't. . . . Well, you know what I mean!"

Everybody laughed. Travers laughed, too.

"You see, it's about Cross. He's gone out for a bit. If you remember, Bland went out for a bit, round about this time, on the evening of September the fifth. I expect you'll find a lot of things to remind you of that evening. Cross—I should tell you—is very sensitive. He's here this evening to do us a good turn, but he refuses to discuss anything with you people. He's got the idea that he doesn't want anybody's blood on his head." Travers looked round rather belligerently. "Personally, I agree with him entirely. I sympathize with his point of view. All the same, he sees no harm in going over this evening, here in this flat, what he knows happened in Bland's house that night. After that you must make the best of it you can. . . . Anything we talk over will be finished by the time he gets back."

"You're going to solve the problem for us?" asked Scott. There was no pettiness in the question. Scott was far too big a man for that.

Travers shook his head. "I can't say. That'll be for you people to decide when this evening's over. It's really—" He broke off. "Still, that would be anticipating! . . . You people any news? Seen the maid?"

"I saw her this afternoon," said Wharton. "We rather guessed something might happen to-night— though we never expected to find Cross here."

"Might I guess something? Did she say her clock had had an accident?"

"Yes—and no. When she came down after dressing that afternoon the clock had stopped and she couldn't get it to go again. Bland said he'd have it seen to, and in the meanwhile she could easily have a look at the grandfather."

"And what happened when Bland rushed into the kitchen to tune in to the *Bolero* music?"

"He told her to go upstairs and get him a clean handkerchief."

"Anything else unusual?"

"Don't think so. . . . Cross had been there a few days before, and everything had gone on precisely the same."

"Yes. Cross told me that . . . Bland didn't send the maid out at all? For a walk or anything?"

"No. She was there all the time. Mrs. Bland found her a couple of books to read as she didn't want the noise of the wireless. And she told her she could go to bed when she liked, as she wouldn't be wanted again after she'd washed up."

Travers nodded. "That's interesting! . . . And nothing else has turned up?"

Nothing apparently had, so they sat and yarned till Cross got back. The vicar drifted in with a diffident little smile, and found everybody conspiring to put him at his ease. Travers got out a chess problem, and the party gathered round. Then at 7.40 he suggested airing the room for a bit and adjourning to the library for a short drink. It was Cross this time who shepherded them in. Travers was the merest moment late. Wharton gave him a suspicious look as he came in.

Travers smiled and opened the door again.

"It's all right, George! I haven't altered the hands of the clock. You can see for yourself!"

They disposed of the short drinks and retired to the cloak-room. Travers was highly amused. The faces of his guests were continually being overcast with doubts. One could see them straining to keep track of the time; to check their own ideas of the passing of the minutes against the time as shown by the grandfather in the dining-room when they should next clap eyes on it.

It was 7.50 when they came in to dinner—a cold but excellent spread, and an extra waiter drafted in to lend a hand to Palmer. The meal doesn't matter; what happened at the end of it was much more important. It was 8.12 when Cross, who had been waiting for a lull, nipped in with his remark.

"What about a spot of music from this wonderful new set?"

"Not a bad idea," said Travers, with the speed of an echo. "Palmer! see if you can find the *Radio Times*."

The copy was handed to Wharton, who looked at the clock and then at the programs.

"London National—orchestral music. Not very exciting. Regional—military band. Midland—a play. 'The Three Brothers'."

"What's the orchestral music?" asked Travers. Wharton said afterwards that he knew perfectly well he was forcing a card; the thing was he saw no point in refusing to take it.

"Orchestral music . . . Overture to *A Midsummer Night's Dream*. That's probably on now."

"What about a little dance music?" asked Norris.

"Nothing about it!" said Travers. "You're a grown man and an officer of the law—and your mind needs improving! So do the minds of every man-jack of you! . . . What do you say, Cross?"

"Well, I'd like to hear the *Overture*."

"Good enough! . . . Palmer! tune in to the National and bring in the speaker!"

There was a moment's silence as if everybody knew something was going to happen; then Travers began to talk effusively about that overture; the shimmering of the violins; the pomp and circumstance of the brass, and the hee-haw of the enchanted ass. Palmer entered carrying the mysterious box from which the music came.

Travers leaned for a moment over Pitt's chair and whispered; gave a cheerful nod to everybody and slipped out to the library. Palmer and the waiter moved round silently, and the men sat there listening. The vicar's face was ecstatic as he sat with chin on knuckles, nodding his head in time. He whispered in Wharton's ear:

"Wonderful! So utterly expressive of the play!" Another minute and he whispered again: "Travers seems a long while! . . . Excuse me a moment." He moved his chair back quietly and went over to the library door. Every eye followed him. His voice came fairly clear.

"Hallo! You're a nice sort of fellow! Putting on a piece of music and leaving us to listen to it!"

Travers' answer could be heard as a mumble, and no more.

"Back in a minute! . . . Splendid! Right! I won't disturb you!"

The vicar closed the door and tiptoed back to his seat, nodding and smiling as if all were well. Within half a minute Travers had followed him. He, too, nodded and smiled as he sidled to his seat. Then he beckoned Palmer and gave him a letter. Palmer left the room as if to post it.

They all sat there like that for another ten minutes, then the violins shimmered for the last time. Cross held up his hand as if to command an even austerer silence. The last chords rose slowly—were held—and died away again into moonlight.

"Magnificent! Perfectly magnificent!" The vicar looked round. "Well, what did you think of it?"

The tension gone, there was a positive Babel. What with one thing and another it was nine o'clock before the table was clear and everybody in the mood for the rest of the evening. Travers looked at the clock.

"Time the chess began! . . . You two had better sit over here out of our way. This is our table. The drinks shall be on this table in the middle, between the two. . . . And don't forget, padre; my money's on you!"

Cross and Pitt got down to their game. At the other end of the room the poker players gathered. Scott knew very little about the game, and Wharton still less, so a quarter of an hour had to be spent on explanations and trial trips. Then they prepared to begin in real earnest.

"What about stakes?" asked Norris.

"There aren't any," said Travers. "The winner gets a box of cigarettes and the runner-up a half-pound of tobacco. Bottom man puts half a crown in the box and the last but one a bob." Then he laughed.

"He's on a good thing!" said Kenton.

"Don't you believe it!" said Travers. "I was merely hoping this place could get raided!"

They played till ten, then halted for drinks. It was all very amusing, with the novices the keenest of the five. Wharton had the devil's own pile of chips. As for the chess players, they were still going at it steadily.

The poker had been resumed about twenty minutes when the chess came suddenly to an end. Travers, looking up from a couple of pairs of which he evidently thought a lot, noticed Pitt at his elbow.

"Hallo! Who's won?"

Pitt smiled. "He carries too many guns for me! . . . Still, we had a capital game."

The vicar, hiding modestly in the background, was brought into the circle, and the two sat watching the poker-players. At

10.30 by the clock Travers, who was banker, suddenly called in all chips.

"One more hand," said Kenton, "and the cigarettes are mine!"

"Sorry!" smiled Travers. "There may be a job of work to do in a minute or two. Pass over that pile of yours, George!"

By the time it was all settled up the clock showed 10.40. Wharton passed round his newly-acquired box of cigarettes.

"Quite a good game, this! Next time I play here you might have my initials printed on 'em beforehand!"

Then the door bell rang. Half a minute and it rang again. Then a third time.

"What's happened to Palmer?" asked Wharton.

"Probably gone out," said Travers. "Er—Cross, would you mind? You're nearest."

The vicar moved at once. Outside in the lobby voices were heard. The door opened again and Cross appeared.

"Some people. . . . They say they want to see you!"

"Show them in!" Travers looked round. "Sit down, everybody! And don't forget to tell the truth, the whole truth and nothing but the truth!"

Behind Cross came two men—a constable and a small man with a sandy moustache, holding his cap in his hand. Travers regarded them amiably.

"Er—you want to see me—about something?"

The small man nodded to the policeman. "That's him!"

The policeman coughed. "I'm given to understand, sir, as how you came into this man's shop tonight"—he took out his notebook and consulted it—"William Mace, tobacconist; and deliberately smashed a clock. Is that correct, sir, or is it not?"

"Of course it's correct!" That was Mace.

"Now you keep quiet for a minute!" the other told him. "You'll have your chance when the time comes."

"At what time was this alleged offence?" asked Travers.

"Eight-thirty!" snapped Mace. "You know it well enough!"

"Will you keep quiet!" He turned to Travers with heavy deliberation. "Eight-thirty it was—as you're supposed to know."

"And where did it happen?"

"It happened in this gentleman's shop—33, Lisbon Street, off Portugal Street." He moistened the pencil. "Now, sir; did you do it or did you not?"

"Wait a minute!" said Travers. "All I gather is that at 8.30 to-night I'm supposed to have gone to this—er—gentleman's shop and broken a clock." He looked round at the company. "Perfectly extraordinary story!"

"Officer!" said Scott quietly, "wouldn't it be as well if the complainant told us exactly what happened?"

"Well, sir . . ." He hesitated, then nodded over at Mace. "You hear that? Tell them what you told me!"

The tobacconist addressed himself to the company generally, and by the end of his story he had worked himself up to a mightily indignant state.

"What I told this gentleman here, is this; that just before half-past eight, this gentleman here come into my shop. I was behind the counter, see? Then he says to me, 'Got any de Reskes?'—like that, see? Then before I could say a word he points to the clock what I have behind the counter on the wall, and he says to me, 'Is that your clock?' he says; then he ups with what looked like one of these here golf-sticks and smashes the face and was out of the door like lightning, see? By the time I'd got to the door he was out of sight."

The policeman's voice followed on without interruption.

"And you identify him as this gentleman here?"

"Didn't I tell you so as soon as we saw him!"

He nodded and turned to Travers with pencil poised.

"What's your name, sir?"

"One moment!" Travers looked really perturbed. "You sure this took place at 8.30, Mr. Mace?"

"Yes . . . and so are you!"

"Your clock was right?"

"Never mind about my clock! My clock was eight-thirty."

Travers smiled. "Here are six people, every one of whom will swear I was in this room at eight-thirty. They'll swear I was here long before that—and that I haven't left the room since!"

The policeman stared at him, then decided apparently that he was in earnest.

"There you are, Mr. Mace! What have you got to say to that?"

"I say he's a liar!"

The policeman's gaze shifted inquiringly.

"That may be," said Travers. "But let me tell you this. If you bring this case into court, there's only you to swear that I did a certain thing at a certain time. I've got six people to prove I was elsewhere."

The policeman had a brain-wave.

"You got a brother, sir?"

"I'm afraid I haven't. . . . But I might have a double. You know—somebody impersonating me for a joke!"

Mace looked at him. "That *would* be a joke!"

Everybody laughed, except the officer. Travers seemed particularly amused. Then he stopped his raillery.

"Look here, Mr. Mace! To save all unpleasantness. I may know who did it and I may not; but I don't want it brought into court. . . . What was your clock worth?"

Mace looked at him suspiciously, lowered his eyes, licked his lips—and thought.

"It cost me ten bob."

"And that'll satisfy you?"

Mace thought again. "And what about my time?"

"Say a pound then!"

Mace shot another look at him. "All right, sir. That'll do me!"

Travers took out his case and passed over two pound notes.

"How's that?"

Mace touched where his hat usually was. "Thank 'ee, sir!" He had another look at the notes. "And if you'd like to have another go any time, sir, you can do so on the same terms!"

Travers laughed. Scott came over.

"Just a word, officer!"

He drew him away to the corner. Travers approached the decanter. "Now, Mr. Mace; what about a spot of whisky?"

"Thank'ee, sir! Don't mind if I do!"

Travers poured it out. "By the way, what do you make the time now?"

Mace looked at his watch. "Just short of eleven, sir—like that clock of yours!"

. . . .

No sooner had the door closed on the two visitors than Cross turned to the company.

"If you gentlemen will excuse me, I'll turn in. . . . It's been a great pleasure to have seen you all."

He shook hands all round, nodded to Travers, then disappeared in the direction of the cloak-room.

"What do you think of him?" asked Travers. "Delightful fellow, isn't he?"

Wharton's voice was the only ungenerous one. "That remains to be seen. . . . How'd you do it? —that clock business. Palmer impersonate you as he did once before?"

Travers shook his head. "All Palmer did was to go to Mace and tell him he knew the bloke who smashed his clock. Palmer brought him and the policeman along here."

Wharton went over to the grandfather. "Some juggling here?"

"Look for yourself!" said Travers. "All come and have a look!" He opened the clock door for them. "There you are! Entrails and all! Do what you like with it!"

They swarmed round it like ants. Even Kenton saw nothing wrong with it. Then Norris had an idea.

"What about that wireless of yours?"

Travers pushed the bell for Palmer.

"Oh, Palmer! Take Inspector Norris to the set and tune in to anywhere he asks!"

They stood there a moment or two, then the music came—a jazz-band. Just as Palmer and Norris reappeared, the number ended. "You have just been listening, ladies and gentlemen, to Lester Layne and his . . ."

"Satisfied?" smiled Travers.

Norris shook his head. "It beats me!"

"Of course it does!" Travers told him. "It beats all of us. The only one it didn't beat was Cross." He looked round. "Fill up your glasses and I'll tell you all about it."

CHAPTER XX
ARC—AND FULL CIRCLE

Travers drew his chair in close. The lowering of his voice and the quick glance he gave towards the bedroom anticipated his explanation.

"Cross was the one who saw something fishy. But for your running into him that night, George—literally as well as metaphorically—he'd probably have gone on smelling out the unclean thing; then he'd have kept it to himself. He's a strange mixture really; not what I might call *personally*, but in his principles and inhibitions. That's why he won't discuss the matter with anybody. He's doing it through a third person—myself. I got him up here because I sent him a message that intrigued him. Once he got here I had to use all sorts of arts and blandishments. Still, that's nothing to do with it.

"As you're all aware, he was a great reader of detective stories. He had also an unusually open and inquiring mind—and he was a mathematician. The mere fact that he should know a murdered person was the impetus that set him off. As soon as you called on him, George, he knew there was something in the wind. The original evidence showed murder as almost certain, so he cast about in his mind for who might have done it. Anybody in the house he set aside; the methods would have been too crude and obvious. But he did remember something— something that you, Colonel, mentioned at the conference—that all the while he was at Bland's house that night there was a curious and most unnatural insistence upon time.

"He tells me he regarded those first suspicions as something to be ashamed of; something that had to be entertained furtively, as it were. Bland he'd never liked or disliked, in spite of knowing him pretty well. There always seemed something down below that he couldn't get at. Mrs. Bland he had to be very wary with. When the Cross family first came to Barlcombe and Cross called on the Blands, Mrs. Bland became rather a nuisance at Barlcombe Vicarage. Mrs. Cross found her too harassing." Travers fumbled at his glasses. "I must say I quite understand that. But as I was saying, Cross felt he wasn't doing the right thing exactly, and it was really against his better instincts that he went on with his hunch. He tried out first—as you did, George—the time required to get from Bland's house to Combe Cottage, cut a throat and get back again. That night you caught him, George, was when he was having a second go at it. It might interest you all to know that he estimated he could do it in three minutes.

"When you called on him the following morning, George, you told him definitely that it was murder, and it had taken place at 8.30. That got him going again on a problem he'd already been toying with. He set out to call at blacksmiths' and ironmongers', beginning at Tiverton and Exeter. Then he tried Taunton. He finally got what he wanted—the information that is—at a blacksmith's shop between Taunton and Mulberton. Details I'll give you later. The secret of the whole thing is extraordinarily simple."

In the bureau he found some sheets of paper and handed them round. Kenton buttonholed him as soon as he clapped eyes on his.

"Wait a minute, Colonel!" said Travers. "I knew you'd spot it straight away. What about you other people?"

"I seem to remember something," said Pitt. "Damned if I know what it is!"

"Well, it's this. Kenton will excuse me if I put the whole explanation very simply. What you're looking at is a formula:

$$t = \pi\sqrt{\frac{l}{g}}$$

"I'd forgotten it because it's years since I was concerned with dynamics. The colonel had no use for it because the matter didn't enter his head. You'll all pardon me if I say there is nothing abstruse or mysterious in it. It's the property of every schoolboy who does applied mathematics. It's the formula for finding the time taken by a pendulum to swing between two points; the pendulum of a grandfather clock, for instance, between the tick and the tock!"

"What do the letters stand for?" asked Scott.

"Well, it is the time required. You get it by multiplying π, that is 22/7, by the root of a certain fraction which is the length of the pendulum in feet, over g, the force of gravity; represented by the number 32. The answer will be in seconds. For instance, suppose you have a grandfather clock with a pendulum exactly three feet long. You say to yourself, 'I wonder if every tick represents a second?' You can soon find out. T here equals 22/7 multiplied by the root of 3/32. If you work that out you'll find the answer is approximately 66/70 of a second. That is to say, your clock is taking just the merest fraction short of a second between tick and tock!

"It was the mention of that formula that intrigued Cross. You might have been amused if you'd seen the face of the girl who took my telegram, when I described the formula as 'tea is pie, and so on.' Still, Cross spotted it and that's all that counts. And now for the application of the formula as far as we—and this case—are concerned.

"We all know how to regulate a clock that has a pendulum. If the clock loses, then we shorten the pendulum; if the clock gains, then we lengthen it. Some of us know that isn't so easy as it sounds. If a clock is practically correct and you want to make it perfectly correct, you have to make an exceedingly fine adjustment. The slightest turn of the screw does it.

"When I was in one of the big stores the other afternoon, I saw that grandfather you see there. I had in my hand at that moment a length of iron rod which I'd just bought. The sight of the clock told me what the rod was for. We'll come to that in a moment or two. The point is, I bought the clock because it was of a certain type. You notice how wide the case is, particularly at the base. Then Cross and I regulated it, using a fine chronometer, till we got it what might be called correct. Then came the real problem!

"First of all you must clearly understand that the figures given are merely approximate. If you decide to bring a case against Bland, you'll have to employ a first-class mathematician; a man whose name will impress the public and the jury; and he'll have to do the experiments in court. That should be child's-play.

"Let's go back to a grandfather clock. You say your clock loses, so you shorten the pendulum. But suppose you want your clock to lose. You want it to lose *as much as five minutes per hour*! How will you do it? If you have an elementary knowledge only of mathematics, you'll still be able to use the formula to find out by exactly how much you must lengthen the pendulum. You find it to be about one-fifth of the length of the pendulum; that is, extra to the length of the pendulum when the clock was correct. Again, you want to make your clock gain no less than five minutes an hour. By the formula you find you must shorten the pendulum by about five and a half inches.

"Now the trouble with lengthening a pendulum is that the pendulum wouldn't be long enough to get the required effect. What you'd have to do, therefore, would be *what Bland did*—make a very long pendulum of your own. You buy a length of iron rod, put on the bob at one end and the suspension spring at the other. Cross and I bored a hole in the rod so that we could put a pin through to keep the bob in position. Any simple device of that kind would do. In an ordinary grandfather, of course, the bob screws up and down; but the possible variations to ensure regulation don't amount to more than an inch or two of length—and therefore an inch or two of *threaded* length.

"Now something else. Suppose you want your clock to lose five minutes an hour, and you therefore make your special, long pendulum. That longer pendulum will swing through a bigger arc. Let me show you! . . . Unless the case of the clock was very wide, the pendulum would now hit the side when it swung. If you remember, George, Bland's clock had a very wide case. I bought this clock, as I told you, because it had a sufficiently wide case to admit of a pendulum swinging through a big arc. In that context it might be profitable to inquire precisely when Bland *bought his clock*! . . . While you're here you notice the two holes in the rod through which you slip the pin to keep the bob in the two positions required. You see, if I'd had the rod threaded all the way up, it'd have taken the devil of a time to screw the bob up or down. Using a hole and a pin you can drop the bob as quick as blazes."

"If I've got the right hang of things," said Wharton, "it all amounts to this. When we entered this room at five o'clock this afternoon, the clock was dead right by our watches. The pendulum was set, however, for the clock to lose at the rate of five minutes an hour. We hadn't any watches, but we had the clock under our noses—"

"And if you don't mind my saying so, you could never have suspected the clock. The tick wasn't abnormal. Also people think a clock is in a bad way when it loses or gains an hour a week. To suspect a clock of gaining or losing five minutes an hour is a manifest absurdity."

"Quite! As I was saying, the clock loses till just before 7.45, when all you have to do is put the bob to the short position—I did that as we went into the library!—and the clock thereupon proceeds to gain what it lost. At somewhere about 11, it's perfectly right again!" Travers smiled.

"To use your own expression, George, you've got it in one!"

"But what about the music?" asked Scott.

"Just a moment!" smiled Travers. "We'll clear up the clock first. You do see, don't you, that when Bland's clock was 8.18 or thereabouts, the correct time was 8.30. Now at 8.18 Bland came out of the study where he'd been ostensibly writing a letter. He was in the study for three minutes. The problem for you is what happened in those three minutes!"

There was a moment's silence, then a babble of voices. Every one seemed to have his own point to raise.

"One other thing might be mentioned there," broke in Travers again. "You've got a witness to help clinch things. He'll be an awkward witness for you, and counsel may give him a very thin time—I refer to Daniels. Daniels said he heard—by his watch—a certain remark made after nine o'clock. Cross says that by Bland's clock, the remark was made ten minutes or so earlier. In other words, Bland's clock was still ten minutes slow at 8.50—which, by a simple calculation, you can see it must have been."

"That's right!" said Wharton. "Daniels'll be the corner-stone of the clock evidence. If he weren't such a bad witness I'd say the case was over."

"We'll face that trouble when it comes," said Scott. "The case looks good enough to me as it is. If we hadn't known something was in the wind tonight, and if Mr. Travers hadn't removed all our watches, we should have been properly bamboozled over the tobacconist's clock. . . . Now, what about the music?"

Travers smiled. "Ah! the music. That's rather absurd. First of all you can take my word for it that the set we have here is the same as Bland's. It's extremely powerful; four-tubes, all-electric is what Palmer calls it. He's the expert, and he's the one who solved that part of the problem. I called him in here and put the question to him. I said, 'You're a wireless expert and all that. How would it be possible for me to create an alibi with a set? I mean, you listen to a piece of music from London at 8.30 and yet it isn't 8.30!"

"That rather flummoxed him. He suggested the music was late perhaps; a talk or something had held it up. I told him that didn't operate in this case because we'd assumed that the B.B.C. had been asked and they'd reported the music as being on time. By the way, I did understand you to say that, didn't I, George?"

"You did. The *Bolero* music was dead on time."

"Good! Well, Palmer thought again and thought wrong, then he got it. 'Perhaps it wasn't coming from London after all. Perhaps it was from some other station!' Now you see it. We immediately looked up the *Radio Times* again, and then got *World Radio*, as Palmer suggested. There was a concert from Rome that night—and Palmer tells me it's a very easy station to get. The *Bolero* music came from Rome, where it was timed for about 8.15. Bland tuned in with the ear-phones, and he didn't plug in the speaker *till the music had begun*. He took care there should be no risk of the announcer's voice. He sent the maid upstairs in case she should notice any unusual twiddling of the knobs. When the music had begun, he brought the speaker into the room. Who was to imagine it wasn't coming from London, as the *Radio Times* plainly said? After all, the language of music is cosmopolitan!—and universal!"

"In other words, what you sprang on us to-night!"

"Well . . . yes! If you go through the English programs on one of those many nights when there's an orgy of music, you're dead certain—so it seems to me—to find a Continental station broadcasting one of the same items at least, and at the same time.

"Cross and I spotted one at once. The *Midsummer's Dream* Overture was coming from Paris. We chose it because it's somewhere about the length of the *Bolero*. I may say we also chose to-night for our little dinner because it was the one night when we could get a piece of music coinciding with anywhere near the time we wanted for an exact reproduction of what took place on September the fifth."

"Damn clever!" said Pitt, then hastily: "Not you, Ludo . . . I mean I was thinking of Bland."

"One other thing. The maid didn't listen in that night. Mrs. Bland," he gave the words a peculiar emphasis, "lent her some books—and told her she could go to bed early."

"You mentioned Mrs. Bland," said Wharton, who'd been scribbling down notes as fast as he could write. "I take it there's no use shutting our eyes to that side of the problem? We're aware that the case stands or falls on her complicity?"

"Why not?" smiled Scott. "Mr. Travers may have been sufficiently chivalrous to gloss over that side of the case. Some of us here are too hard-bitten for chivalry of that particular kind. Besides, she'll have her loophole. She can plead she didn't know what she was doing things for."

"And get away with it, sir!"

"She almost certainly will, Norris!" He looked round. "Anything else, because I think Wharton will agree that some of us are going to have a busy night."

"Yes, sir!" said Norris quickly. "I've one point to raise. You imply that when Mrs. Bland looked in the study she imitated her husband's voice!"

"Mumbled or muttered!" corrected Scott. "Just a growl or anything. The same as Cross did with Mr. Travers here. Isn't that so, Travers?

"Well, that was our idea."

"And she suggested the *Bolero* music?"

Travers nodded.

"And suggested it should stop before it did?"

"That's right. . . . That was arranged. She pretended to be so nervous in order that Bland might turn off the music promptly—before the announcer's voice gave the game away." He hesitated for a moment. Something was on his mind and the words were difficult to find. "I'll mention this and leave it to you. That night I went to dinner with Mrs. Bland, she went over every detail of the case with me—and I didn't know it. I sensed there was something; what it was I didn't know. She pretended Combe Cottage was further off than it was; she insisted on my seeing the wireless set—or hearing it; she told me all about the *Bolero* music; she said the clock was a wonderful timekeeper, and she even showed me the study. She set out to spike every possible gun—and she tried to spike me in addition." Wharton nodded, then had another look at his notes.

"Only one thing strikes me as presenting any difficulty. Suppose Daniels and Griffiths hadn't panicked. Suppose it'd been clear to both of them that neither had done it. Wouldn't their natural instincts have made them call up Bland? Then what would have happened to Bland's alibi?"

"We thought of that," said Travers. "Some moments must have elapsed before they phoned. Phoned, remember! They wouldn't have fetched him. Bland would have answered the phone himself. He'd have said to Cross, 'Sorry, but I've got to go to Combe Cottage. Something urgent.' That mere act of telephoning *after* the murder established his alibi, since he hadn't left the house. . . . Cross and Mrs. Bland would have waited for a bit, then Bland would have rung them up. The evening would have been off. Later on, if there was any question of times, all that could be said was that Daniels watch was wrong. In any case, Bland was all right. He couldn't have been in two places at the same time."

Scott was whispering in the A.C.'s ear. Wharton, who'd been nodding away for all he was worth, wrote his last note and put away the book.

"Nine to-morrow suit everybody? . . . And what about Cross?"

"He won't be here," said Travers. "If you want him at a trial he'll give his straightforward evidence like a man and a citizen. The rest he's turned over to me."

Pitt suddenly began to clear his throat lustily.

"Putting aside all—er—business, perhaps I might—on behalf of everybody here—thank Travers for the really magnificent way he's done us to-night. We always have known him to be an excellent fellow—"

"The very best!" cut in Wharton. Travers thrust himself into the small opening.

"Just a moment, gentlemen! Sorry to interrupt the A.C. and all that—thanking me for nothing and so on. But I'd just like to ask one simple question— a very personal one. I've been doing the devil of a lot of talking to-night. Er—do you people consider me an orator?"

"Orator!" said Pitt, and looked round. "Well, you're a damn good speaker—and a clear one!"

Travers smiled. "But you wouldn't put me in the same class as—say—Mark Antony!"

Pitt didn't quite know if his leg was being subtly pulled or not.

"Well, not quite so good, perhaps. You're pretty good—mind you!"

Travers laughed. "The point is this. Mark Antony—as you know—had to address a gang of the toughest citizens of Rome. He got their attention by mentioning Caesar's will—and what they'd get out of it. Then he switched off to something else—the real thing this time. He did it so well that when the gang finally departed, they'd forgotten all about what they'd been so interested in—the will!" He smiled round benevolently.

"Well!" said Wharton. "What's the joke?"

"There isn't one," said Travers. "Except perhaps that you people are going off without your watches!"

....

On the morning when Bland was hanged, the wheel had moved full circle. Travers, in fact, was once more standing in Lord Zyon's library, discussing certain matters with his lordship, and particularly the allocation of a certain reward.

Lord Zyon—pink, plump and suave as ever—had just come in. The usual compliments had just been exchanged, the weather mentioned and the final platitudes disposed of. Then his lordship came to the point.

"Now this reward business you were phoning about. I thought I had settled Cross was to have it! Everybody agreed—Press and public opinion generally—that he'd contributed most."

"I'm afraid Cross is out of it, sir," said Travers. "I got a letter from him this morning. He mentions your letter, as you see. He feels it a matter of principle."

"Principle? The man's earned it! . . . Hasn't got too much money already, has he?"

"No!" said Travers. "He hasn't got too much money."

His lordship adjusted his glasses, read the letter and passed it back.

"Hm! Bit of a crank! . . . What's that 'Aceldema' allusion?"

"But didn't you suggest that if he didn't want all the reward he might at least purchase a playing field for the village? Sorry if I'm wrong, but I understood that."

"What's that got to do with it? What's he mean?"

Travers almost smiled. "Well, the word itself means—er—the field of blood—or something like that."

"Blood! . . . But he wasn't killed in the field, was he? I mean, he was murdered in the house!"

Travers smiled demurely. "Mr. Cross is an eccentric character, sir. Almost as eccentric as myself."

The other gave a quick look. "Well, I suppose he knows his own mind. . . . What's going to be done about it? The *Record* is waiting to publish!"

"Scotland Yard will let you have their opinion to-day, sir. They requested me to inform you to that effect."

"Good!" He fidgeted for a moment, then thought of something else. "You've been very helpful in this affair, Mr. Travers. There isn't anything I can do for you in any way?"

Travers smiled dryly. "I'm afraid not, sir. . . . Very nice of you, of course. . . . How's the League going?"

"Splendidly, Travers! Splendidly!" He craned up his neck and whispered impressively, "We've got the government on the run!" Travers nodded violently. Lord Zyon moved over to the door. As he took the pudgy hand, Travers thought of something.

"One thing you might tell me, sir. . . . Is there any truth in those rumours about the *Evening Echo*?"

"What rumours?"

"Well—er—that your group was purchasing."

"Hm! Yes. As a matter of fact we are." He spoke with no particular enthusiasm. "Three evening papers are enough for London."

"You're scrapping it?"

"Hm! . . . Not immediately. . . . Ultimately of course." He held out his hand again. "You must come to dinner some time."

"Thanks!" said Travers. "I'd love to."

Outside there were no sunblinds—and no begonias in the window boxes. The wind cut clean and the air seemed heavy with snow. As Travers descended the steps he shivered in his heavy coat—then paused for the merest second. That groove in the gravel. Could it have been made by the feet of somebody who'd leaped from the window all those months ago, when the begonias were in bloom and the sunblinds had fluttered gently? Before the winter was dreamed of and—he smiled gently—before the government had been on the run?

THE END

Lightning Source UK Ltd.
Milton Keynes UK
UKHW020654201218
334319UK00009B/166/P

9 781911 579779